Calculated Collision

Book Three
Crossing Forces

CALCULATED COLLISION

CROSSING FORCES BOOK THREE

USA TODAY BESTSELLING AUTHOR

C. A. SZAREK

Calculated Collision
C.A. Szarek
Crossing Forces Book Three

Paper Dragon Publishing
North Richland Hills, TX

eBook ISBN: 978-1-941151-27-3
Paperback ISBN: 978-1-941151-26-6

Published in the United States of America
Second eBook Edition: January, 2018
Second Print Edition: January, 2018

Other Books by C.A. Szarek

<u>Crossing Forces — Romantic Suspense</u>

Collision Force (Book One)
Cole in Her Stocking (A Crossing Forces Christmas) — *FREE read!*
Chance Collision (Book Two)
Calculated Collision (Book Three)
Collision Control (Book Four)
Superior Collision (Book Five)
Incendiary Collision (Book Six) — *Coming soon!*

<u>The King's Riders — Epic Fantasy Romance</u>

Sword's Call (Book One) — *Also in Audio!*
Love's Call (Book Two) — *Also in Audio!*
Rogue's Call (Book Three) — *Also in Audio!*
Fate's Call (A Novella from the World of the King's Riders) — *Also in Audio!*

<u>Highland Secrets — Historical Fantasy/Time Travel</u>

The Tartan MP3 Player (Book One)
The Fae Ring (Book Two)
The Parchment Scroll (Book Three)
Highlander's Portrait (A Highland
Secrets Story) — *Coming soon to Audio!*
Highland Valentine (A Highland Secrets
Story) — *only .99*
The Princess and The Laird (A Highland
Secrets Prequel)

Highland Treasures — Historical Fantasy/Time Travel

Highland Oath (Book One) — *Coming January 2018!*
Highland Essence (Book Two) — *Coming soon!*

Anthologies

Deep in the Hearts of Texas — *FREE read!*
    Story: Promise (A Crossing Forces Companion)

Crossing Forces

Small Town Texas doesn't always mean small time crime.

Welcome to Antioch, population fifty thousand.

With a police department full of detectives and officers who are good at what they do, throw in the occasional FBI agent, and the bad guy doesn't have a shot, no matter how big the crime.

They work together and fight together. Relationships will be forged and changed along the twists and turns.

When fate intervenes, love and happiness can be found in unlikely places.

Dedication

WOW! Book three! How did that happen? I am so grateful to so many people. Without them, this adventure never would have happened.

To my husband, Shane. Thanks for helping me with this series and letting me read it to you. Thanks for your input, too.

For this one, I need to thank my Judge, Mike. Thank you for all the help with the lawyerly stuff. Had I not been able to ask you questions, I would've been lost!

Thanks to Holly, once again, for your continued support, explanations and FBI stuff. I'm pretty sure since you were an NYC FBI there's a little of you in Lee. She's a tough chick like you!

Thanks, as always, to my critique group. Michelle, Jen, Clover, Gina. You're made of awesome and you've made my writing stronger.

Thanks, Susie, for critiquing and reading for me at the drop of a hat. Your interest and help keep me going in this world.

Jo-Anna and JoAnna, you both know I love you to bits. Thanks for always being there for me, listening to me rant and whine about writing and helping me through the rough spots.

Carrie, thanks for letting me talk your ear off: you know audible plotting helps, and I always appreciate your input and patience. Love ya!

To my new friend/motivational writer buddy, Christine: you're totally awesome. Thank you for the constant encouragement, check-ins and long chats! Thanks for the input, too! You keep me going, and as you know, sometimes I need that!

Thanks to my constant cheerleaders, Amee, Alanna, Toni, and Kerry! If I didn't have you guys to be excited about new words, new scenes and new chapters, I don't know what I'd do. Love you guys!

Chapter One

Sweat broke out on her brow and Lee gripped her Glock tighter instead of wiping the moisture away. She bit back a curse.

What's taking so long?

They should've already heard shouts of, "Federal agents!"

She *hated* being in the back.

Being *back-up.*

Lee and her partner, Clint Downs, were the lead agents of their unit, and usually headed raids.

Not today.

Their boss, Special Agent Olivia Barnes, wanted them — her in particular — to take a breather from going hard and fast.

Nothing wrong with the passenger seat, right?

Maybe if she kept telling herself that, it'd sink in.

Hard and fast was all she knew. How she got the job done.

But...even her partner had reminded her there were *sixteen* members of their human trafficking unit. They were *all* partners.

Ugh.

She'd rather hang a *'Doesn't play well with others'* sign around her neck.

"You good?"

Her partner's gravelly voice made Lee tense. "Yup." She didn't look his way.

"You seem shaky."

"I'm good." Flexing her fingers on her gun's grip, she inched forward. "Wanna get this done."

Downs didn't have a chance to answer; the battering ram exploded the door in front of them and wood splinters went flying.

Collective shouts of, "Federal agents!" coupled with "FBI!" surrounded her and she rushed forward behind her teammates. In correct formation, head in the game.

We're doing this.

Screams and whimpers greeted her ears. Lee's heart used to jump with the fears of the victims every time they did a raid, but not anymore. Instead it was steel, and her gut made of iron.

She was used to seeing tears, and hearing them cry. What she'd never get used to were the bruises and skimpy clothing on kids that were less than half her age.

Babies. They're all babies.

Most weren't even sixteen, yet in a lot of cases they'd been bought, sold and forced to have sex with more pieces of scum than she could count. The lucky ones got *owners* that didn't beat them, but a sex-slave was still a sex-slave.

Bastards.

They all needed to die.

The relief on the girls' faces when they first realized they were being rescued was always a reward. Reminded Lee she was a good person—why she did the job. If only the sentiment lasted in her mind.

A shot rang out and her instincts kicked in. She

dropped to the dingy carpet and rolled to the nearest cover—a dark-colored couch.

Someone returned fire just as her partner crouched beside her. "Shit," Downs spat. "It's going south, fast."

She smirked and raised her Glock. "Nah, we got this." She popped up over the couch for a quick survey.

A bullet whizzed overhead and her partner yanked her back down.

"Don't be reckless."

When he flashed his perma-scowl, Lee almost rolled her eyes.

How many times had he said that?

Wellllllllll, for today it's probably the first time.

Orders to drop weapons went unheeded as more *bang-bang* made her ears ring. She risked another look over the couch.

Other members of their unit had taken cover, but several were returning fire.

One of the girls screamed again and Lee looked that way. Three—no, four—teens were huddled in a corner, arms wrapped around each other, but they were out of the line of fire.

Good.

Today's group of fine, upstanding human traffickers was made up of illegals from Mexico.

She and Downs had been after these guys for months. The fact they'd hooked up with Tony Caselli's outfit had been dumb luck.

The other object of today's raid—Giovanni Nicci—was shooting a big .45.

One of the assholes he was supposed to sell girls to

lie in a pool of blood about five feet from him. Dead Mexican's partner returned fire next to the Newyorker scum.

If—no, *when*—the FBI gained control of the situation, their unit would score double. According to the morning's intel, Nicci was supposed to be meeting up with Russians. They'd have to find out why there'd been a change in plans later. It had to mean something.

Lee took a shot, hearing her partner curse next to her. She ignored him and pulled the trigger again.

Nicci shouted something in Italian and grabbed his arm. She'd hit the bastard, but it wasn't mortal. He backed up quickly, retreating down the hallway.

"Least let me cover your ass!"

Downs' shout sounded behind her as she scooted around the couch to pursue Nicci.

Gunfire in the front room came to a halt as members of their unit fell in behind Lee and her partner.

Out of the corner of her eye, she saw Evan Roberts wrench the second Mexican's arms behind his back to cuff him after kicking the guy's forty away.

The short and stocky man started cursing in Spanish. He gestured and told the FBI agent to lick his balls.

She smirked when Roberts answered the man's insult with something appropriate in Spanish.

Mexican Two snapped his mouth shut.

Didn't expect the white guy to speak the language, huh, scum?

Lee kept moving, sensing her partner's large frame

at her back.

He inched forward and they made eye contact for a split-second. Downs nodded toward the master suite of the apartment and she moved beside him to the right.

Another one of the guys moved in to cover their asses and her partner kicked the door in.

Nicci fired a shot even before the wood slammed into the wall.

Lee didn't hesitate. She pulled the trigger of her forty not once, but twice.

The Italian thug grunted and winced. He dropped the gun as members of her unit swamped the room. "Fuck me. All-*fucking*-right!"

"Hands up." She smirked and gestured with her Glock. "C'mon, I don't need an excuse to put another hole in you, Nicci."

"I got witnesses, bitch."

"Yeah, yeah. Shut it," Downs ordered.

Her partner holstered his Glock and Lee kicked Nicci's weapon away. With the help of Agent Bobby Smythe, Downs hauled the injured piece of scum to his feet.

"Hey! I have rights!"

Lee laughed and holstered her gun after the click and slide of her partner's cuffs shouted the human trafficker was secure. "Yeah, rights. Like those little girls out there. You're real concerned about rights."

"Fuck you."

"Not in a million years."

"Partner, I got this. Why don't you see about the girls?" Downs arched a dark eyebrow.

She narrowed her eyes, but nodded.

Did he think she was going to attack Nicci or something?

"I'll get the medics on the way for His Highness here," she said on her way out.

Smythe snorted.

Lee palmed her cell and turned on her heel, shaking her head. She made the call. Medics would be there in a few.

She took one look at the four petrified teens huddled in the corner and swallowed back a curse. They should've let Nicci lie on the floor and bleed.

Lee sucked in a calming breath and approached the real victims of the raid.

"The girls are all Mexican. Two are fourteen, one fifteen and the other, sixteen. They won't tell me their last names, but they're not legal. They were supposed to be absorbed into Caselli's organization." Lee shook her head and met her partner's crystal blue gaze.

"Child Services are already on the way."

"Good. But that's going to scare the shit out of them even more. They don't speak English. Hope we get a bilingual responder, or I'll have to ride down there with. Not on my list of fun things to do. Anyways, what did Nicci give you? Anything?"

"Some chatter about one of Caselli's big deal attorneys getting kicked to the curb, but nothing else," Downs said.

"Didn't we already know that? Angelo Fiato or

some shit?"

He nodded. "Right. But rumor is he's hiding upstate now, and there's a pretty heavy-duty purse on him."

"Can we confirm it?"

"Roberts and Stewart are already on it."

"Good deal. Hope the guy's good at hiding. When Caselli takes out a hit on you, it's nothin' to play with. Did he say anything about the Russians?"

Her partner shook his head. "Nope. Denied there was a meet scheduled."

"Damn. Either we got bad intel or he's a liar. I'm leaning toward liar. Maybe we'll get it out of him later." Lee studied her partner's expression when he didn't remark.

Downs sighed and ran his hand through his graying-brown crew cut. He had about ten years on Lee's thirty-six, but the ex-Marine wasn't washed out.

He was still as tall and muscled as the picture on his desk of him in fatigues from twenty years before. Broad-shouldered and handsome, he always wore a neatly trimmed moustache.

They worked well together—for the most part. But *'reckless'* and *'Lee'* in the same sentence were his two favorite words.

Didn't matter what order.

His silence shouted that he wanted—no, *needed*—to lay into her. It was a normal part of their after-raid debrief.

"Go for it," she said.

His eyes flashed—she hadn't missed her mark.

"One day you're gonna get killed. It won't be because you're a shitty agent."

Lee opened her mouth, but he put his hand up.

"You know what you're doing. We *both* know that. But it's really fucking amazing that after a year and a half, I *do* have to remind you I'm your *partner*."

She stared. Her proper, rule-following partner had dropped the F-bomb?

Lee blinked. "Look, I'm—"

"Don't tell me you're sorry, Special Agent Selena Dawson. *Show* me. Quit shitting on me."

Jesus. Where the hell is this coming from?

"Just remember you're my responsibility, as much as I am yours," Downs said when she still didn't speak. "You put yourself in danger so, I have to do the same to go after you. You might live alone, but I have a wife and two kids who are pretty fond of me coming home at the end of the damn day."

Yup.

That about defined '*asshole*' and '*partner*'. Both suddenly synonymous with '*Lee Dawson*'. Succinct, even.

"I'd ask you what happened when you went to Texas to go after Marchetti, but you'd just tell me to go to hell, so *I'll* just tell *you* to get over it and stop being a loner. It's been six months."

Damn straight.

Six months, or six days, she wasn't talking to *anyone* about Nate Crane.

"I don't want to be forced to have a sit down with Barnes," he said.

Ice raced down her spine. It wasn't a threat her partner had made—it was a promise. A man of only necessary words, Downs never said anything lightly.

Normally she would've cracked a joke, teased him, but as Lee looked into pale eyes that matched her frozen veins, she couldn't utter a thing.

It's starting. Dallas all over again.

"I like working with you," she managed.

His shoulders relaxed, that big chest heaving as he sucked in air. "I believe you. But you need to get it together before you get yourself hurt. Or worse."

"Before I get you hurt, you mean." Her throat was tight, painful as she forced her statement past her lips. Her heart thundered, her temples throbbed.

Downs' eyes widened and his large hand clamped down on her forearm.

Lee would've pulled away, but her vision wavered, her legs wobbled.

"Dawson?"

Her mouth moved, but no sound came out. She fought the darkness swamping her vision.

"Holy shit, you're hit!"

Blackness swallowed her whole.

Chapter Two

"I shouldn't even be here, but I needed to talk to you." Angelo looked around the fancy hotel lounge as if nothing was wrong, but Nate didn't miss his old friend's damp forehead or how his dark eyes darted all over the place.

"What's wrong, 'Lo?"

The old college nickname made one corner of the guy's mouth lift, but Angelo didn't relax an inch. Broad shoulders tight, he was hunched on the bar stool. "I'm in trouble."

"What kind of trouble?"

His friend's Adam's apple bobbed as he swallowed. He reclined on the barstool, but the action was forced. His long legs were tense, and he tapped one foot on the carpeted floor, the other foot perched on the bottom rung of the stool and shaking.

"That bad, huh?" Nate asked, sucking in a breath when his buddy remained silent. Seeing the confident — some would say egotistical — high-powered attorney rattled was enough to make *him* shake in his cowboy boots.

Angelo Fiato had done very well for himself after Colombia Law. Starting off as a prosecutor for the District Attorney's office in New York City, he'd rarely lost a case. Then he'd decided there was more money in defense, and had crossed to the dark side, as their buddies teased.

He'd done even better on his own. His firm was huge now — partners, junior partners and associate attorneys galore. He'd been after Nate to leave the county DA's office in Dallas for years. Even offered him partner at his firm right off the bat. When Nate had refused repeatedly, Angelo had accused him of being too idealistic.

'Lo nodded, patting his forehead with a silk handkerchief before shoving it back inside his jacket. His hand shook. "You were right, my friend."

"About?" He arched a brow.

"I shoulda stayed with the DA's office."

Nate paused as the wheels turned in his head. "You pissed off a client?"

"You could say that. I agreed to *assist* the FBI. In a certain matter. It got back to him, and… Well, let's just say, taking a risk to see you is putting it mildly."

"Tax fraud?"

Angelo shook his head. "Much bigger than that."

He shoved his hand through his hair. "What can I do to help?"

A bitter laugh greeted his ears when he met his friend's gaze again. "*No one* can help me now. I'm fucked."

"Then why — "

Angelo's olive skin drained of color and his expression screamed horror. He was glued to something over Nate's right shoulder, but a woman's shriek and a *boom* made his ears ring before he could react.

Two more shots reverberated before he processed

what was happening.

A starburst of dark red was born on Angelo's dress shirt, spreading fast. His friend grabbed at his chest and toppled off the barstool.

Nate whirled, but the gunman was already retreating at top speed, a blur of dark clothing. "Son of a bitch!"

People scattered, several with cellphones already pinned to their ears. "I'm calling 9-1-1," a woman shouted.

"Thank you!" He spit curses that rarely exited his mouth, and knelt next to his college roommate. "Angelo! 'Lo, answer me." He shook his shoulder, but the man's eyes were rolled to the back of his head, whites showing, his arms slack at his sides.

Blood dominated his chest.

The only part of his shirt still white was his collar.

"Angelo!"

This time he received a grunt, and hazy dark orbs struggled to focus on his face. Angelo lifted his arm, and Nate grabbed his hand, squeezing.

"C'mon, buddy, stay with me. Medics are on the way."

"N-Nate."

"Shhh, don't talk. Just hold on. You're gonna be fine." He swallowed against the lump in his throat.

Lying through your teeth.

His friend was dying. The knees of Nate's jeans were already soaked with Angelo's blood.

The pool was growing.

"L-l-listen… Pl-please."

"I'm listening." he bent low, his ear right over 'Lo's mouth.

"Caselli."

The word was clear and rocked him to his soul.

"Son of a bitch."

"What the *hell* are you doing here?"

"Nice to see you too, partner." Lee grinned at Downs, setting his coffee on the desk in front of him, since he'd neglected to take it from her hand.

She'd got into the habit of grabbing java for them on the way into the office.

Usually the guy was grateful.

"Go. Home. Dawson."

"No. Way. Downs." Three days off had been enough. She'd been going stir-crazy alone at home, but she wouldn't tell him that.

She sat at her desk after a healthy sip of hazelnut cappuccino, ignoring the burn in her side. Lee pressed the power button and waited for her computer to boot up.

Also ignored the imposing figure of her large partner behind her, even though she could feel the irritation coming off him.

"What do we have going on this morning?" She ensured she was pleasant, as normal as she could manage.

When a good minute had passed and he didn't answer, she spared him a glance over her shoulder.

His pale gaze scorched, and his mouth was a hard

line. Downs tilted his head to one side, crossing his thick arms over his broad chest.

Lee smirked. "You might be a foot taller than me, and twice what I weigh, and you might intimidate the shit out of most people, but *I* am not most people, Clint Downs."

One of his eyebrows shot up. "How are you feeling?"

She swiveled her chair around. *That* was the last thing she'd expected him to say. "Fine. You?" Couldn't quite decipher his sigh.

He shook his head. "You're fixin' to kill me, as you would say."

"Wow that sounds *wrong* when you say it. Please don't. *Ever* again." She laughed and her partner's frame loosened a little. "Oh my God, are you smiling? Is that what passes as a smile for you, partner?"

"Oh leave off, Dawson. Can I say anything to get you to go home?"

Lee pretended to think about it. "Nope. I need to work."

"There are fifteen other people in charge of the same thing you are. *We're* not idiots, you know." He thumbed his chest.

"Did I say you, or any of the others, were? No. *My* need to work is on me. Nothing to do with them."

Downs stared until she had to force herself to sit still.

Evan Roberts popped his head into the office with a knock on the doorframe. "Oh, Dawson, you're here."

"You bet."

"There's a Sergeant Kowalski from NYPD on the phone for you."

"Okay, transfer him to my line. Thanks." Lee sucked in a breath when the phone rang.

Please, let it be work-related.

She'd had a fling with Ryan Kowalski over a year before—not long after moving to New York City. He'd wanted more than she could give. She'd shot him down repeatedly, until he'd finally got the message and stopped calling.

He'd better not be up for round two, because I'm sooo not.

Nate Crane's smiling face flashed into her mind. Lee frowned and gripped the receiver tighter. "Dawson."

"Hey, Lee. How're ya?"

Her heart sank.

Be polite.

"Fine. You?"

"Pretty good. I tried to call your cell..."

I wouldn't have answered your call anyway.

"Oh? Sorry, it's on silent, I guess." She glanced at the screen of her ever-present cellphone.

Yup, two missed calls.

"No worries. Something's come up and I thought you'd want to be in the loop. I know you're still on the Caselli case. Are you familiar with an attorney named Angelo Fiato?"

Work stuff. Thank God.

"Yeah. Hold on, my partner's here." Lee hit the speaker button and set the receiver in its cradle.

"All right. I'll cut to the chase. I'm down at *The Seasons*, the big five-star downtown. Waiting for homicide."

She exchanged a glance with Downs.

"Standing over the body of Angelo Fiato."

"Shit. Witnesses?" her partner asked.

"Yes," Kowalski said.

"What happened?" she asked.

"Gunned down inside the bar, lobby level. One shooter, in and out. No one else was harmed. Just popped him. One to the chest did him in. He didn't have a chance. The guys on the streets will be on the lookout, but you know how these things go. It was professional. They know how to disappear."

"Anybody get a good look?" Downs asked.

"Yeah, one or two," Kowalski said. "We're talking to them. Homicide will want to as well, and I know you will. Everyone's been told they need to stay put."

"Good. Thanks for the heads up. We'll be right there." Lee ended the call and met her partner's eyes.

"So much for being upstate." He shook his head.

"Poor bastard."

Chapter Three

Sergeant Ryan Kowalski was still tall, broad and hot.

When their eyes met, Lee could see he was just as interested in her as before. She bit back a sigh and ignored his obvious perusal.

Nope.

Not even tempted. Not even one little tingle when his blue gaze traveled her frame. Not like when Nate looked at her.

Shit.

She needed to get the Texas Assistant District Attorney out of her head.

Stat.

Sixteen hundred miles and six months since he'd touched her hadn't done the trick so far. Lee hadn't been with anyone since Nate, either.

She hadn't wanted another man.

Her partner stepped up, and she introduced them. Downs stayed close, as if he hadn't missed Kowalski's stare.

She should thank him, but she didn't need his protection.

"Nice to see you again, Agent Dawson."

Lee snorted at his formality, but accepted the sergeant's handshake. "What's changed since we talked?"

"Not much. Detective Reed is running things. Told

him I gave you a call. He's talking to Fiato's friend. The guy saw him go down, but didn't get a good look at the shooter. They're over there." Kowalski gestured, and she glanced over her shoulder.

A tall blond man had his back to her as he talked to an older, dark-haired guy with his head bent.

The detective wrote in a little notebook as he listened, nodding from time to time.

Her heart plummeted to her stomach.

The broad shoulders and tapered waist were familiar. As was the nice ass filling out tight, dark jeans. Cowboy boots visible from a mile away.

No. Can't be.

There were tons of guys with fair hair and a lean, muscular build. Over eight million people in New York City, right?

"Dawson? You okay?" Downs rested his hand on her forearm and squeezed. "You're white as a sheet. Your side bothering you?"

"Her side?" Kowalski asked, brow drawn tight.

"Never mind," Lee barked. She ignored her former lover and her partner and marched to the two men.

" —had on dark clothing. Sorry I didn't get a better look. Someone else saw him. The lady that dialed 9-1-1, I'm pretty sure."

The soft Texas twang made her heart stop and her feet pause, but she pushed forward.

How *dare* he be in New York?

Nate Crane's gorgeous hazel eyes widened when he caught sight of her.

She couldn't look at him.

Lee ignored her zinging pulse and made herself focus on the detective. "Special Agent Lee Dawson, FBI." She thrust her hand out and he shook it.

"Detective Hank Reed."

"Nice to meet you."

"Lee," her attorney whispered.

Her name on his lips was breathless.

A tremor shot down her spine. She clenched her jaw and looked him in the eye. "Counselor."

God, he looked the same. Sinfully handsome. High cheekbones. Gold, green and light brown all wrapped together to make up the most beautiful pair of hazel eyes...ever. His nose was regal, his clean-shaven fair skin giving him a youthful air.

Way hotter than Kowalski.

His body held the defined lean muscle of the swimmer he'd been in high school and college, before he'd pursued a career in the law. Nate Crane was an idealist. He was logical, moral and a hell of a prosecutor.

The best lover she'd ever had.

Memories of them entwined danced into her head and Lee's body warmed. Heat crept into her cheeks.

Do. Not. Go there. Texas is over and done with. No going back now.

"You two know each other?" the detective asked.

She cleared her throat. "Yes. He prosecuted a case I was involved in down in Texas."

Nate's gaze burned her face. *'Is that all?'* it demanded.

"Ah. Something to do with this here?" Reed

gestured to the scene with his pen.

The Medical Examiner's team had arrived and were already hovering over the body with crime scene techs.

"Maybe." Lee glanced at the detective. Refused to look back at Nate. Her stomach jumped.

"Well, you won't hurt my feelings if the FBI is going to take over here," the detective said.

"That's the plan. Thanks for your cooperation, in advance."

"I'll finish gathering statements, grab my partner and get you my initial report by the end of the week."

"Great, thank you." She handed the detective her business card and he nodded before shoving it in his pocket and giving her one of his.

"I'll leave you two to talk."

Please don't.

Reed slipped away, meeting with her partner, who was talking to a petite blonde woman.

"She called 9-1-1."

Nate's voice made her jump.

Lee swallowed hard and made herself look at him. "My partner will get her statement."

Duh. What an idiotic thing to say.

She shifted on her feet. "Wanna tell me what happened?"

"You look good." He moved closer.

She tried not to fidget. Could feel the heat coming off his body. Wanted him even closer. "Let's just keep this business."

"Let's not." His gaze bored into her. "I didn't plan

on seeing you like this, but I *did* plan on seeing you."

"You're a witness now, in my case. Your friend had ties to Caselli, did you know that?"

"He told me."

"Tell me what happened."

"I will. But let's be clear about one thing, Selena Dawson."

"Let's not," she repeated, but Nate didn't stop talking.

"Before you left Texas, I told you we weren't done. This is me *showing* you."

Her gorgeous dark brown eyes widened, but she schooled her expression fast. Squared her shoulders. Lee's locked jaw dared him as they faced off.

His little FBI agent wasn't going to win this one.

Nate wasn't going anywhere.

He bit back a smirk.

Fate was on his side today, despite the loss of one of his best friends. He'd mourn Angelo for a long time. He was determined to do what he could to help get the attorney's killer, whether she—or the FBI—wanted his help or not. She couldn't deny he was a valuable resource. He was familiar with Angelo Fiato *and* Tony Caselli.

Working with Lee—he'd never be *just* her witness—was going to be what they both needed.

His heart skipped into overdrive as their gazes collided again.

She crossed her arms over her generous breasts

and Nate couldn't get the image of her bare in his bed out of his mind.

Nothing had changed for him over the past six months.

He wanted her as much as he ever had. Had planned to see her again. Like he'd said.

"I'm not going into this with you again." Her face tightened. "Especially here. This is my crime scene. My case."

He'd show her how wrong she was.

Nate itched to touch her. Pull her to him and take her mouth. His tongue tingled with the memory of her taste. He sucked in a breath and chided himself to calm. "I'll never be *just* your case, Selena Dawson."

Lee dropped her arms to her sides. "Nate." When her eyes clouded with some unnamed emotion, his stomach fluttered.

It was gone so fast he could've imagined it.

"Lee."

She pursed her lips and shook her head. "Tell me what happened."

Right.

Nate needed to focus on Angelo, anyway. He ran his hand through his hair and replayed the event in his mind. "It was quick. I only saw the guy from the back. Heard the shots and the screams and saw 'Lo fall." Pain burned his throat as it hit him.

The click of a gurney being raised and locked into place caught his attention.

His friend had been placed in a black bag, but the pool of blood still saturated the carpet.

Nate couldn't look away, and his gut clenched. "I guess, with everything, it's only just sunk in for me."

Lee put her hand on his forearm and squeezed, taking a step closer. "I'm sorry you lost your friend."

His breath caught for a different reason, and he screamed at himself to calm down.

Idiot, horrible friend. Think of Angelo, not Lee.

"Thanks. We were roommates, and frat brothers, back in college."

She nodded, her expression serious. "What do you know about him?"

"Cut to the chase. You mean what do I know about Angelo and Caselli?"

"Yes."

"Nothing until today." Nate frowned and shook his head. "His firm got huge fast."

"With dirty money."

"Hey, he was a good lawyer."

Lee's brow furrowed. "Like he didn't know what Caselli was up to? A good lawyer wouldn't deal with scum like that."

"Are all *your* friends perfect?" He watched as more emotions flickered across her face, but she said nothing.

"He didn't cooperate with the FBI until the shit hit the fan."

"Damn. So that's why Caselli had him killed."

She nodded.

"He was telling me someone was ticked at him when the shooter burst in. '*Caselli*' was his last word." Nate winced at his shakiness.

"Oh, Nate. I'm really sorry you had to find out like

this, and see him die."

When Lee took another step toward him, he wanted to yank her into his arms. She was petite—he had a foot on her—but she was warm, and he remembered it well. He made tight fists at his sides, instead. If he touched her now, it'd only piss her off.

She surprised him when she reached for his hand and squeezed.

"Thanks. That means a lot, really." He stopped short of entwining their fingers.

"Dawson." A tall, broad-shouldered guy with a crewcut strode to them and Lee dropped Nate's hand as if he'd burned her. The man noticed, his eyes darting to her as he stopped in front of them.

She cleared her throat and shifted on her feet, opening her mouth before the older man had a chance to speak. "Downs, this is Nate Crane. He was the prosecutor on the Maldonado case a few years back down in Texas, as well as involved with the Marchetti case. He's familiar with Caselli, and an old friend of Fiato. Saw him go down. Nate, this is my partner."

"Clint Downs." The FBI agent stuck his hand out, and Nate shook it.

"Nice to meet you, Special Agent Downs. Cole Lucas has mentioned you a time or two."

"I'm sure." He nodded, one corner of his mouth lifting, making his moustache shift. "How's my old friend?"

Nate smiled. "He's great. Married to my brother's partner. Two kids. Took the shift from FBI agent to small town detective with no problems."

"Still bossy," Lee muttered.

Downs shot a look at her but said nothing.

Nate smirked. No doubt the guy was thinking, *'Look who's talking'*.

"I've talked to Ms. Pressley. She got a look at the shooter, but unfortunately is pretty sure he saw her, too. Roberts is going to take her to the office, finish up, then we need to keep her protected."

Lee nodded.

"I'm headed to the security office. There're cameras all over this place," the older man continued.

"Good deal," she said.

"Hopefully there's a good view of the guy," Nate said. "I'd like to see the footage, if you don't mind."

Lee opened her mouth, but her partner beat her answer.

"No problem with me."

"Thanks."

Her glare burned him, but he flashed a smile and followed her partner out of the lounge.

Chapter Four

Lee's partner hadn't said much after cajoling the hotel's head of security to cooperate.

Reluctant pretty much said it all, but the manager and his officers hadn't refused the huge, dark-haired FBI agent who currently stood over the camera operator's shoulder, studying the moving images on the wall of computer monitors.

Agent Downs had his arms crossed over his massive chest. Even if the guy wasn't being intentionally intimidating, his stance pretty much screamed *'just do what I tell you'*.

Nate snorted.

His cell blared from his pocket and he looked away from the screens in front of him. Pete's photo and number popped up on his phone.

"Are you all right?" his older brother barked even before Nate could say hello.

He stepped into the hallway outside the security office. "Hey, big brother."

A sigh echoed in his ear. "Thank God. What happened?"

"How could you have possibly heard already?"

"Cole. He talked to one of his former teammates today. It came up in passing like it was no biggie. Are you okay? What the hell happened?"

"I'm fine. Angelo's dead, though. Right in front of me."

"Damn, I'm sorry. I know you two were close. I'll try to keep things on the down-low for now, I don't want Mama freaking if she watches national news."

Nate swallowed back a groan. "Right. But a high profile attorney with ties to organized crime getting gunned down, hitman-style, at a five star hotel in New York City is gonna be reported nationally."

Pete's silence lasted a few seconds too long. "Organized crime?"

"Caselli was on 'Lo's client list."

"Shit."

"You're telling me."

"You need to come home, now." The guy's order was firm. "Shit, you can't. You're a witness. Double shit."

"Right. I'm a witness. I'm gonna be fine. Didn't get a good look at the shooter anyway."

"He probably saw you. You know Caselli. This isn't our first or even second rodeo. He always ties up his loose ends."

"Texas isn't any safer than New York, Pete."

His brother said a few more choice words. Including *'fuck'*, which rarely came out of the detective's mouth. He sighed, and Nate pictured his older brother running his hand through his blond hair, like he always did when he was frustrated. "I don't like this."

"Neither do I, but I'm stuck here. I want to help Lee and her partner as much as I can anyways. I've known Angelo for years. I know him best."

"Lee? You've seen her?"

It was his turn to sigh as his stomach fluttered. His brother knew all about his torrid affair with the FBI agent—and how it'd ended. He'd also told Pete he planned to get her back. "Yes."

"And?"

"Went as well as could be expected."

"Crap. I'm sorry, little bro."

"Hey. I'm not out just yet. Now she's stuck with me."

Pete chuckled. "That's my brother." Then he got serious. "Tell her to slap you in a safe house and we'll feel a hell of a lot better."

"We?

"Me, Cole and Andi. And your sister-in-law is pretty damn fond of you, too."

He laughed. "Wow. Married a month and she already goes from Nikki to the ol' sister-in-law."

"Oh, all right, *my wife* then." The pride in his brother's voice made Nate smile, but envy settled in his gut.

He wanted with Lee what his brother had found with the tall, slender redhead.

"Regardless, I don't like that you're all the way up there, witnessed a shooting and lost a friend who happened to be killed by a very bad dude."

"I know, but I'll be fine. Pissed at me or not, Lee and her team will cover my ass. I feel safe with them. Seriously."

"I'd feel better if you had a gun."

"I know it. But don't worry about me. Please. And I agree, *don't* tell Mama."

Pete laughed again. "You got it. I might call Pop to give him a heads-up. Maybe he can keep her from the television."

"And the Internet."

"Crap, I forgot about the iPad."

Nate shook his head and grinned. "Her latest obsession. She knows how to surf the 'net on it."

"Never would've believed it if I hadn't seen it myself. Look, stay safe. I love you, Nate. Call me when you can with updates."

Shock rolled over him. Sure, he knew his brother loved him. But for Pete to say it…

Shit.

His brother was more worried about this situation than their conversation had let on.

He cleared his throat. "I will. Love you, too."

There was a pause before the guy disconnected, but neither of them filled it.

The steady hum of Nate's voice rolled over her when she turned the corner to head to the security office. Lee had followed the directions of the helpful concierge, but her stomach was churning at the news she had to share with her partner…*and* Nate.

Her phone conversation with her boss, Special Agent Olivia Barnes, had gone badly.

Protective custody.

The phrase bounced around in her head.

She'd be *trapped* with Nate.

Evan Roberts was the lucky one. He'd been

assigned to the blonde woman, Savannah Pressley. Liv wanted Lee with Nate. Because she was familiar with the attorney, her boss had said.

She was going to do her best to convince Downs he owed her one, but their boss had settled Nate in *her* lap. Said her partner would be working from the office.

The safe house was ready for their arrival. Roberts and Ms. Pressley would be sent to a separate secure location.

Shit.

"…love you, too."

The three words made her heart skip.

Who did he love?

Six months is a long time.

Maybe he'd moved on. Fallen in love. Lee ignored the pain that seized her gut. It didn't matter anyway.

They'd had a fling.

It'd ended badly.

There was no going back. Besides, if he'd found someone else, would he have got in her face and declared they weren't done?

Forget it. Right. Now. You focus on this case. Work.

Keep him safe so she could send him back to Texas and he could truly be out of her life.

That was what she wanted.

Nate turned and their gazes met. When he smiled, her stomach flip-flopped and her mouth went dry. Lee wanted to bark at him to stop looking at her like that, but the guy was being normal… Friendly.

Don't be a bitch.

He'd lost his good friend today. A smile was an

accomplishment.

"I need to talk to you and Downs." She bit back a cringe, but if he noticed her cracked sentence, he didn't react.

"He's watching video." The attorney thumbed toward the ajar office door behind him.

Lee nodded. "Get anything?"

"Not sure. I stepped out to take a call."

"Ah." She wanted to ask who, but didn't. None of her business. She walked past him, ignoring his familiar heat when she turned to go into the office with 'Security' on the door in white lettering. Her spine tingled and she cursed her traitorous body. The scent of his clean, masculine aftershave tickled her nose. The same as it had always been.

"What's up, anyway?" Nate stopped her entrance with a hand on her arm.

She fought a shiver. "Don't wanna repeat myself." Lee had to break their physical contact. Couldn't deal with the memories it brought back. She tugged and her skin burned when his fingers slipped away. She wanted to beg him to maintain his hold. Pull her into his arms. Kiss her again.

Knock it off, Selena Dawson.

His jaw clenched, but he nodded and stepped out of her way.

Lee entered the office in time to see her victim slip from the stool and Nate rush to his side. Other cameras had caught the shooter's image, but the man was no stranger to keeping his head low.

He wore all black. Ball cap covered his face, low

brim. Oversized dark sunglasses shot any last chance of a good look to hell.

His movements were quick and efficient, but he didn't run on his way out. The son of a bitch was an expert.

"Again," Downs ordered, his gaze glued to a different monitor.

"Damn," Nate's curse was low and full of emotion that made her want to reach for him. He, too, was watching the footage.

Instead, she slid to her partner's side, leaving her ex-lover just inside the doorway.

"One more time, I want to see the exit again. And I need you to burn these for me," Downs told the camera operator.

"I'll have to check with my boss."

"You do that." Her partner scowled and the young guard looked away as he hit rewind.

"We need to talk," Lee said.

Downs glanced away from the screens, one eyebrow up. "You okay?"

No.

"Yup. Case stuff. Just got off the phone with Barnes."

"Okay. As soon as I have our DVDs." His voice rose to make a point to the pimple-faced camera operator, but the kid ignored him, didn't look their way.

He did, however, reach for the phone and dial his boss.

Lee shifted from foot to foot, ignoring the dull ache

in her side. The bullet wound had been shallow; a clean in-and-out, but she wasn't good at following doctor's orders. She'd viewed *'take it easy'* as an ignorable suggestion. Her two mile run that morning was one she probably should've forgone.

"He said okay, so I'll get these burned for you, and label which camera view is which."

"Thanks." Downs shook the guy's hand and guided her away from the bank of monitors. "What's up?"

She tried not to look at Nate as he moved closer.

Both men regarded her with curious expressions as Lee fought for a coherent sentence.

God, I don't want this.

"Spoke to Special Agent Barnes."

"And?" Amusement rippled across her partner's face as he appraised her. He couldn't know *why* she was uncomfortable, but he could see it.

Dammit.

"Roberts is going to take Savannah Pressley to a safe house. His partner will handle things at the office and help him when necessary."

"All right. Good." He crossed his arms over his broad chest. "What else?"

"You and I..." Lee cleared her throat and pretended Nate wasn't standing next to her. Pretended she couldn't feel his eyes on her and the warmth of his lean form. Ignored the skip of her heartbeat. "You and I are in charge of Nate."

"Protective custody as well?" her partner asked.

"Yes." She blew out a breath and rushed the rest.

"Liv said the place I'm supposed to take him to is ready. As soon as we're settled, you can head back to the office. You're supposed to check in later."

Downs looked at Nate, and her pulse thundered in her temples. "I know you're here on vacation and you didn't get a full look at the shooter, but trust me, this is for your own safety."

Her ex nodded and glanced at her, a smile playing at his lips. His expression was smug, and Lee cursed him to hell and back. "Believe me, I understand. We can't take my safety for granted."

Chapter Five

Darth Vader's entrance march sounded and Jeremy made a dive for his phone from the end of his desk.

His partner arched an eyebrow over the pretty witness's head.

He ignored them both and dashed into Downs' and Dawson's shared office. Prayed no one saw him as he enclosed himself in the dark.

"Stewart," he barked.

A deep laugh greeted his ear and Jeremy cursed.

"I've told you not to call me at this number."

Of course, the ringtone had given away who was on the other end of the phone. He shouldn't be surprised the crime boss had oversized balls.

"And I have told *you*, you work for *me*, and not the other way around, *Special Agent*."

He cringed and cleared his throat. "You pay me for information, nothing more."

"I tell you what I pay you for."

Jeremy clutched the cell closer. "I told you where the attorney would be today, did I not?"

Another laugh. "Worried you won't be rewarded?"

"No, never that, not from you."

"Right. I'm glad our arrangement is still satisfactory. I would hate for you to be…disappointed."

Like I have a choice.

"What do you want?" He stopped himself from barking the man's name. He was at the office. Needed to remember that.

"Follow-up information."

"There's nothing to tell."

"Don't lie to me, Special Agent." Caselli was low and deadly, but Jeremy didn't flinch.

"Fifty thousand."

The man laughed long and hard. "Don't try my patience, my friend."

"I'm not your friend."

"How many witnesses?" The man ignored his irritated statement.

"Like I said before, more information equals more money."

"Do I need to remind you I know where you live? I know all about you. I know about your family. Your beloved, poor, cancer-ridden mother. Your beautiful ex-wife. Two daughters. They're gorgeous, like their mother. Even their dog, what's he called? I believe your oldest named him Scout."

Jeremy's heart took a dive for his stomach. "This is between me and you, not them."

"As long as you and I are on the same team, you are correct. Don't double-cross me, Special Agent. I have more resources than you."

"Then why the fuck are you calling me?"

"Everyone needs insider information once in a while."

"Hire an investigative reporter."

Caselli chuckled. "I don't need a reporter. What I

have is better. I have *you*. Now tell me what I need to know."

"I'm not lead on this, and neither is my partner."

"Somehow, you'll get me what I seek. You always do."

And people always die.

"There's video surveillance."

"Have you determined what's on it?"

"No. Like I said, I'm not lead. But when I get a chance, I'll check it out. We'll debrief as a unit, like always."

"You do that."

"Don't call me again," Jeremy warned. "I'll contact you when it's time."

"Are you threatening me, Special Agent?"

"We're done."

He went to end the call, but crime-boss barked his name.

"What?"

"You have not told me what I need to know."

"I told you all *I* know."

Caselli *tsked* as though Jeremy was a kindergartner who'd messed up his alphabet. "You know how I feel about liars, Special Agent. Angelo Fiato lied to me. Look what happened to him."

A terrified shiver shot down his spine. "What do I have to tell you for my money?"

"The truth."

"Like I said, fifty K."

"Done. It will be in the usual drop. Tomorrow morning."

He gripped the back of the chair in front of him until his fingers smarted.

Why had Caselli relented so easily to his outrageous amount? He'd been bluffing—well, sort of. He could always use the money.

"What do you need to know?"

"How many witnesses?"

Jeremy closed his eyes, sweat breaking out on his forehead and dripping down his cheek. "Two."

Caselli laughed long and hard for the second— *irritating*—time. "I think it's time we changed the terms of our arrangement."

Lee scowled as she watched Nate stuff his belongings into a huge black duffel bag.

He was humming.

Humming.

"Hey, can we knock off the *'whistle-while-we-work'*?"

Her ex glanced over his shoulder and grinned. "Why? Afraid I'll start calling you Grumpy?"

"Jesus," she muttered, shaking her head.

"You're short, but I never would have gone straight to dwarf."

She glared.

"You need to take a breather and lighten up." Nate zipped the bag and draped the strap across his torso.

She tried to ignore how the extra weight tightened his shirt and outlined his pecs. "Says the guy who lost his friend today."

His expression sobered as he straightened. "Ouch. Low blow."

Guilt rushed up and she pushed off the wall by the doorway; moved closer. "Sorry. You're right."

Nate reached for her hand, and she couldn't pull away after just being a jerk. She let him entwine their fingers.

"I just want to make the best of our situation. I want to help you catch this asshole."

Lee nodded. "I know. Hafta admit, your input will help."

He smiled and her heart skipped.

She had to clear her throat. "Let's go. Boss said the house is ready."

"My buddies and I rented a place about forty-five minutes north. A big townhouse with five bedrooms," he said.

"Sorry you wasted your money. What's the occasion, anyway?"

"Every January I get together with my friends from Columbia. We swap law war stories, and the married ones complain about their wives." He winked.

Right.

He'd gone to Columbia Law. He'd mentioned his annual trip when they'd been together in Texas. How had she forgotten that?

"Hope you cancelled."

Nate nodded. "I sent emails. Fortunately, they weren't supposed to arrive until Thursday anyway. I got in early to meet with Angelo. Last week, he asked if I could move my flight up. Now I know why." He frowned. "'Lo…was the only local."

"Did you tell them about him?"

"No. I'm not stupid, Lee. I kept it vague, just that something had come up."

"Good. They're not coming anyway?"

"No. But they'll hear about Angelo on the news."

"Right. But you won't be able to take calls."

He sighed.

Lee dropped his hand and glanced around the hotel suite. "Got everything?"

"Just have to grab my suit from the closet, but yeah. Only got this place for one night, so I hadn't really unpacked. The house wasn't ready until today."

She led them out the door after he'd grabbed a garment bag and slung it over his shoulder. "You should've told me you were in town, this place is expensive." It was out without thought.

Nate paused, and his smile was wicked. "Yeah. That would've happened."

Her stomach flip-flopped. "You're probably right. My place is small—not up to your standards, anyway." She smirked.

"Hey, are you calling me a snob?"

"Never."

His place was huge. Had to be thirty-five hundred square feet of sprawling two-story. She'd only visited once, because it was about an hour from Antioch. They'd spent most of their tryst at *The Covington*, the fancy new hotel in the small Texas city.

A vision of them entwined in the big bed made her shiver.

Get your mind out of the gutter.

He stared as if he could read her thoughts, and Lee squirmed.

"Your house is huge is all," she muttered.

Nate shrugged. "Got it for a steal. It was a foreclosure. It's more than I need. For now." He quirked a fair eyebrow, hazel gaze even more intense.

She ignored him, slipping in front of him in the hallway. "Don't watch my ass."

He laughed and she couldn't help the smile that curved her lips, but she wouldn't turn to look at him.

Couldn't.

Because if she looked at him, she'd do something colossally stupid, like kiss him.

Chapter Six

"Where are we going, anyway?" Nate asked when his things were tucked safely in his rental.

They'd opted to take his car. It wasn't like the vehicles that belonged to the Bureau, so they could blend in better. Not so obviously law enforcement.

"I'll drive."

He rolled his eyes, not the least bit surprised about her assertion. "Umm. My car."

"Do *you* know where we're going?" Lee countered.

"I would if you told me. I lived here for several years, remember? I'm familiar with the area."

"Kids, do you need to be separated?" Her partner's question was wrapped in amusement, and his moustache twitched.

She scowled and snatched the car keys from Nate's hand. "Just let me drive."

He let it slide and looked at Agent Downs.

The large man had his arms crossed over his broad chest and he was observing Lee with one dark eyebrow arched. He reclined into the passenger side of his standard-issue, unmarked, navy blue Dodge Charger. The vehicle screamed, '*I'm a cop car*'.

"Let's get moving. I'll follow at a distance and stay alert. When we get to the place, you can run home to get your things, Dawson. I'm sure Crane and I can last without you for a little bit. I'd say go now, but we need to get you secured, Counselor."

They both nodded, then Lee glanced at Nate. "As silly as this might sound, it's necessary. But you're familiar with Caselli's work, so it shouldn't surprise you."

"Hey, no argument from me. I get it. Precautions are necessary. I want to make it home alive and well, not in a box."

She winced, but schooled her expression so fast his stomach flip-flopped. If she cared about what happened to him, could she care *about* him?

He watched her suck in a breath and exchange a few more words with her partner.

When Downs went around to the driver's side of the Charger, Nate got into his rental's passenger seat and yanked on the seatbelt.

Lee's expression was smug when she started the Honda, but she wouldn't turn his way.

"I think you like to fight," he muttered.

She shot him a look, brow knitted. "What?"

"You argue over every little thing. You don't always have to be in control, you know."

"Yes, I do. I have to keep you safe."

"You will." He grabbed her hand and squeezed. "I trust you, Lee. I feel safe with you."

Her cheeks flushed pink and she swallowed.

Nate bit back a groan, burning to kiss her.

"Stop looking at me like that," she whispered.

"Like what?"

A horn blared, and they both jumped. Lee cleared her throat and looked away, grabbing the shifter.

"Impatient ass."

He chuckled and glanced over his shoulder in time to see Downs gesturing for them to move.

The Charger was behind them, waiting for her to back the Accord out.

Nate chided himself for getting lost in her dark gaze and ordered his heart to calm. He thumped his head back into the headrest and closed his eyes.

"We're not going far. Just outside the city."

He didn't answer but lifted his head in time to squint against a clear winter sky as Lee pulled out of the parking garage. He shivered, missing the mild North Texas winter.

The temperature was in the thirties, and more snow was due later that night, supposed to fall up into the morning.

"You cold?" she asked.

"I'm good. But thanks." He watched her eyes dart to the rear-view mirror, as well as discreetly to the side mirrors.

She wasn't checking for traffic — she was absorbing their surroundings.

Downs might've mentioned he was in charge of keeping his eyes peeled, but Lee was alert.

She flexed her fingers as she turned the wheel, straightening her shoulders and repeating her checks.

Nate couldn't stop watching her.

Gorgeous.

Fully in control.

"Do I have something on my face?" she murmured. Her jaw tightened.

His little FBI agent didn't like to be observed.

He smirked. "No. I just haven't seen anything so beautiful since I left Texas."

Lee snorted. "Right. Since when did you become a pick-up line kinda guy?"

Laughing, Nate shook his head. "I'm not. Just stating the truth. You're gorgeous, Lee Dawson."

And I missed you.

"Are you sure you're not cold? This is my second winter here, but I'm still not used to it."

"I'm fine." He let her subject change go. Last thing he wanted to do was argue. "But if you're cold, turn on the heat."

A slight nod was all the response he got as she turned right at a traffic light.

They'd only been in the busy traffic of downtown a few minutes before Lee's attention darted to the rear-view mirror again. "We're being followed."

"Are you sure?" His heart skipped.

"Downs already noticed. Black SUV about three cars back."

"Caselli standard issue," Nate breathed.

Lee went left, slipping between a truck and a car. A horn screamed, but she kept maneuvering the Honda in and out of traffic even after they'd moved out of the city and entered the freeway.

His heart didn't care that she was in complete control. It thundered with every new car she sped by. "A million miles an hour isn't going to help," he complained.

"I wanted to lose him in the city."

"Did you?"

"Not sure. I can't spot him right now, but Downs kept up."

"Could it be FBI? Don't y'all have the same standard-issue black SUVs?"

"Hmm, maybe," she said without looking his way. "Doubt it. Downs and I were the only two from the team on scene."

Nate didn't answer, just gripped the seat with white-knuckled hands.

"Relax, we'll be there soon."

Her voice was calm, and it grounded him, but he closed his eyes again, blocking out the rushing scenery.

"I didn't know you got car sick. You okay?"

No.

"It's not the car. It's…everything about this situation. I take a vacation for the first time in months. I even worked through Christmas this past year, much to my mama's chagrin. Then I see one of the best friends I ever had gunned down. Now someone's after me? I didn't even get a good look at the shooter."

"Nate."

His name on her lips made his heart thunder for a different reason.

Lee stayed locked on him longer than she should've before refocusing on the road. "It'll be okay."

Nate sighed and relaxed into the chair. Three little words, and some of the weight lifted off his chest. He believed her. *Trusted her*, like he'd said before they'd left the parking garage. "I'm glad I'm with you."

Although she didn't answer, the slight upturn of

her luscious mouth was enough.

For now.

They didn't talk for the remainder of the drive, but she kept checking to see if they'd lost the black SUV. She pursed her lips every time her gaze darted. If she'd spotted something, she didn't mention it.

Like she would, stupid.

After his little soliloquy, she probably thought he couldn't handle it.

Not very macho of you, Nate Crane.

He snorted.

"You say something?"

"Nope."

The click of the turn signal filled the car as Lee exited the highway, and Nate took a moment to look around.

They were in New Jersey now.

She pulled into the vast parking lot of an apartment complex.

Surprise rolled over him as she followed a curve. It narrowed to a road that led behind the first and second rows of buildings.

Lee slowed the Honda, rolling to a stop in front of the biggest building on site. It had three rows of three balconies climbing up the front of the brick façade, as well as sizable enclosed porches on the ground level.

If the backside was the same, it'd have to house at least eighteen apartments. It was farthest from the road, with woods surrounding it. Somehow it seemed secure, and separate from the rest of the place.

"Apartments?"

"The Bureau owns this whole building."

"Ah. People actually live here?"

"Yes. Undercover agents from time to time, as well as transfers. I stayed here the month before I found my place in the city."

"But… It's safe? Secure?"

Lee nodded and Nate stared.

If she was irritated by his questions, he couldn't tell.

"Why is the roof almost…flat?"

"Indoor pool. It's heated. There's also some really nice workout equipment up there. Locker rooms, too. You know, the Bureau wants us fit and comfortable." Amusement rippled across her beautiful face.

He had trouble focusing on her sarcasm. "So, it's not common knowledge who owns the place?"

"Nope. I'm sure it's a cover of some sort. The government is good at that kinda shit. As far as the rest of the complex is concerned, *Building F* is just like the rest, just with double the units. C'mon, let's go."

When Nate looped his duffel's strap over his body, Agent Downs came striding across the parking lot. He must've parked the Charger in front of the next closest building.

The big man shook his head and jogged to close the distance to them.

Nate stood by Lee at the trunk of the rental car.

"I don't like this," Downs said, running a hand through his jarhead-style buzz cut.

"I'm pretty sure we lost them." She crossed her arms over her breasts and Nate tried not to stare.

"I wish I could've gotten a better look." Her partner shook his head.

"Nate made a good point. It could've been a Bureau vehicle."

He frowned. "As much as I'd like to believe that, I don't buy it. But that, at least, I can confirm. When I get back to the office I'll check into it. They were with us for a while before *and* after you played Nascar."

Lee smirked.

"So, there's no guarantee?" Nate asked.

The man's crystal gaze settled on him. "Right. It was either someone not all that great at tailing, since we lost them so easily, or we weren't followed at all."

"Knowing how to tail someone is Caselli one-oh-one," his ex remarked.

Downs sighed. "I agree."

"Just let me know what you find out when you look into the FBI vehicle possibility." Lee reached into the backseat and grabbed the garment bag containing Nate's suit. She folded it to get a better grip, ignoring his protest that he'd carry it.

"I'll keep you posted. Let's get Crane inside." Downs gestured for them to head into the building.

She tugged his jacket when Nate made a go for the elevator, nodding toward the stairwell.

The jog up to the third floor was a blur. The FBI agents kept him moving his feet—all three of them silent. Both looked around, cataloguing every detail, and they ran into no one.

Nate's skin crawled.

If this place is safe, and the FBI owns it, why are they so twitchy?

They put him between them as they arrived at apartment three-twenty-four.

The reality of his situation sank in as he felt the heat coming off Downs' big body at his back.

This is real. Your life is in danger.

Lee faced the door, quickly punching a code into a number pad below the door handle. She breathed an audible sigh as soon as the three of them spilled into a sizable living room.

"You guys freaked me out more coming up here than the drive in. Worse than the threat of being followed," Nate admitted.

His duffel slipped from his hand to the floor with a *thud*.

The older guy smirked. "Sorry. We didn't want to run into anyone, FBI or not."

"Ah."

"Liv and the team are the only ones who know your location." Lee unzipped her brown leather bomber jacket, but didn't slip it off. "The master's the farthest room down the hall. You take it. I'll take one of the smaller bedrooms."

"Run home and get your things, Dawson." Her partner spoke before Nate got a chance.

"Good thing is I can keep an eye out on the way back into the city. Maybe determine if we really had a tail."

Downs nodded. "Sounds good to me." He looked at Nate. "Get comfortable, Crane, you'll be here for a while."

Nate tried not to groan.

"So what did you do to my partner?" Downs flipped through channels on the big screen as if he hadn't just asked an invasive question.

The apartment was fancy — full-sized kitchen with table and chairs, as well as a formal dining room right off it. The living room had two oversized recliners and every video game system known to man to go with the huge television. A teenage boy's dream.

Nate hadn't spent much time in the master suite yet, but the attached bathroom was spa style, walk-in shower with *three* showerheads. It even had a separate Jacuzzi tub.

He'd grumbled about taxpayer dollars, and Lee's partner had chuckled.

She'd been gone about twenty minutes, but had assured them she wouldn't be gone more than two hours. She'd even promised to cook dinner.

He spared the man a glance, his stomach fluttering. "What?"

Downs didn't look at him, but one eyebrow shot up. His posture was relaxed, large frame reclined into the plush maroon couch, long legs stretched out in front of him. He bent one knee and perched his boot on the edge of the coffee table in front of them. Somehow, even though his big body was loose, the FBI agent was still intimidating. "Okay, I'll sit here and pretend I'm stupid."

A laugh escaped Nate and he shook his head.

"You're not stupid."

Clear blue eyes were aimed right at him. "Then?"

"I'm just surprised you're asking is all. She sure as hell wouldn't want me airing her—our—dirty laundry."

"Ah. So *you're* the reason she came back from Texas different?"

"Different?"

The FBI agent sat up, nodding. "Dawson was never talkative, but *loner* gained a capital *L* after she came back. Figured it wasn't case-related. Of course, my tight-lipped partner won't tell me a damn thing."

"Doesn't surprise me."

"She's reckless."

Nate blew out a breath. "That doesn't surprise me, either."

"She's gotten worse in the last six months. Like she doesn't have anything to live for."

Shock washed over him, and pain settled in his gut.

My fault?

Who'd been left with a broken heart?

"Damn."

Downs stared, boring into Nate. "You care for her."

"Yes." He didn't bother denying it.

"Good." The man gave a curt nod and turned back to the TV, saying nothing more.

Nate smiled slowly as the approval of the FBI agent settled in.

They didn't speak, but it didn't bother him.

The guy channel-surfed for a while before finally settling on an all-sports network. A highlights show predicting who'd win the Super Bowl flashed picks and the season's best moments. The announcers had a healthy debate about their favorite teams.

"She needs something to live for," Downs broke the silence.

He startled on the edge of the couch.

What could he say to that?

He'd give *anything* to be Lee's reason to live.

Her past was like a horror movie. And she'd kick his ass if she found out Nate had done his homework after she'd crushed him in Texas.

How much did her partner know?

Six years ago, Lee had lost her husband and young son in a car accident. They'd been killed by a drunk driver.

The bastard perpetrator was rotting in jail.

The deaths of Russell and Dylan Dawson were his third offence.

Nate wanted to visit him just to beat the shit out of him.

His ex-lover had quickly turned to alcohol, jeopardizing her job at the FBI when she'd received a DWI his own office had swept under the rug.

The officer's dash cam video Nate had open-records requested had revealed a Lee he didn't know. Belligerent and angry, she'd flaunted her FBI status all the way to jail. Had almost fought with the cop.

He suspected the charge's disappearance and her sudden transfer out of state were the only things that'd kept her employed with the Bureau.

Someone had gone to bat for her. He hadn't figured out who. Perhaps his own boss, the District Attorney, but why?

Lee had been placed on probation, and the judge's orders had included treatment, completing a twelve step program.

Did she still go to meetings?

"Nothing to say?" Downs' deep, gravelly inquiry made him jump again. When their gazes brushed, the FBI agent's moustache twitched as if he was fighting a smile.

"I suppose I can't tell you it's none of your business?"

The man laughed. "It's not. God knows, she'd threaten me at gunpoint if she knew I'd broached the subject."

"Right." Nate grinned.

"Well?"

"Like you said, I care about her. You do, too, it seems."

He nodded. "You can't be partners with someone for over a year and not feel something. She's aloof, and I don't know her as well as some of the guys I've worked with over the years, but I know she always has my back. So yeah, I care about her."

"I'm glad she has *you* at her back."

"One day she's going to get me shot in the ass."

"Reckless." The word rolled off Nate's tongue like it had from her partner.

Downs appraised him. "I won't pry. Just don't give

up on her, okay?"

"I won't."

I came here to get her back.

But he wouldn't tell her partner that.

His answer seemed to satisfy the agent, and Downs turned his full attention back to football highlights.

Nate felt awkward, fidgety. "What about you?"

"Put in twenty with the Marines before I joined the FBI. Married, two girls, eight and ten."

"Semper Fi," he whispered.

Downs smirked. "You?"

"Nah." He shook his head. "My dad's older brother. He was killed in Vietnam. Pop hit the police academy instead. I'm the only male in my family that didn't do either."

"I won't hold it against you."

He stared. Lee's partner sounded even, no hint he'd been joking.

Then the man smiled. "I like you, Nate Crane, even if you are a lawyer. I hope my partner keeps you around."

Chapter Seven

She was going out of her way to avoid him—eye contact, and most definitely touch. Even the barest brush from his hand made her jump away as though he was a leper.

It was driving Nate crazy.

Downs had left not long after Lee had returned to the apartment with her things. The big man had declined the offer to share dinner with them, and Nate had watched her deposit her things in the bedroom closest to the end of the hallway—also the front door—with an amused expression.

She'd picked the room farthest away from the master suite where he'd sleep.

He was torn between hurt and laughter. Perhaps a little insult, too. Did she think he'd pounce on her? As much as he wanted to, his woman *was* armed.

Nate sat across from her at the small table and willed Lee to look up at him as she ate the food she'd prepared.

She wouldn't.

Awkwardness settled over them and he swallowed back a groan with the next bite of delicious *carne asada* she'd prepared. Nothing to do with the quality of their meal.

He'd never felt uneasy around her. Their time had always been spent in light-hearted fun. Laughter. Kisses. Making love. Never the seriousness that surrounded them now.

Despite the fact he was in danger, he wanted things the way they'd been between them.

He forked some meat and let the sauce roll around on his tongue. Damn, she was a good cook. She'd joked about making a Mexican dish, which happened to be his favorite. Lee had assured him it came with the heritage.

"Do you think Downs'll call tonight and let us know what he found out about us being followed?"

Her head shot up, eyes wide. As if she'd forgotten he was there.

Ow.

Nate fought the urge to rub away the ache in his chest.

Lee took a drink of water and set her cup down with too much vigor. Clear liquid sloshed as the glass wobbled.

He made a go for it at the same time she realized it was about to topple over.

Their fingers bumped.

She yanked her hand away as his grip encircled the rim. Steadied it on the table.

"You gotta stop that." It tumbled out unplanned.

Her eyes went even wider. "St-stop what?"

He frowned. "Acting like my touch burns you. It's insulting. I'd never hurt you."

She looked away from his face and back. "Sorry," she muttered.

Nate sighed and shook his head. "Don't worry about it. I'm sorry you'd rather be somewhere other than with me."

"I didn't say that."

"You don't have to *say* it."

Shock rolled over him when Lee reached for his hand and squeezed. Her touch wasn't unwelcome.

Nate entwined their fingers, daring her to pull away. When she didn't, his heart skipped.

"I'm sorry. My mind is going a million miles an hour. This...case is getting to me. I want to break Caselli's organization—really *break* it—so bad. When I think we have a handle on it and the end seems in sight, the shit hits the fan."

"I get it. And now I'm mixed up in it, too. More than I ever was when I prosecuted Maldonado's murder cases in Texas."

Lee nodded.

They sighed at the same time, but she maintained his gaze.

Nate ordered himself not to slip into her eyes. "Thanks for dinner, this is good." He loosened his shoulders when she smiled and he couldn't help but smile back.

"Not too hot for you? I like it spicy."

He bit back his instinct to tease Lee about *her* being spicy. It'd just piss her off. "Hell, no. I'm a Texas boy," he said instead.

To emphasize his point, he grabbed a whole jalapeño and popped it into his mouth. Lee had cut the ends off, so he didn't have to worry about a stem. A slow burn started as he chewed, but he loved the flavor bursting on his tongue. The seasoned beef only made it better.

She grinned. "Couldn't forget that. It's my favorite thing about you."

Nate paused and his stomach flip-flopped.

Act natural. She meant nothing by that.

He winked, and Lee's grin widened.

"Anyway, you asked about Downs. Yeah, he'll call if he found anything, but most evenings he goes off grid. I only bother him in an emergency."

"Ah. He did mention he's married."

"Right. Total family man. Married kinda late, after the military. Kids are little, and he spends all the time he can with them. Great girls, too. I love his wife."

"Total opposite of you, huh?"

"What's that supposed to mean?" Lee snapped.

"Nothing. Just that you never go off grid." His head spun. The scowl she wore took him off guard from the casual direction of their conversation.

"Doesn't mean he's not dedicated."

"I didn't say it did." Nate put both palms up. "Look, I didn't mean to upset you."

She glared then looked down at her plate. Lee stabbed a piece of beef and pushed it into her mouth. Wouldn't look at him, turning her face away as she chewed and swallowed.

"I'm sorry, Lee."

His FBI agent didn't answer.

The rest of their meal was heart-achingly silent.

Nate called himself every name in the book for putting his foot in his mouth.

But what exactly did I say? Why'd she get

so…defensive?

He'd been trying to compliment her, not insult her or her partner. He looked up when she shoved her chair back from the table and popped to her feet.

Still wouldn't look at him, even as she gathered utensils, plates and her empty glass from the table. Lee made it to the sink and turned on the water. Her every action was jerky and stiff.

He sighed and grabbed the bag of tortilla chips, then reached for the bowl she'd poured some in so they could have chips and salsa.

Nate would help her clean up, and maybe salvage their evening.

"I'll get that," she said even before he could take the clip from the plastic bag.

"I want to help — you cooked."

"I'd prefer if you didn't. It'll be quicker. I don't want you in my way."

Ouch.

Like he was a little kid. "Lee—"

"Just… I want to be alone, Nate." Lee glanced over her shoulder, meeting his gaze for the first time. Her full mouth was a hard line.

Salvage their evening?

Yeah right.

What he'd said had obviously hurt her, but the apology fizzled out on his tongue before it could pass his lips.

Where was the constant amusement he'd got so used to when she was in Texas?

She was a jokester like his brother. A witty

wisecracker. Always wore a smile and a smartass remark.

The woman before him was a different person.

Do you know her at all?

Her partner's words about her being a loner haunted his thoughts.

Nate ached for Lee. Wanted to hold her. Kiss her. Wipe that look off her face.

Defeat washed over him. Nothing he could say would help right now. But he *could* give her what she'd asked for.

Space.

He cleared his throat so he wouldn't choke. "I'll be in the living room."

Lee sucked in a breath.

He was gone.

She'd been a total bitch. "Good job, Selena Dawson." The whisper made her cringe when it greeted her ears.

She knew *exactly* why what Nate has said hit home. But *he* didn't. He couldn't.

He hadn't deserved her biting his head off. She was the one who'd called her partner a family man. His response had been an innocent observation.

It wasn't like she'd explain herself, anyway.

Lee never told anyone about Russ and Dylan. Especially ex-lovers.

Family.

Who knew it was such a visceral word?

She snorted and shook her head.

Anyone who's lost them, that's who.

"Fuck me," she said, clenching her jaw until her teeth smarted. Refused to cry at the safe house. She hardly ever cried anyway.

She needed to stop thinking about what she'd lost and *start* thinking about her case.

Protecting Nate.

Getting Caselli, investigating *and* solving her case *while* keeping her attorney safe, actually.

She needed to get with Downs. Lee needed to text him to see what he'd discovered, if anything. They needed to determine if they'd been followed.

Compromised.

Shit, she didn't even want to contemplate it. However, it was prudent to consider. If they *had* been followed, Nate was a sitting duck.

They'd have to move him to another location ASAP.

She made a mental note to check in with Roberts and Stewart, too. See if they'd made it to their location free and clear. If either of her fellow agents suspected *they'd* been tailed, then all four of them needed to compare notes and move their charges. Savannah Pressley was their best chance at identifying the bastard. She'd seen him from the front.

Lee squared her shoulders and shut off the faucet. She bustled around the kitchen, putting away leftovers and starting the dishwasher.

Planning always made her feel better.

If only she could get out of facing Nate in the living

room when she was through. Owed him an apology even if she wouldn't say *why*.

He shot off the couch as soon as she entered the room. "Sorry." The apology was rushed, and his gorgeous eyes were wide, sincere.

Her heart hit overdrive and she shook her head. "Sorry I snapped at you."

"It's okay." Nate came to her side and grabbed her hand.

Lee made the mistake of looking into his face and stilled, unable to pull her fingers out of his. She was poised to order him to stop looking at her that way. Stop touching her. Stop everything.

But when Nate lowered his head, *she* closed the distance between their mouths.

On a groan, she went to him, her breasts pushing into his chest even before she stretched to wrap her arms around his neck.

He deepened the kiss, rubbing his tongue against hers. He pulled her closer, squeezing her ass with both hands and rocking his pelvis against her. Nate was already hard, his erection evident, and her sex throbbed in response.

God, it's been too long.

She moaned and kissed him harder. Lee rocked her hips into him, wanting him to know she wanted him as much as she ever had. Wanted him to read her mind. Know she was sorry for more than just snapping at him about things he didn't know.

Lee cared about the Texas ADA.

Wait.

No.

You can't.

She put her hand to his chest and shoved. "No, Nate. I'm not doing this." She panted, her whole body a live wire for him.

He still lit her up from the inside out.

With one kiss. Made her *feel* more than any man ever had.

Kissing him was the same— No, it was better.

Desire unfurled low and hot, and she struggled to breathe. To forget. Fought the urge to move back to him and let him take her mouth again.

"Why?" Nate put his hand on the wall as if he needed to steady himself. His chest heaved as he sucked in air. His cheeks were flushed with color and his mouth open.

Lee shivered when his tongue darted out to moisten his bottom lip. She swallowed. Hard. Shook her head. "Just…not going there."

"Why, Lee?" He grabbed her shoulders, but he didn't hurt or scare her.

He forced her backwards until she hit the wall outside the kitchen. Nate pressed forward, trained on her like prey. He dipped his head low as if he would kiss her again, but stopped, lips hovering millimeters over hers.

She gasped, her heart kicking up a notch. "It's…different." The hesitation was forced, cracked.

"How?" His warm breath was minty, tickling her mouth, her cheeks.

Her lips parted of their own accord and she

struggled for coherent thought. He was too close, and she wanted him. Seared for him. "H-h-ow?" Her repetition fell out fragmented.

Nate put one palm flat to the wall above her head, and the other at her waist. His chest wasn't touching her breasts like it had been when he'd kissed her, but she could feel every inch of his body as if they were melded together.

Lee ached for him.

"How is now different than when we were together in Texas?" His voice dropped, but his tone was even, calm.

In complete control.

Somehow, it enflamed her even more.

"Nothing's changed except venue. We were only fucking, remember? Can't we *fuck* in New York?" he said what she'd flung at him with a straight face.

A flush lit her from head to toe and she trembled. She'd hurt him when she'd said it to him the day she'd left Antioch. She'd hurt herself, too.

Because it was a damn lie.

When he'd told her he felt something for her, he thought they could make a go of a real relationship, she'd had to get him away from her. Had to make him change his mind — put him in check.

Lee didn't need a reason — then or now — to admit the unwanted feelings Nate brought out in her. She'd had six months to get over him.

Yeah, that'd worked.

"Nate." She meant to shout, scream, order him to move away, but his name came out as a croak. Strained.

Wanton.

"Lee." His mouth brushed hers. Tender. Soft.

An inquiry.

Lee fought the urge to close her eyes. Agony, confusion, guilt, desire—all rushed her at the same time, making her head spin. It took all she was made of to turn her face away.

His second kiss landed on her cheek.

"Don't, please." Once again, the demand came out as a whisper.

Nate stilled. He searched her face when she managed to look at him again. His jaw was tight, expression unreadable.

And there you go, you hurt him again. What a winner you are, Selena Dawson.

"You still want me, Lee." This was even lower.

A tremor slid down her spine. What could she say?

If she lied, he'd call her on it.

Nate was an excellent body language interpreter. He'd told her once he pretty much detected deceit for a living. It made him a damn good prosecutor, but a crappy former lover. He was too in tune with her.

"Don't tell me what I want."

He smirked. "I don't have to. Your body is screaming at me. *For me.*"

Like he read my mind.

He dragged two fingers down her bare forearm to her wrist. Nate caressed her knuckles and squeezed her hand.

Goosebumps rose and she shivered. Both reactions she couldn't hide from him. "No."

"No? I see it. Straining nipples. The rise and fall of your gorgeous breasts. You're panting. Flushed cheeks, swollen lips. I see you tremble and beg for my touch. You can't hide it, Selena Dawson. You. Want. Me."

Nate's hand fell to his side, but he didn't have to touch her. His words rolled over her body like a caress.

Lee bit her lip so she wouldn't moan. Glued her back to the wall so she wouldn't lean in to him. Arch and rub her aching nipples against him. "Don't tell me what I want." She put more force behind second denial.

Like that would help.

"Get out of my way before I knock you on your ass." She buried her shoulder in his chest and shoved.

Air whooshed out audibly as he stumbled backwards.

She whirled on him, glaring. Her body screamed a protest, but she ignored it, mustering all the anger she could.

He'd put her in a corner, backed her into a wall, literally.

Made her lose control.

Fuck. That.

"When I say *no*, I mean it," Lee barked.

Nate shook his head. "You're a liar." He mirrored her now. Gone was the calm she'd seen moments before.

Rage roiled her gut and boiled over. She made two tight fists, planted them at her sides so she wouldn't hit him. She wanted to scream. Shout. Tell him how wrong he was.

If you do, you prove him right.

She growled and narrowed her eyes. Then turned on her heel and fled to the bedroom she'd picked, calling herself a coward the whole way.

Chapter Eight

Nate cursed under his breath and whipped the towel off the rack in the master bathroom. He yanked up his swim trunks, ignoring his half-hard dick. With a groan, he adjusted himself to a more comfortable position. His cock throbbed but he wasn't even tempted to find release with his hand.

He left the room open when he was through. When he'd made it into the hallway, he glared at the closed door to the bedroom she'd hidden herself away in.

She ran from me.

Lee could stay in there all night as far as he was concerned.

She was lying to him, to herself.

The hurt in those dark orbs had told him what he'd said had hit home, but for the first time she'd shut him down instead of rising to his challenge.

Of course, his little FBI agent wouldn't admit she had feelings for him — back home or now.

Her eyes spoke of…something.

Nate's stomach jumped. He wouldn't read into it — couldn't. He'd been crushed by her already. "If you're afraid of getting hurt, why did you bother coming here?" The statement in his head made its way out of his mouth and he straightened his shoulders.

Pete had told him it would be the greatest risk of his life. His older brother had reminded him it'd be worth it in the end. But the guy had won — got the girl.

What if Nate *couldn't* because Lee didn't feel the same?

He sighed and shook his head. Needed to blow off some steam. A dozen hard laps in the pool should do it.

Tell her you're stepping out, his mind chided, but the hurt in his heart won out.

Screw it.

Let *her* find out he'd left if she gave a damn.

Cool air greeted him when he exited the apartment. A chill crawled down his spine and Nate regretted his attire of only flip-flops and shorts. The towel over his shoulder did nothing for winter's bite in the unheated hallway. A reminder that he was far from home.

He surveyed the wide corridor, all the apartment doors. No one in sight. If there were cameras, they weren't overt. He jogged to the elevators. Couldn't be certain how many floors were between the third and the pool.

The question was answered when he stepped inside the mirror paneled elevator. He punched the button labeled '*Pool*' and sighed.

What was he going to do about Lee?

Having her stuck with him wasn't supposed to end in arguments after stolen kisses.

"What did you expect?" His own scorn made him cringe.

But what *had* he expected?

For Lee to rush into his arms, declare she loved him?

If she felt that way, she would've never broken his

heart on her way out of Texas.

Dammit, Nate. Grow a pair.

He yanked one of the glass doors to the pool entrance open with more force than necessary. The sharp corner of the long handle caught the side of his hand and bit his skin.

"Shit." Nate inspected the burning spot. Blood seeped from a small cut. Nothing serious, but the chlorine of the pool water would sting like a bitch.

He didn't care. Maybe physical pain would counteract the agony in his chest.

Humidity from the vast pool wrapped around him like a cape. The familiar scent of chemicals and mugginess brought back memories.

He closed his eyes, hearing the rush of the crowd at many a competition. Nate had been a Longhorn, burnt orange and white all the way.

Full scholarship for his undergrad at the University of Texas at Austin because he'd been a hell of a swimmer. Could've made the Olympic team at one point, but he'd turned down the opportunity to attend try-outs after earning the spot.

He loved swimming, competition, but the law had always been his passion. So he'd completed his four-year degree in three and had made the decision to come to New York before the acceptance letter from Columbia Law had even been cool from the heat of a Texas summer afternoon in his parents' mailbox.

Nate had only gone up from there. Valedictorian of his class, and hired as a county prosecutor in the DA's Office at the tender age of twenty-four.

Winning his first case on his own—a horrific double murder—had been the start of the fame in his office, and had sped him to the top of the podium. The District Attorney, Dean Foreman, his boss and mentor, had seen him as the star of the office.

Now a lead prosecutor at thirty-two, he didn't care about recognition or prestige, not really. Growing up had shed his need for such feelings. It all boiled down to justice for the victim and putting the bad guy away. He thrived on it. What was good. Right. His career.

He slipped out of his flip-flops and dropped the towel on a lounger, then shook out his arms and jumped in place. He'd neglected to hit the locker room for a rinse, but this was about blowing off steam, not having a proper workout-swim.

Nate went to the deep end and jumped in the water, banishing all thought.

No Lee. No work.

No dwelling on the sadness of losing Angelo. Not even fears of Caselli and all the man was capable of.

He swam down, letting the water caress his body as he sliced through it, traveling to the bottom of the twelve foot depth. Wanted to touch the bottom. Feel the roughness of the textured surface with both hands.

Maybe it would help reality wash away.

Put him back to simpler times, when he'd thought he'd known everything. When he'd had a naïve outlook on life.

Before he'd been crushed by what he wanted most.

"Nate?" She hollered at the encroaching panic to leave her the hell alone when he didn't answer her second or third calls.

Lee had pissed him off. Hurt his feelings. She didn't blame him for ignoring her.

She made her way into the master bedroom. His duffel was on the bed, open. The green shirt and jeans he'd worn all day lay next to his bag on top of the black comforter. Cowboy boots on the floor, one standing and the other on its side.

Was he in the shower?

But it was quiet—too quiet—and the bathroom door was open.

When she'd searched the whole apartment and failed to find him, terror came back full force. Visions of him lying bloodied and broken danced into her head, then morphed to a twisted SUV in the middle of a Texas four-lane state highway late at night.

Six years ago.

Glass everywhere.

The scents of burnt rubber and engine oil were real, in front of her face, like yesterday. Steam rolled off both vehicles.

Cops everywhere.

She'd flashed her FBI ID. But as soon as the first detective had realized who she was, he'd tried to get her away from the scene.

Lee had started screaming even before the Medical Examiner's van made scene. Knees had buckled and she'd hit the pavement. Ripped her pants and a rock broke the skin, but she didn't give a shit.

Dylan and Russ...

Some local cop she didn't know had wrapped his arms around her and hauled her to her feet, but numbness had taken over her by then.

"It's going to be okay, Special Agent."

The lie hadn't given comfort, because her gut had told her it *wasn't* going to be okay. It *hadn't* been okay since that night.

Until Nate.

Lee shook herself as her whole body quivered. "No." She cleared her throat. "No!" The denial was a shout this time.

The six-year-old memory melted into the background, and she panted until her breathing regulated.

She scanned the living room of the large apartment. Big screen TV, matching maroon furniture—couch, loveseat and two recliners. Dark wood coffee and end tables.

No Nate.

Eerie silence burned her ears and her heartbeat kicked up all over again.

"Where the hell is he?" Lee's hand hovered over the Glock at her waist. She ran to her bedroom and grabbed her small rolling suitcase. Ripped the zipper open and grabbed her backup pistol, a smaller version of her duty weapon.

She perched her foot on the trunk at the end of the bed and strapped her ankle holster on. Yanked her jeans down over it, commanding herself to calm.

Sucked in a breath, then another.

He couldn't have left on his own. Nate wasn't stupid. He, too, was familiar with Caselli's proclivities, so he couldn't be far, either.

Maybe he'd gone for a walk.

"No," she whispered.

The pool.

He'd gone up to the swimming pool. Nate had been a swimmer in high school and college. Swimming was a part of his normal workout, even now.

God, please let him be up there.

Lee was torn between relief and anger. He hadn't told her he was leaving the apartment. She looked for a note in the living room and kitchen.

Nothing.

She snorted.

Do you blame him?

Ignoring her conscience, she bolted out into the hallway, yanking the apartment door shut with a *thud*. She jogged to the elevator, her stomach somersaulting on the aggravating two floor ride.

She shut down the *'what-ifs'* churning through her head. Disregarded the shaking in her limbs and the shortness of her breath. She could ream him all she wanted later. Had to find him first.

Lee encountered no one as she walked down the long corridor to the pool.

Artificial light reflected off the glass double doors. She opened the one on the right, the splash of water greeting her ears even before she saw his long, lean form slicing through the water.

She tore her eyes off Nate, surveying the vast area.

No one visible. Her gaze darted to the entrances to the locker rooms. Quiet. Still nothing.

Good.

They were alone.

The pool was large, three different depths, with two diving boards at the end. There were lounging areas, picnic tables, as well as two covered hot tubs on the far end of the room.

It was dim, no overhead lights were on, but the underwater lighting inside the pool made the water glimmer, a different hue denoting each depth.

Nate was in the deep end making long strokes on the surface of the water. He disappeared below as he turned his body to go the other direction.

Laps.

He was swimming back and forth, going fast.

Humidity made her shirt damp, but the room was warm, had an inviting feel. However, safety was an illusion, even in a federally-owned building.

His skin glowed golden because of the pool lights, and Lee couldn't look away as he moved up and down the deep end. He hadn't seen her yet, but her feet were frozen. She couldn't move closer. Didn't want to leave, either.

Nate disappeared again as he flipped around, but he was swimming toward her now. He slowed in the water, then made his way to the side of the pool, head and shoulders bobbing up and down. "Lee?" His voice echoed in the cavernous room.

"You left." Instead of the accusation she'd intended, the phrase was a cracked whisper.

He didn't answer, but pushed himself up and out of the pool, water flowing off him as he walked to her.

Rivulets played around his pecs, running to his trim waist, and Lee swallowed against the sudden lump in her throat.

His sparse golden hair was soaked and flat to his chest, but she trailed down, and she shivered at the small strip of tight curls dividing his defined abs. It disappeared into the waistband of his swim pants.

Her fingers itched to touch him.

Yellow trunks were plastered to his body, outlining powerful thighs, hugging his package.

She tried not to look there. Tried not to remember what he'd felt like. Tasted like. How he'd made her combust when he'd been moving in and out of her.

"Lee."

She looked into his eyes. The emotion staring back at her made her whole frame shake, but she ignored what she couldn't acknowledge and tried to glare. "Don't leave like that again."

"I'm sorry. I was angry. I'm not sorry I came here, but I should've told you."

Lee shook her head. "I'm supposed to protect you. I can't do it if you disappear."

"I didn't disappear. I knew *you'd* know where I went." The ghost of a smile played at his lips and twisted her stomach. "You know me well."

She didn't deny it. She did. And it was killing her. "Nate, this is serious."

"I know. I didn't leave the building."

"It doesn't matter."

"You said the FBI owns this building."

"So?" Lee made a cutting gesture with her hand. "Agents *undercover* crash here. Who knows who could be around? Sometimes cases have to come home, too."

Nate sighed, shoving his wet hair back. "I didn't run into anyone else. Did you?"

"Doesn't matter, like I said."

His shoulders sank. "I don't want to fight with you. It gets us nowhere."

"You said you understood."

"What?" He arched a fair eyebrow.

She frowned. "You said you understood what had to be done because of Caselli."

"I do."

"Then let me do what I need to do to protect you."

"I plan on it. I am."

"That doesn't include taking off."

"Lee, I said I was sorry for not telling you."

Hands on her hips, she glared. "Doesn't. Matter. Promise me you won't take off again. Getting mad will happen. God knows, you piss me off."

Nate smirked. Then laughed. "*I* piss *you* off?"

She fought a smile. The look on his face was gorgeous, his laugh infectious. "Yes." She bit her lip to keep the giggle inside.

He growled and grabbed her, pinning her to his wet chest.

"Hey! Let me go!" Her protest was weak, and they both knew it.

"You need to loosen up." His mouth hovered over hers, and Lee's breath caught when he didn't kiss her.

"You're getting me wet."

Nate lifted his head and grinned. "Not touching that."

I wish you would.

Lee searched his face, but no words would come.

"Come swim with me," he whispered.

"W-w-w-what?"

He brushed his lips over hers in a tease that wasn't nearly enough.

Her libido kicked up and she fought the urge to grind against him.

"Let's get in the water. It's warm."

"I don't have a suit."

Nate waggled his eyebrows and beamed. "You don't need it."

Chapter Nine

Jeremy buried his hands in his hair and tugged until pain made his temples ache. He stared at the forty caliber Beretta lying on the bed of the safe house. Hiding out in the back bedroom wasn't going to change what he had to do.

He was running out of time.

His partner, Evan Roberts, had only run out to get food for them and their witness, Savannah Pressley. Even in New York traffic, the hour and a half he'd been gone was pushing it.

He dug his cell out of his pocket and sent a quick text to his buddy.

Where ya at?

Stuck in traffic. Bad accident. Looks like I'll be a while. Sorry.

The answer was quick, even before he could slip his phone away. "Thank God." The whisper was anguished, and Jeremy's stomach twisted.

Info for cash that resulted in someone's death was different than pulling the trigger.

I have to.

Caselli would kill Beth and the girls.

The bastard had been *at* his daughters' school when he'd called the day before. Childish laughter had filled the background. After they'd disconnected, his phone had received four pictures of his kids.

His own children.

The crime-boss had been within twenty feet of them.

"That fucker." He gripped the *gift* the gangster had included with his fifty thousand dollars and a tremor shot down his spine. The note included read *'Welcome to the family'*. A Beretta was Caselli-standard issue.

He'd have to get rid of it as soon as the pretty blonde was dead. Hope to God he didn't get caught.

Jeremy was fucked either way.

Not only Angelo Fiato, but he'd also been the reason for the location and murder of two other Caselli witnesses.

Twenty-five years at best.

Not including the minor bribes he'd taken to pay back his gambling debts. He'd been stupid to think Caselli wouldn't find out he was FBI. He'd been an even bigger idiot to play tables when he'd known the mob boss owned his three favorite locations.

He should just kill himself

No, couldn't do that to his mom. Or Beth. They might be divorced, but his ex's father had committed suicide when she was a teen. He couldn't put her through it again, let alone their daughters.

"Fuck."

Jeremy squared his shoulders and attached the suppressor to the end of the Beretta. His FBI-issued Glock stayed holstered at his waist as he silently made his way down the hall.

The extra effort wouldn't totally erase the bang of the weapon, contrary to what Hollywood tried to convince the world, but hopefully no neighbors would dial 9-1-1 until he was ready.

God, let my plan work.

He needed to kill the woman, ditch the Beretta and make it look like a break-in. There were no cameras in the duplex Evan and the witness were staying in. Another point in Jeremy's favor.

I won't get caught. I'm being smart about this.

He chanted all the way down the long, narrow hallway, and into the living room.

She sat at the dining room table, her back to him, laptop in front of her. Absorbed in her work, the tap-tap of her fingers flying over the keys was the only sound that greeted his ears.

The witness was in real estate, and Evan had told her she could work from the safe house as long as she didn't disclose her location or tell anyone what was going on.

Jeremy held his breath as he raised the gun. Pretended his hands weren't shaking and there wasn't sweat soaking his brow, dripping down his temple. He flexed his fingers on the grip of the unfamiliar weapon.

Pulled the trigger.

Even muffled, the sound of the gunshot bounced around the walls of the open floor plan.

Savannah Pressley slumped over her laptop. The machine screamed a beeping protest from all the keys the weight of her head had depressed.

The bullet had torn through the back of her neck.

Blood darkened her fair locks and was spattered all over the wall and glass table top. All over her white shirt.

A pool was starting to gather beneath her, and one of her arms had slipped from under her, dangling like the dead weight it now was. Blood ran down and dripped from her fingertips to the floor.

Something—maybe a paper bag—rattled and thumped to the hardwood floor in the foyer.

The scent of fast food tickled his nose.

"Jer." Evan was even, calm. "Drop the gun and turn around, slowly."

Jeremy crushed his eyes shut.

"C'mon, partner. Don't do this the hard way, please."

He whirled, whipping his arm up, aiming the Beretta straight at Evan's chest.

His partner's Glock was pointed right back at Jeremy.

"Jer. Buddy. What've you done?" Evan's voice dropped, but his arms were steady. A promise his partner would do what he had to, as much as *Jeremy* would.

"I didn't want to." The confession was unwanted. Unplanned.

The guy nodded. "I know. I know. But it's gonna be okay. Put the gun down, and we'll sort it all out. I promise."

A bitter laugh exited his mouth and he shook his head. "I'm fucked. I'm fucked, Ev. Just *fucked*."

"No. Jer, it'll be okay. Stop now, and it'll be okay.

We'll work it out. Talk to Barnes, get you a good lawyer."

Jeremy paced and waved his Beretta around. "No."

"Jeremy. Put the gun down. I don't want to shoot you." There was an edge to his partner's orders now, and he zoned in on the man's face.

Blue eyes widened. Implored.

The Glock remained trained on him.

Evan Roberts.

His partner of four years. The one and only partner he'd had since transferring from white collar crime to human trafficking.

His friend. His *best* friend.

Been beside him through a nasty divorce. Through the gambling. Cleaned him up after drunken nights. Forced him to get help.

"I'm sorry." The apology caught in his throat.

Jeremy pulled the trigger.

Lee thrashed in bed, ripping the thin sheet from her body. She'd pushed the comforter off already — it hung, hovering above the floor.

Hot.

She groaned and stretched as she came around from the vivid dream. Her body scorched, throbbing.

After blowing out a breath, she popped up, yanking the white ribbed tank top straight.

In bed. Alone.

Only a dream.

She looked around, frowning as unfamiliar surroundings greeted her groggy morning mind.

Right.

She wasn't at her own place.

Nate.

Sighing, Lee slipped out of the borrowed bed and arched her back, spreading her arms and shaking her body loose. She yawned.

Her side smarted and she glared down at the patch of gauze. She lifted her shirt, slowly peeling the bandage away, hissing when she ran her fingers over the line of stitches. Still too tender.

However, they were dry and tight, the skin no longer angry and puffy. If she'd taken time to heal, she probably could've had them out already. Would most likely end up ripping them out anyway.

Sex wouldn't help her healing wound, but she *could've* been waking up next to him. Down the hall in the master suite of the apartment. In his arms. Her body under his. Her tongue entwined with his as they moved together.

A tremor shivered its way down her back and legs.

Knock it off.

Lee curled her toes into the plush, tan carpet and clenched her fists at her sides. Needed to get her attorney out of her head. Scratch that—she needed to get away from him.

Stay away from him.

He's not your *attorney.*

Her partner had damn well better show up as he'd promised the night before. Downs hadn't been able to determine if they'd been followed, but he'd assured her he'd check in with Roberts and Stewart and get back to her. He'd see at least one of them at briefing in the office that morning.

Lee had run from Nate by the pool the previous night.

Fled for the second time.

She'd declined the offer to swim with him, even though her body had wanted nothing more. But if she'd shed her clothes and got in the warm water with him, they would've finished what they'd started in the living room.

Lee couldn't do that again. Already felt too much for him. If she let him back into her body, he'd end up even closer to her heart.

When the case was over, he was going back to Texas and she'd lose him. *Again.*

She could never go back to Dallas.

So she'd barked at him to get his things and get back to the apartment.

He hadn't argued, but Nate hadn't rushed right back, either. He'd shown her he couldn't be ordered around.

As much as it made her anger boil that he hadn't followed immediately, she admired his balls. He wouldn't let her push him.

When he'd entered their temporary home a good twenty minutes later, he'd gone straight into the master bedroom.

Hadn't slammed the door, but Lee had *felt* shut out.

Nate hadn't come out of the room for the remainder of the evening, and staring at the door had failed to will it open.

Failed to bring him to her side.

Jesus. You rejected him, but you're hurt?

Get over yourself.

Lee growled and slipped out of her black bikini panties. She ripped the tank off and tossed it to the carpet. A glance at the clock told her it was early—just after seven. She had time to hit the shower and mentally regroup. She needed to before she had to face him again.

After a long, hot shower that did nothing to calm her, she dressed quickly in jeans and a blue long-sleeved button-down. She strapped both her guns on and stuck an extra mag in her in-the-waistband magazine carrier.

She checked both her weapons, even though she *knew* they were both loaded with one in the chamber.

OCD much?

When Lee made it into the bright, welcoming kitchen, he was already sitting at the table, a computer tablet in front of him, propped on a multifunctional folding case. Fresh coffee and food mixed with the clean masculine scent that was just Nate tickled her nose.

"Morning." He smiled and her stomach flipped.

"Morning." She made her mouth echo the greeting, but she had to clear her throat.

"Sleep well?"

"Yes, you?"

Nate nodded. "I made coffee and breakfast—yours

is in the microwave keeping warm. I didn't know how long you'd sleep."

"Thanks."

The small talk about killed her. Lee had never felt so distanced from him, sitting four feet away.

She shoved scrambled eggs into her mouth, but she couldn't taste them. The bacon was crunchy, but her usual favorite breakfast item was also tasteless as it passed her lips and she forced herself to chew. "Hey, um…" she started.

His gaze met hers, and she fought the urge to squirm.

"Yeah?" he prompted.

"I… I'm sorry about last night." Heat rushed her cheeks. Lee broke their eye contact and rubbed the back of her neck.

"You were right," Nate said.

"I was?" She shivered. Prayed he wouldn't notice.

He nodded. "I should've respected you, not pushed you." His warm hand settled over hers and squeezed. "I'm sorry."

No, you were right. I want you. I need you more than I need to breathe.

She couldn't say it. Wouldn't.

Lee bit her bottom lip and made her eyes stay locked onto his. "I-i-it's okay."

He flashed a smile that kicked her heart into overdrive. "At any rate, I wanted to start over with you this morning. Truce?"

She nodded, but numbness rolled over her and she tried not to quiver in the chair. Did this mean he'd back off?

Stop *showing* her they weren't done like he'd promised at the hotel?

No.

Wait. That's what you want. Right?

His fingers slipped away from hers, and Nate's focus was intense on the screen of his iPad.

Lee swallowed against the lump in her throat. The food was like a brick in her stomach. "What are you doing?"

Normal. Just be normal.

He glanced up. "Reading the news."

"Ah. Be careful if you're planning on emails."

"I will. I know how to be tight-lipped. But I'd like to call my brother later."

"Sure. Might not be a bad idea for me to get a hold of Lucas at some point, too. Maybe he'll recognize the shooter, since neither Downs nor myself were able to."

"What about the rest of your team?"

Lee nodded. "Good point. Unit briefing is this morning. I'll see what Downs says, he should be here afterward."

"Ah."

She didn't get a chance to answer him.

A gunshot shattered their morning.

The front door split in two as it crashed open, still half attached to the doorframe and hanging at an angle.

Wires from the electronic lock sizzled and smoked.

Chapter Ten

"**G**et down, now!" Lee's shout made Nate flinch, but he did what she'd ordered.

She returned fire and said a few choice words. Two big guns fired back.

One had to be a larger caliber than the other, because he heard *bang* and *pop*. His ears rang as the sound reverberated off the walls of the apartment.

Her gun was louder because she stood next to him, and he fought the sense of surreality threatening to envelope him.

This is happening. Someone's shooting at us.

He crouched behind his chair, looking around frantically. They were up shit creek in the kitchen. There was no cover, no protection other than a flimsy wooden table.

Lee's breakfast and plate went flying as she knocked the table to its side in front of them. She fired her weapon two more times before lowering her body beside him.

"We need to get to the living room," Nate said.

"Just stay down." She peeked over the edge but didn't stay up long.

The kitchen window shattered over their heads and he grabbed her, shielding her from the flying glass.

"Let me go! I'm the one with the gun!"

He shook himself and released her. She was right, *damn* his protective instinct. Holding Lee down could get them both killed.

Bullets kept flying, until one of the shooters cursed.

Nate wanted to look over the table to see who was hit and where, but she kept him blocked with her body. Amusing, considering she was half the size of him.

And she isn't wearing a vest.

He held panic at bay that she'd get hurt protecting him. It might be her job, but he'd never get over it if she was harmed *because* of him.

"Federal Agent! Drop your weapons!"

The shout jarred him, and Lee jolted forward as if it had shocked her, too.

The male voice was unfamiliar. Wasn't her partner.

True to the scum they dealt with, the gunfire increased instead of ceased.

When there was finally a pause, she stood and held her Glock high, but didn't fire. She was probably checking for the location of her fellow FBI guy.

The sickening thud of a body hitting the ground sounded and she threw him a look. "Stay here."

"You're not wearing a vest," Nate said.

"Neither are you. Stay put. You're the important one."

"Wrong."

But she was already gone.

At least the gunshots had stopped.

Grunts and the shuffling of booted feet suggested there was a physical scuffle and he cursed. He'd kill whatever bastard had the nerve to put their hands on Lee.

Nate wanted to go to her, help her and the mystery

agent, but he couldn't see anything from his position. Hated to admit it, but *she* was in control and he'd have to respect her orders.

She *would* keep him in one piece.

He trusted Lee completely.

Staying covered is smart.

"Dammit." He made a fist and shook his head. Nate had a concealed handgun license in Texas, but New York didn't recognize it. He hadn't brought his Sig with him anyway. He wished for his forty now.

A pool of blood was visible at the edge of the room, stopping at the threshold of where carpet met linoleum floor of the kitchen. The body wasn't in sight, but couldn't be far, not with all that dark red on tan.

"Son of a bitch!" Lee's shout accompanied a gun shot that racked him to his core.

It was closer, louder, than the others.

He popped to his feet, ignoring the stinging in his legs and hopped over the table. Nate almost tripped over a pair of legs clad in black, but he was able to jump over the injured or dead shooter without falling on his face.

His ex-lover had her Glock trained on two men who were wrestling over a single gun. She couldn't get a clear shot.

There was a semi-automatic handgun lying on the carpet about ten feet from them. He rushed forward and kicked it farther away. He knew better than to touch it.

He retreated behind Lee.

She was still trying to get a clear shot, but the

bigger guy cold-cocked the other man, and he tumbled to the carpet.

The man on the floor had gained control of the weapon.

"Stewart, shoot him," she shouted.

The assailant backed toward the bare doorway, pointing at the male agent. "You. Are. Dead." Then he whirled and fled the apartment.

"Fuck!" Lee darted out behind him.

The other FBI guy—Stewart—made it to his feet. He looked at Nate. "Stay here. Call 9-1-1." Then he was gone, pursuing Lee and the bad guy.

Nate's whole body shook.

Lee was gone.

Out the door. *Without a vest.* After some unknown, Italian-looking-thug.

It didn't matter that it was her job or that she did it every day.

She could get hurt. Shot.

Dead.

Shit.

He shook his head and looked around.

The guy on the ground was big, probably even taller than Nate's six feet three inches, and his skin was pale, drawn. Shoulders broad, frame packed with muscle.

He couldn't tell where the man was hit, but his shirt and jacket—covering his whole chest—were soaked in blood. Dude looked Italian as well.

Did Caselli do an ethnic background check before he hired on? Or were they all born into the organization?

He'd heard the gangster's father had been in '*the business*' for years before him.

Nate felt for a pulse, but failed to find one. His knees knocked together as he gained his feet. He locked his legs so he wouldn't fall over. "Right. 9-1-1."

He hurried into the kitchen and made a grab for the cordless on the wall. His hand shook as he dialed the three numbers. Reaching for all his inner strength, he calmly explained to the dispatcher what had happened, and that he was with two FBI agents.

Both of whom were in foot pursuit of the remaining shooter. Told the woman there was a man down, no pulse. No, he didn't want to stay on the line until the police arrived.

He hung up, the click and dial tone making his ears ring all over again. As loud as the gunshots had been.

Nate dragged his hand down his face and blew out a breath. In all the years he'd been a prosecutor, all the pictures of crime scenes he'd had to show juries, nothing was like seeing a body first-hand. Blood. Torn skin. The stench of released bodily fluids, the pallid tone of bloodless flesh. He'd visited scenes, of course, just by the time he'd been there, the body was always gone.

At least this was a thug he didn't know, not a long-time friend. He wouldn't have been able to withstand losing two people he cared about, and witnessing it. Angelo was enough.

He'd received a few death threats at the DA's office for cases he'd won or lost, but it'd never been so close to home. Not like this. Not two guys bursting into an apartment where he was supposed to be in protective custody. With the FBI covering his ass.

Bile rose and he swallowed against the sudden lump in his throat. His stomach threatened to toss his breakfast.

Get it together. Now.

What the hell had happened? How'd Caselli find out where he was? And what about the other witness? Was she okay or had he found her, too?

The jumble of questions with no immediate answers came to a halt as Lee came back into the apartment. Curses spewed from her mouth that would make any trucker proud.

The other agent was on her heels.

Both wore expressions of fury.

"He got away," Nate said. Not really a question, but she nodded and came over to him.

His gaze ate her up, and he wanted to sweep her into his arms, feel every inch of her body to make sure she was okay. He didn't. They weren't alone.

"Driver was waiting. They peeled out of the parking lot even before we could get the plate. But it was New York, not Jersey. Black Cadillac Escalade. Guy musta run a hundred miles an hour down the stairs. Damn, he was fast."

The other agent's words were lost when Lee's eyes locked onto him.

He couldn't move as she stared, appraising him. "Are you all right?" she demanded. She didn't touch him, either. But her expression shouted concern.

Nate's heart flipped. "I am. Are you?"

She gestured as if it was an afterthought, but nodded again.

"Police are on their way," Nate said.

"Thanks. So are our guys," the other agent said, coming closer to them.

"Jeremy Stewart, Nate Crane," Lee said, holstering her weapon. She stared at her fellow agent. "Stewart— Not that I'm complaining, but what the hell are you doing here?"

"I was headed to meet up with Roberts at the other secure location. But I caught notice of a familiar vehicle—Caselli-issued—and decided to follow instead."

"They were headed here?" Dawson said. One dark eyebrow arched, as if she could see the lie coming out of his mouth for what it was.

Jeremy's heart skipped. "I was shocked, too. As far as I know, no one knew the locations but us. Just our unit."

"Did you check in with Roberts?"

"Not yet. Obviously I was busy here." He swallowed his urge to defend his actions. He needed to act *natural*. Had to get away with this.

His answers *had* to make sense. Give him an alibi.

The text messages he'd exchanged with Evan danced into his mind, but he tamped his rising panic. They wouldn't suspect him. There was no reason to think he'd lied. No reason to pull phone records.

He'd grabbed his partner's cell and destroyed it, anyway. Ditched it along with the Beretta Caselli had given him.

Jeremy ignored the reminder; he'd made an effort to take the phone, his team was likely to wonder *why* it was missing. He'd probably just put a spotlight on it.

Shit.

It's gonna be okay.

He chanted it, trying to ignore the way Lee Dawson was appraising him. His palms were clammy, and he fought a bad case of the shakes.

No doubt his forehead was sweaty, but Jeremy could always blame that on the adrenaline dump from their recent run. Combined with the stress of a shooting, of course.

"Jesus Christ." The curse fell from the mouth of Special Agent Clint Downs.

"That about says it all," Dawson said as members of their unit poured into the apartment.

"What the hell happened?" Downs asked.

Bobby Smythe and his partner fanned out, surveying the damage and taking a look at the dead guy.

They had the *'do you recognize him?'* convo, before Smythe's partner dug out the guy's wallet and held up a driver's license belonging to one Michael Bellini.

Jeremy didn't know the guy, but he'd known the other shooter. Hopefully Dawson wouldn't attach any significance to Terry Agosti's parting threat—no, *promise.*

Caselli would see his actions as a betrayal.

Might even send guys after *him* now.

When he'd seen the black SUV, anger had made his blood boil. He didn't need back-up to handle his business—he'd already taken care of the first witness, and his partner.

Fuck Caselli for checking up on me.

It would bite him in the ass in the end, but Jeremy would show Caselli he'd deal with this situation on *his* terms. And hell, he'd inadvertently saved Dawson's life.

He hated to admit it, but killing an innocent woman and having to shoot his partner had been too much. He could've stomached killing the other witness—after all, he'd *had* to—but not Lee Dawson. Not *another* member of his team.

He'd wept like a pussy when he'd staged the scene to look like Evan had been surprised by shooters at the front door. Jeremy had made sure to steer clear of his partner's blood. No footprints, no fingerprints. Wiped everything as clean he could—but not *too* clean.

So his choice to shoot Caselli's man had probably fucked him, but at least Dawson was alive. He'd call and promise the crime boss he'd get the job done. Make up a story about what'd happened. He *had* to convince the man to leave Beth and the girls alone.

If Caselli went after his family, he'd never forgive himself. He should call Beth and tell her to take their daughters to her sister's place in Maryland. With his luck, Caselli would find out. Plus his ex would demand things he couldn't answer.

Jeremy ignored the thundering of his pulse. Made

himself focus on Dawson's and Downs' conversation.

"Don't even tell me, Lee. Seriously. Just get him out of here."

"What?" He stepped closer to his teammates.

Both looked at him.

The tall, blond witness hovered, worry written all over his face.

Jeremy averted his gaze. He didn't want to look at the man. Having to tell him to call the police had been bad enough. If he and his family were to survive Caselli, he still had to kill Nate Crane.

Downs gave him a long look. "We have a leak." His voice was low, deadly serious.

His stomach twisted into knots. He cleared his throat. "One of *us*? No way."

"Nothing else makes sense," Dawson said. "Radio and cell silence until we find out who the bastard is and make them pay."

"I agree. I'll call Liv. Not even she gets to know where you take Crane. Stewart, call your partner," Downs ordered.

Jeremy nodded and backed into the kitchen. He dialed Evan's cell phone. Felt like one hundred eyes were burning him. Right to voicemail. But that's what happened when a device was smashed in the sewer. He swallowed hard and called two more times before making eye contact with Downs. "I got nothing."

"Shit," Downs and Dawson said at the same time.

FBI crime scene techs came into the apartment along with two paramedics with a gurney and a woman from the Medical Examiner's Office of the local county.

"Son of a bitch!" Smythe trotted over to Downs and Dawson at the same time Jeremy joined them.

"What is it?" Downs demanded.

"Kirk and McCall headed over to the other apartment when Barnes heard Stewart was here. Roberts missed morning check-in, too. Savannah Pressley is dead. Roberts was shot twice. He's in critical."

"Fuck," Dawson shouted, making a fist.

A flush rolled over his body as four sets of eyes landed on Jeremy.

Evan isn't dead.

Chapter Eleven

"Y ou all right?" Lee barked, slamming the driver's door to the rented Honda shut. They didn't have another transportation option, as much as it burned. Now she didn't doubt that they'd been followed yesterday.

Or was it the rat?

No matter, she needed to get Nate to safety.

Pray they wouldn't be followed again.

Going cell and radio silence twisted her stomach, but it was necessary. She'd do what she had to do to keep him safe. Prevent another attack. Even though it left her on her own for a little bit.

"I'm good. Promise." His sounded calm, unlike her. "You, however, I'm worried about."

Lee's heart tripped and she tried to smile as he snapped his seatbelt into place. "Sorry. Don't worry about me. I'm so fucking sorry about all this." She shoved the key into the ignition and cranked the engine.

I could've lost him today.

He could've been shot. Hurt.

Killed.

If Stewart hadn't shown up—

"Hey."

She blew out a breath and put the car in reverse, ignoring Nate.

They needed to go.

Now.

"Lee. Stop the car and *look* at me."

His command had her pausing without thought.

Hand on the gear shifter, she met his eyes.

He cupped her face and kissed her hard.

It was over before she could sink into him. Her stomach somersaulted.

"It's gonna be okay."

How could he be so sure? So *trusting* after a shootout?

No. The question is — why the hell are you so rattled?

She nodded, because she didn't know how else to answer. "You cancel your house rental?"

Nate smiled, slow and sexy, and her body heated. "No, ma'am. Didn't have time. I told my buddy I'd handle it. I have a rapport with the owner, and Nick wanted to see if I could get his deposit back."

"Good. You know the address?"

"Yes, ma'am."

Lee grinned. The timing was horribly off, but the Texas twang when he said *'ma'am'* made her heart gallop. Made her want him. She didn't even chide herself this time.

"So I guess calling my brother is out, huh?"

"For now."

"What about a prepaid cell? Untraceable and all that."

"We could go that route. Not a bad idea. I can keep in contact with Downs that way, too."

They stopped at the first Wal-Mart off the freeway and were in and out of the store with their new phone in about ten minutes. Nine minutes too long, as far as Lee was concerned. If she'd had her way, she would've made Nate stay hidden in the car, but she hadn't wanted to leave him alone, either.

After bickering about who would drive—again—they made it back on the highway headed toward upstate New York.

"Still stubborn," he muttered, but he was amused.

She harrumphed, and tightened her hold on the steering wheel. "*Stubborn* will keep you alive."

"You drive me crazy."

"Feeling is mutual."

"Feeling? You have those?" One corner of his mouth lifted.

Lee glared. "Irritation. Annoyance. *Those* are feelings. I think both are commonly associated with how *you* make me feel."

"Hmmm…about the same thing. Limits your emotional range, if you ask me."

"Nate," she growled.

He laughed. "Geesh, I'm teasing you! Relax, angel."

Her heart fluttered a little. *Angel?* Not even close, but for him to… Mixed emotions rolled over her and she gripped the wheel even tighter. Until her knuckles whitened.

"Lee?"

His concern made her glance at him.

"What?"

"You okay?"

"Yes, will you quit asking me that?" She tore her

gaze away, gluing it to the road and ordering herself not to think of Russ.

He'd been the only man to ever call her anything other than her name, but he'd refused to call her *Lee*. Said it was a man's name, and he'd certainly not married a man.

Most often, he called her his *chilosa*, or hot, sassy one. He didn't have a drop of Hispanic blood in his veins, but the man had spoken Spanish as well as Lee.

After her husband, she'd never let a man call her anything but her name. *Honey, baby, sweetie*. She'd shut it all down.

Why's Nate different?

Lee wanted to be his angel.

Dammit.

"Sorry I snapped," she whispered.

"It's all right. We've both had a crappy few days. Understandable that tensions are high."

She didn't answer because she didn't know *what* to say.

The rest of the ride was mostly silent, but she could *feel* his eyes on her. She screamed at herself to remain still in the driver's seat. Not let him know he was affecting her comfort level.

"You can turn into the development on Hatcher. It's coming up soon. It's a back way in, easier than going to the front entrance." Nate sliced through the quiet.

Lee jumped.

A smile played at his lips.

"Don't you dare ask me if I'm okay."

"Well, I've never seen you so…nervous."

"I'm not nervous." She cringed at the sharpness of her denial.

"Okay…jumpy?"

She frowned.

Yeah, that's a good word. Unfortunately.

Lee cleared her throat for the hundredth time of the day. "So you know this place?"

"Yeah. Either me or one of my friends rent the house every year. This year Nick, my friend from Alabama, grabbed it, but it's not a problem if we use it. Like I said, I didn't get a chance to make that call for him. Even though we all know the owner well now, he's most familiar with me." Nate's gaze searched her face, but at least he'd let her subject change slide.

How can someone interrogate with a look?

She swallowed and sat higher in the driver seat. Damn the man for making her feel odd in her own skin. "Frat brother reunion?" She forced the inquiry out, striving for *normal*.

He laughed. "Something like that." He sighed. "Angelo was after me for years to come work for him. Offered me partner at his firm so many times I've lost count."

"Can you even do that?"

"I love being a prosecutor, putting the bad guys away, even if there's more money in defense. But yeah, actually, I'm licensed to practice law in New York state."

"Really?" Lee hadn't known that.

What else don't you know about him?

Do you know him at all?

"Yup. New York and Texas. When we graduated, me and all my buddies ran to take the New York bar exam. And whaddya know? I passed. Kept it valid all these years. I dunno why."

She mulled over everything, making a right turn on the road he'd indicated. Visions of Nate in a New York courtroom flashed into her head. Then in her apartment, at her tiny table sharing a meal with her. In her bed.

Wrapped up in her.

"Turn on Victoria, and it's the third house on the left."

Lee jolted forward and her hand almost slipped off the steering wheel. "Shit," she muttered.

Idiot. You're an idiot with a wild imagination.

"Something wrong?"

"Nope."

His expression shouted disbelief.

She ordered herself not to look at him. Studied each road sign, willing '*Victoria*' to appear and chanted, *third house on the left.*

If she didn't get out of her own head, she was going to scream. Needed to get away from Nate for her own sanity. Now she was even more *stuck* with him.

Alone with him.

Burner phone or not, they needed to keep their outside world contact limited. All they had was each other.

Damn, it was going to be a long day.

Nate sighed and shook his head. No matter what he said, he pissed her off or made her shy away.

Skittish. Rattled. Unlike the Lee he knew.

Could the shooting really be the only cause?

As soon as they'd entered the house, she'd ordered him to stay in the living room so she could survey, check the perimeter and familiarize herself with the place. So she could defend them if she had to.

But she wouldn't look him in the eye.

After she'd returned to his side, she'd added the minute card to their prepaid cell and glued it to her ear, pacing the room and keeping her back to him.

So much for a truce.

Nate felt every inch of the distance between them. *Hated it.*

He wanted to pull her into his arms. Calm her. Make her talk to him. Find out the real reason why she was so jittery. Remind her he was there for *her*, too. They were in this together, they *needed* to communicate.

Besides, they both could benefit from a mental debrief of what they'd been through that morning.

"Downs has our number now, but he said to keep contact sporadic and to the point. I agree. So, when you call Pete, keep it short." Lee handed him the phone.

He set it on the end table in the big living room. "I'll call him later."

"All right. We should get settled. Pick rooms and make a plan. We need a plan." Her words were rushed, eyes wide.

"A plan? For what?"

"Safety."

"Lee, you got me to safety. This—" Nate gestured to the living room, then toward the whole house—"*is* safe. Literally no one but you and I know where we are. It'll be okay."

"We can't take anything for granted."

"I agree, but—"

Lee turned away before he could finish, crossing the vast room. Headed to the stairwell leading to the bedrooms. "So you know the layout pretty well."

He followed. Wasn't about to let her ditch him. "Yes, one bedroom down here, the rest upstairs. Five in all. You know where the kitchen, dining room and everything else all is from your walk through, right?"

"Yeah. This place is big." She nodded curtly. "Okay, good."

"Lee."

"What?"

"Lee."

She finally paused, glancing over her shoulder. "What?" Brow drawn tight, her expression screamed annoyance.

"Slow down. Take a breather."

"Are you telling me what to do again?"

Nate laughed. "I thought we'd called a truce?"

Without an answer, she whirled away with a glare, but he grabbed her wrist and snatched her tight to his chest.

Couldn't help it. The need to touch her won out over everything else. He needed to make her talk to him; tell him what she was thinking. Help them both process the shooting.

Nate burned to kiss her, but she fought him, and they tumbled down against the stairs. He cushioned their fall by wrapping his arms around her.

She landed beneath him — just where he wanted her.

"Damn, I missed you."

He pinned her wrists against the side of the step. However, Lee didn't fight him as he moved closer, inhaling deeply and pressing a kiss to her neck.

She scowled up at him. "Get off me." Her clean scent tickled his nose. The top two buttons of her shirt were open — the barest hint of her perfect breasts made him want her more.

His ploy at breakfast, the plan to play into her denial of wanting him and back off for a bit dissolved. He'd hoped it would draw her out to rise to his challenge.

Nate wasn't going to have to wait after all.

Not if the dare in her face was any indication.

"We both know if you didn't want to be under me, you'd put your knee in my balls."

Lee smirked. "Wanna try me?"

"C'mon, angel. You would've done it already."

She didn't call him on his statement, but she lifted her knee and pressed it into the crotch of his jeans. Instead of hurting him, she rubbed his erection until a groan fell from his mouth.

"Nate."

His name on her lips made his need to taste her

surge.

"No more denial?" he whispered, making himself wait. He wanted to hear her admit it.

She shook her head.

"What about last night?"

"Truce, remember?" Irritation was nowhere in sight. Lee's eyes were heavy-lidded, desire in the deep brown depths. Her breathing uneven, the rise and fall of her breasts was more pronounced. She lifted her face and brushed her lips against his.

It was all the invitation he required.

Nate dipped his head down and deepened the kiss, twining his tongue around hers.

She kissed him back with a demand he wasn't about to refuse. His cock pounded against his zipper.

He needed inside her.

"Let go of my hands," she breathed into his mouth.

"Are you going to kick my ass?"

"I need to touch you."

The phrase came out as a moan that sent an unmanly shiver down his spine.

He'd waited too long for this. He wanted her. Needed her. Once he got her again, Nate wasn't going to let Lee go.

After releasing her hands, he put his own to work. He pulled her shirt out of her jeans and opened all her buttons.

Lee lifted so he could shove it off her shoulders. When her arms were free, she yanked his shirt out of his jeans and unbuckled his belt.

He skimmed her gorgeous frame.

Her black bra barely encased her full breasts. Her nipples strained against the fabric.

Nate itched to taste every inch of her beautiful, light brown skin again. He froze when he spotted the large bandage on her right side. "Lee?"

"It's nothing." She shook her head, working his zipper.

"Doesn't looking like nothing." He clenched his jaw, but when he went to move off her, she wrapped her legs around his waist.

"I don't want to stop."

"I don't either, angel. But I don't want to hurt you." He caressed her cheeks.

"You'll hurt me more if we stop. Blue balls are no fun."

Nate laughed and kissed her again. He thought better of mentioning the pair she'd left him with last night. "There's my Lee."

She paused, their eyes locking. When she swallowed, he wanted to kiss her throat.

He waited for her to call him on the possession, but she didn't.

"We can find a bed. Whatever room you want," he whispered, his mouth hovering over hers.

"I'll take you anywhere I can get you."

His heart skipped, but he chided himself not to take stock in that. His woman wasn't hearts and flowers in the least. Desire and passion didn't always mean honesty, especially since she'd been so firm in her denial the night before.

Take what you can get for now.

"What happened here?" He distracted himself with the reality of her wound. Nate laid his hand over the white gauze.

"I got shot."

"Shit, Lee. Then we shouldn't do this now."

Once again he tried to pull away, but she held him tight with her legs and wrapped her arms around his neck.

"I'm fine. I want you, Nate Crane."

His head spun with what he'd longed to hear from the moment he'd seen her in the hotel lobby. But he wanted her heart and soul along with her body.

"I don't want to hurt you." The repeated phrase sounded lame as it fell out fragmented, because Lee chose that moment to trace his lips with her tongue.

She crushed her mouth into his and rocked her hips against him, hitting his cock in just the right spot to make them both groan.

The kiss went on until they both shook with need.

"Too many clothes," she whispered, tugging on his shirt.

Nate pulled away for a split-second and ripped the tee off. When he turned back to her, she'd lost the bra. His mouth went dry. "God, you're beautiful."

"You've seen me naked before," she scoffed, rolling her eyes.

He ignored her, skimming his hands down her torso. He caressed her breasts, teased her nipples, and dragged his fingers down her stomach until her muscles jumped under his touch.

Lee squirmed, but he ignored her, slowly lowering

her zipper and pulling her jeans down. Her panties were simple white bikinis, making her naturally bronze skin stand out even more.

Nate ran his hand over her covered sex, groaning at her heat. She was burning for him. It made his blood sing. He teased her through the thin material, rubbing her clit. Feeling the moisture beneath.

She was soaking wet already.

"Nate," she panted, her perfect breasts heaving. "Quit being a tease."

Flashing a smile, he dipped in for another kiss.

Lee kissed him back, shoving her hand into his boxers and gripping his cock. She stroked him until he was gasping against her lips.

"Who's a tease, angel?" he breathed.

She kissed him in answer, squeezing his dick. "Lose the rest of your clothes and I'll show you how to seal the deal."

He yanked her panties down and pushed his jeans and boxers off his hips. Was back in her arms in seconds, regretting not taking a moment to look at her laid out before him, fully naked. "Oh, I know how to seal the deal."

Lee smirked and nipped his bottom lip. "Prove it."

With a growl, he shot forward, filling her completely with one long stroke.

She moaned and arched her back, pushing her breasts into his chest.

Nate paused. Had to, or he'd lose it like a horny teen. But it gave him the chance to savor every inch of her bare, hot skin against his. Supple, smooth, all muscled curves. She felt the same. Familiar, but just as *right* as before.

Lee was his.

He thrust again and she kissed him, holding him close as they started to move together. The stairs gave him leverage, but he was worried about hurting her, so he lifted her bottom with both hands and planted his knees on the steps. He took their weight and cushioned her head with his T-shirt.

The angle allowed her to take him deeper and she closed her eyes as she met him thrust for thrust.

Pleasure washed over him. Nate was finally back with his Lee.

The rhythm of their bodies took over as she demanded more and he gave her what she wanted. They'd both have bruises later, and maybe a rug burn or two.

Lee dug her heels into his ass as she urged him faster, each plunge more frantic than the last. She moved with him, then against him, their rough tempo giving them both what they needed.

She threw her head back and gripped his forearms, nails digging in. Her body tightened and her jaw clenched.

"Angel, don't hold back. Come for me. Let me see how I make you feel," Nate ordered.

Her body loosened and she whispered his name as her sex clutched his.

His balls jolted and his spine tingled. Orgasm roared over them both. His release shot into her, his dick jerking, tearing a moan from him.

Lee pulled him closer, demanding a kiss.

He pressed his mouth to hers, slanting to taste as much of her as he could. It melted into something more.

Deep and languorous. Meaningful.

When she looked at him, he had to swallow back the three word phrase that threatened to tumble out.

He bit back a gasp. He'd come after her.

He wanted her. But love?

Yes. I love her.

Something of his feelings must've shown in his face, because Lee's expression tightened ever so slightly. An unnamed emotion flickered across her face. Then it was gone, and her mouth curved in a lazy, sated smile. "I guess I missed you, too."

Nate chuckled even has his heart twinged. He couldn't' let it bother him for now. "Let's go upstairs, angel."

"We weren't so good at that the first time."

He grinned and scooped her up into his arms.

Chapter Twelve

nger and grief boiled in his veins and Jeremy roared. He pitched his cell across the room in his apartment, watching it crack and splinter as it hit the wall and slid down, landing on the carpet soundlessly, as if he hadn't just destroyed it.

"Finish him."

The parting words of a conversation that hadn't gone as planned.

For Beth and the girls to live, Evan Roberts had to die.

Caselli had even threatened his sixty-four-year-old mother.

Jeremy's poor mom, suffering from two different types of cancer, and no health insurance. He paid for chemo with the money he'd *earned* from the mob boss.

"Fuck."

He closed his eyes. A tremor started in his spine, spreading over his limbs until his knees shook and he wobbled on his feet. He buried his hands in his hair. Didn't fight the urge to hit the carpet.

The first tears fell as his ass landed on top of his boots. His thighs smarted from the weight, but he didn't move. Didn't try to get comfortable. He didn't deserve it.

Savannah Pressley lay in the morgue because she'd picked the wrong hotel to have lunch in with a potential client. His best friend lay in the hospital with collapsed lungs and a nicked heart valve because he'd been ordered to protect her.

"No way. Own up to it." Jeremy tugged his hair and rocked. "She's dead. He's hurt. Because. Of. You."

Evan hadn't come around yet, either. '*Coma*' they'd said. In some ways it was a relief—unconsciousness meant he couldn't ID him as the assailant.

Jeremy had always been a piece of shit. If he hadn't been, Beth wouldn't have divorced him. He wouldn't have to see his girls only twice a month and every other holiday.

His partner was the only person who could halfway stand him. What did he do? Fucking shoot him.

"Fuck you, Caselli!" he shouted over and over, until his throat was raw and his neighbors were likely to call the police.

He wiped his face and called himself a few choice things.

Jeremy struggled to his feet, clinging to the sting and burn in his legs. He needed it, needed *more*.

Pain.

Yanking the Glock from the holster, he stared at the cool black metal. Imagined all the blood on his white carpet if he were to put it in his mouth and pull the trigger.

He turned the gun over and over in his hands.

"Coward, you can't even do that." He reholstered, blowing out a breath and wiping his face.

Caselli had ordered him to go to the hospital to kill Evan.

'*A man for a man,*' he'd said.

Funny, he didn't give two shits if Roberts woke up he'd identify Jeremy.

The crime-boss just wanted to make him pay for killing Michael Bellini.

The asshole wasn't too pleased about the FBI radio and cell silence, either. He'd ranted and raved about Jeremy not being privy to Nate Crane's new location.

He hadn't had much luck threatening to handle things his way. The company of the bastard's men wasn't at Jeremy's discretion.

'*You don't get to choose.*'

Caselli's command bounced around in his head.

So he had two missions, whether he wanted them or not.

Kill Evan Roberts. Find out where Nate Crane was, report back to Caselli and go kill him.

Leave Dawson alive. Believe it or not, the gangster wanted him to avoid another FBI casualty, but he wasn't to get caught or be tied back in any way to Caselli.

Good luck.

Jeremy snorted. Dawson was sharp and a crack shot. How he was going to get *her* witness was a plan for another day. However, he needed to figure it out.

Fast.

If he failed in either mission, his family was dead. His wife *and* mother. Caselli, the bastard that he was, had said he'd make an *accommodation* for Jeremy's daughters. He would take over their care, he'd termed it.

Translation—he would sell them. For sex.

Another roar filled his living room. He screamed until his throat burned. Dry and swollen, it ached for liquid of any kind. He didn't give in. Wanted to suffer.

Because his duty weapon had been confirmed as the one to end Michael Bellini's life, Jeremy was on administrative leave.

The Glock at his side was a replacement given to him when his had been taken for ballistics testing. He couldn't have it back yet.

Bobby Smythe was in charge of the investigation, and should have it wrapped up in a few days, but until then, he was grounded. Everyone agreed it'd been a good shoot. Hell, Dawson and her witness had backed him up.

No lies required.

Jeremy had to steer clear of the office until he received a call to come back to work. His supervisor, Special Agent Olivia Barnes, had told him to take a few days, and it wasn't a suggestion.

Talk to someone about Evan, because obviously she assumed he'd blame himself for not being there. For his partner being injured and the witness being killed.

Jesus, if she only knew.

Liv had made him an appointment with the shrink for nine a.m. the next morning. Once again, not going wasn't an option. At least he didn't have to fake his grief over Evan. However, he was going to have to watch what he said. He couldn't be discovered as the shooter. Nor could he risk the psychiatrist diagnosing him as being as crazy as he felt.

Jeremy paced, pulling his hair again. He needed to hit something.

No he needed to *be* hit.

Needed pain.

Someone to beat the shit out of him until he bled. Until he felt as bad on the outside as he did on the inside.

Needed his skin torn open and oozing. Throbbing. Damaged.

He rubbed his face and disarmed, leaving his replacement duty weapon on his coffee table. After strapping his backup weapon to his ankle, he tucked his jeans around it, making sure it was concealed.

Jeremy slipped his FBI ID out of his wallet and dropped it beside the Glock.

If he had any balls, he'd leave the apartment without a weapon entirely, but it was against his programming. Not having a gun made him feel naked.

There was a bar down the street. He'd get piss drunk and start a fight. With the normal crowd that frequented *Molly's*, it shouldn't be hard to find someone bigger, meaner than him.

Someone willing to kick him in the face, in the nuts. Anything to make him forget.

Make him hurt.

Maybe something would go right for him today, after all.

Lee stared at Nate's sleeping form and her heart leapt. She shut down her mind's idea of happiness and chided herself.

They'd been at the safe house for three days.

And she'd done it again.

That first afternoon, instead of telling him to go to hell, she'd wrapped herself around him and let him take her on the stairs. Then again in the borrowed bed.

They'd shared that bed all night—and every one since—and she'd been getting the best sleep since she'd been away from her own place.

After day one, she'd promised she'd stay away from him. Keep her hands to herself.

She couldn't let it go. Lee had to have him.

Just like Texas.

They'd met two years ago when he'd prosecuted Carlo Maldonado for killing two of Caselli's goons who'd followed him to Texas when the traffickers had fled the FBI in New York.

She'd been partnered with now former FBI agent, Cole Lucas, who'd ultimately stayed in Texas and married Detective Andi MacLaren, who he'd been working the Maldonado case with.

Lee had liked Nate from the moment she'd met his hazel eyes, despite the fact he was a few years younger.

They'd resisted their mutual draw to each other at the time.

When she'd made it back down to the small city of Antioch to go after another of Caselli's thugs, Luciano Marchetti, they'd run into each other again.

She'd been partnered temporarily with Pete, Nate's older brother. Pete, an Antioch police detective, had invited her to their parents' home for Sunday dinner one weekend.

Seeing each other again had been explosive. She'd taken him back to her hotel that night. They'd fallen into bed and not been far from each other's side for the rest of her stay in Texas.

Until he'd told her he thought they had something other than just sex.

The past is the past. You can't go back. You have him again. For a little while.

The problem was, now that she'd spent three nights in his arms again, Lee didn't want to let him go. She cradled her face.

Why is it different with him?

Better with him?

Why did Nate *matter?*

He made her break *all* her rules.

She never slept over. *Ever.* Sex happened. Then she was out. Couldn't stand to be coddled, cuddled or touched. And no condom? Only with Nate.

Back in Texas, Lee had told him she couldn't have kids, which was true, but still… She *always* used protection, no matter how many times she'd been with a lover. Six months ago, they'd shed the condoms after only being together once. With him, it was a separation from his body she couldn't stand.

Never let a man go down on her, either, even for her pleasure. Yet, here she was, in Nate's bed. He'd tasted her not once, but twice. Before and after the shower they'd shared.

She *wanted* him to hold her. Cuddle with her. Touch her. Put his tongue in places that made her eyes roll back in her head.

Protective custody forced them to stay together, especially after the attempt on his life at the apartment, but like Nate had said, the townhouse had *five* bedrooms.

Lee could find her own place to sleep.

She *should*…but she didn't want to leave him.

Merely looking at him made her want to snuggle into his side, have him pull her close.

Make love to her?

"Angel?" His voice was heavy with sleep, but his gaze was concerned when their eyes met.

"Why do you call me that?" she whispered.

Nate smirked and it made her want to kiss him. "Because you're anything but."

She gave a small smile.

He sat up and slipped his arm around her shoulders. "What's wrong? Does your side hurt?"

"No. Don't worry about me. I'm good."

"I do worry about you."

Unwanted emotion rolled over her. The sincere look on his face was why she didn't do *this*. "I should go. Find another bed." Words fell out. Words she didn't mean.

He glanced at the nightstand on his side of the bed. "It's four o'clock in the morning. Why now?"

She shrugged under his arm. "I just should."

Nate frowned, but kissed her temple.

She told herself not to melt into him. Commanded herself to move away.

But she didn't. *Couldn't.*

When silence settled over them, he shook her shoulders gently. "Hey. What's wrong?"

"Nothing," she croaked.

"Bullshit, Lee. Talk to me. Please."

"I want you," she blurted.

A smile played at his lips. "Right. You look like you want sex right now. Something has you freaked out. What is it?"

It's you. How I feel about you.

She'd cut her tongue out before she said that aloud. Lee wrapped her arms around him and rushed into his chest, burying her face against his neck.

Nate sighed and pulled her closer, rubbing her bare back in large, soothing circles.

She closed her eyes against his warmth, fighting tears.

Really?

God, you're a pussy, Selena Dawson.

He held her as the first moisture leaked out and rolled down her cheeks.

She sniffled, then blinked, but her vision blurred and more tears flowed.

Nate didn't acknowledge what he could surely hear, and for that she was grateful.

The thought of him seeing her as weak twisted her stomach into knots.

"Angel, what's wrong?"

"Nothing. Really. I'm glad to be here with you." Truth hurried out before Lee could censor it, but at least she wasn't looking at him. Heat crept up her neck and she buried her face deeper against him.

"I'm glad you're here, too. I meant it when I said I missed you."

She crushed her eyes shut. She'd missed him, too. Couldn't tell him. Couldn't look at him and admit he did something to her. Made her feel again.

"You don't have to say anything," he whispered, as if he'd read her mind. "I just wanted you to know."

"Thanks for listening to me at the apartment." The rushed statement made her heart pound. Lee needed a subject change. *Now.*

"You got me out alive."

They made eye contact and her answer dissolved when she saw the tenderness in his expression. "I...couldn't let anything happen to you." More truth fell from her lips.

Nate kissed her, pulling her even closer.

Lee melted into the heat of his mouth moving over hers, leaning into his muscled chest.

His nipples teased hers as they brushed, leaving her achy as desire made her core throb.

How could she want him so much?

Over the last three days, they'd already been together more times than she could count.

"Seems like something I should be saying to you," he breathed against her mouth.

It took a minute for the passionate haze to clear her brain so Lee could make sense of what he'd said. She smiled, her lips still flush to his. "I'm the one with the gun."

Nate laughed and pressed tiny kisses all over her face. "In New York. I grew up in Texas with a cop for a dad. I know how to shoot, angel."

"I'll remember that, in case."

He nipped her bottom lip and she slanted her mouth into his.

The tease became another heated kiss that left them shaking in each other's arms.

"You do that." He laid her down into the bed and rose above her.

She didn't resist him, opening her thighs and inviting him to come closer, slip inside her. Lee already burned for him.

"God, I want you." His voice was rough, emotional.

Her stomach flipped, but she ignored unwelcome feelings.

Focus on the physical. Lust. You want him too. Show him.

She reached between their bodies and encircled his erection. Dragged her fingers up and down the length of him, teasing his tip.

Nate threw his head back and moaned as she wrapped her hand around him, starting light strokes.

Every noise he emitted made her sex ache and pulse for him.

"Have me. Fuck me, Nate."

One corner of his mouth shot up. "Oh, angel. You still think we're just fucking?" He grabbed her hand, bringing it to his mouth and lavishing kisses on her knuckles. His gaze remained locked with hers.

Lee shivered at the intensity there. The tenderness, heat and emotions she refused to name.

He gripped his erection without looking away. Positioned himself at her center and filled her with one powerful thrust forward. "I'm sorry you're confused," Nate grunted. "But I'll show you. I promise. This isn't fucking. This is *more*."

I know. That's what scares the shit out of me.

Once again, she couldn't say what was floating around in her head.

She whimpered when he propelled forward, picking up the pace like he knew she wanted. *Needed.*

He could please her without effort or thought.

That scared her, too.

Nate's mouth found hers again. He kissed her into oblivion, moving his tongue with his hips as he explored her, possessed her. His hands roved her heavy breasts as their bodies rocked in rhythm.

Their mouths stayed fused as Lee's orgasm built slowly, powerful waves of pleasure rolling over, sucking her down and pushing her up. There was no urgency, just a consistent sensation as the ride made her feel good.

Intensity swirled around them as his thrusts took her higher.

The typhoon hit them at the same time, and she broke the seal of their lips, throwing her head back and screaming his name.

Lee tightened her arms and legs around him as her thighs shook, her inner muscles taut, contracting and relaxing of their own accord.

He grunted and buried his face against her shoulder. His cock pulsed inside her, and they both moaned when she shifted against him, rocking under his weight.

She caressed his cheeks and pressed her lips to his.

He took control, kissing her until her toes curled and her body lit up from the inside out, even though she'd just had the climax of her life.

The kiss continued until he slipped from her body and pulled her closer. Nate rolled to his back and took her with him, fitting her against him.

Perfect.

As if she belonged beside him like this. Belonged *to* him. Legs entwined. Her cheek to his chest.

Lee willed tears away.

No. This isn't fucking.

Oh, shit.

Chapter Thirteen

"I 've got good news and bad, whaddya want first?" Cole Lucas' deep voice startled her, even though it was good to hear from her old partner.

"Hold on. I'm gonna put you on speaker so Nate can hear you too." Lee's heart kicked up a notch through the pleasantries the two men exchanged. She didn't want to wait on whatever Lucas had to tell her, even for the sake of manners.

A baby's cry broke through their conversation. "Crap, gimme a sec."

"Lucas, we don't have all day," she called. Irritation flared. She looked around the living room of the big house.

It was cold outside, but the bright afternoon winter sun lit up the vast room. Light flowed in through five large windows.

She winced. They might be safe—sort of—since no one knew where they were, but the whole house was too open for her liking. Huge, too. Probably about three thousand square feet. A lot of ground to cover if they were attacked. On the other hand, size could be an advantage—places to run, disappear.

"Sorry, Micah's crawling all over the place and he bumped into the couch. It's okay, buddy." The guy's six-month-old son was close to the phone now, cooing and babbling. He didn't sound upset.

"He okay?" she asked. Wasn't heartless, after all.

"He's great. So fricking cute. I'll send you new pics. He looks like me, but he has Andi's eyes." The former FBI agent murmured to his son and the baby giggled.

Nate threw her a grin that made her body flush and scooted to the end of the cushion on the couch.

She stood by him, but they weren't touching. Lee turned her back slightly and fought the urge to close him out.

Dylan's big brown ones flashed into her mind and she shut them out.

I can never have that again.

She ignored the feeling of loss at the memory of her three-year-old son combined with the pregnancy she'd lost two weeks after he and Russ had died.

It felt fresh suddenly. Painful. Her gut ached.

She tried not to think of Dylan. *Ever.* Next to impossible, but one of the reasons she kept herself busy, so she didn't have time to think. Remember.

Grieve.

He'd be nine now.

It'd been easier when she'd been drinking.

Oh, God. Stop. Right now.

What was worse?

Memories of her son or the baby that could've never been?

Lee had been at her desk at the Dallas FBI office when pain in her lower belly had doubled her over. Her boss had called 9-1-1 and she'd been rushed to the hospital.

Pregnant.

It'd been a tubal pregnancy. No more than four or

five weeks along, it wouldn't have been viable anyway.

Emergency surgery had left her with one ovary and a damaged fallopian tube. They'd had to remove the ovary and tube containing the pregnancy. Doctors said she wouldn't be able to conceive again.

But it'd been Russ' child. Her last link to the husband she'd just lost. She'd mourned all over again.

She'd started drinking the day she'd been released from the hospital. Kept drinking. Until her disaster in Dallas.

Lee still went to meetings from time to time in New York, but only when she couldn't dig herself out of whatever hole she'd got into. She really had no one to talk to about it.

Not that I want to. Not that I ever would.

No one in her unit — including Clint Downs — had a clue. Liv knew — full disclosure of the DWI and her progress was a part of taking her on — but the Special Agent supervisor was nothing if not discreet.

She was alone in her own head. It was better that way. That way she didn't drag anyone else down with her shit.

Alcoholic.

The word would haunt her for the rest of her life.

Lee hadn't had a drink in over two years. Most of the time, she wasn't even tempted. Beer was easy to resist — it only resulted in mild dry mouth. If it was a bottle of Jack...

If her hands shook to hold it and her tongue begged for it, she hurried her ass to a meeting.

One handy thing about being in a city of eight

million people was that AA meetings were everywhere.

Cole Lucas' baby giggled. Teasing. Torturing. It was like background noise in her mind, mixed with Dylan's laugh.

Not that she'd ever wanted another child. She couldn't replace her son like that. He'd been her heart. Her life.

She averted her gaze from Nate.

Another reason she couldn't stay with him long term. He'd never be a father. Lee couldn't give him a child even if she wanted to.

What the hell are you thinking?

"Anyway."

Lucas yanked her from her own mind—damn good thing.

"Spit it out," she snapped.

He laughed. "You don't like me holding you in suspense? It's Saturday. I'm not supposed to be working. Not even on call this weekend."

She growled and Nate laughed.

"You're not *working*. You watched a damn video. What a time suck." Lee rolled her eyes even though he couldn't see her.

Nate smirked.

"Oh, all right. Don't tell me you're no fun anymore, Dawson. You were always fun. Where's my old partner?"

"Your old partner is going to fly to Texas and kick your ass."

"Language, language. There're little ears present," Lucas said, but amusement wrapped his admonition.

She groaned and Nate flashed a grin.

"Well, the good news is I recognized your shooter."

"And the bad news?" Nate asked.

"It's Caselli."

Shock threatened to bowl her over, and Lee had to lock her knees to stay on her feet. "No fu— 'Effing way." She tightened her grip on the prepaid cell until it creaked a protest.

Her lover arched a brow at the altered curse, but his face was pale. "The man himself?" His voice shook so she moved closer. He pulled her down next to him on the couch and threw his arm around her shoulders.

Lee pressed into him.

"Yup," Lucas said.

"Are you sure?" she asked.

"I watched it a dozen times. But yeah, I'm sure. I can't believe it, either. But it's him. Tony frickin' Caselli."

"Himself," Nate said.

"Yup." Lucas' repetition didn't make it sink in for Lee, even as he continued speaking. "You know how elusive he normally is, too. All the time I was under, I only got to see him a few times. As you know from all the pictures we've taken over the years we've worked this, there aren't that many of Tony, Jr."

He was right.

Lee would have to dig through files and remind herself what Caselli looked like. She wouldn't likely recognize him if he passed her in the street.

Not good.

"Why the hell—heck, sorry—would he kill Angelo Fiato himself? He's got an army of thugs!"

"I guess that's what you need to find out, old partner."

Lee and Nate exchanged a look.

"Hey, there's one awesome thing about all this," the former FBI agent said.

"What?" she asked at the same time Nate said, "You got him, now."

"Right. For years we failed to prove him personally guilty of wrongdoing. You caught his hand in the cookie jar, Dawson. On. Video."

Holy shit. They were right. This could break their case.

"One little murder can make everything else snowball." Lucas cleared his throat. "Sorry, Nate. I know the lawyer was your friend. No offense."

"None taken."

She almost didn't hear him. Chaos spun her thoughts. They might have Caselli on video, but he was practically wearing a disguise. They needed someone other than Lucas to ID him. Lee needed a plan. *Now.* "I need to call Downs."

"I'll leave you to it. Nate, I'll tell your brother you're good, dude."

"Thanks," he muttered. He appeared deep in thought, too.

"Hey, Lee."

She paused, her finger hovering over the *end* button. "Yeah?"

"Stay safe. And get this bas—jerk."

Lee snorted and glanced at Nate as the call

disconnected. "What does it matter? Kid's six months old. He can't recognize a cuss word."

He laughed. "Yeah, but we don't want his first word to be *'fuck'*."

She laughed too, shaking her head. "Right. Lucas likes that word way too much, so it's a possibility."

Nate grinned, but his expression sobered. "Caselli," he breathed.

She sucked in a breath and nodded. "I know. Makes me wanna look at case file photos. I need to get a good look at his face again. It's been a while. I *have* to be able to recognize him."

"I don't disagree, but we can't go anywhere. And so much for a short phone call…"

"I know, but we needed to know. Ours is prepaid, and he called from a landline. We're probably okay. I'll see if Downs can email me an encrypted file to personal email or something. I need to tell him what's going on so the team can get on this. Shit. Just… *Shit*."

His chest rose and fell as if he, too, needed a few deep breaths. Nate gave a curt nod. "Angel, it's still gonna be okay. It doesn't matter *who* the shooter was. Just that you get 'em."

Lee couldn't look away. How could he be so calm?

If anything, he should be *more* rattled at finding out *the* Caselli killed his friend. Yet he was trying to make her feel better?

Her heart fluttered and she wanted to kiss him.

"Why would Caselli take the risk of getting caught, being out in the open, killing Angelo *himself*? What did Angelo have on him?" He sounded thoughtful, his head cocked to one side.

Her plan to climb onto his lap fell to the wayside. Letting lust cloud her head was a bad idea anyway. She had a few calls to make and plans to formulate. She only regretted she wouldn't be in on the execution of it all, because she had to stay with Nate. Not that she didn't want to be with him. She *did*. Therein lay the problem.

Oh, shut the hell up.

She considered telling him she couldn't discuss the open investigation with him, but he wasn't just anybody. He was as involved in this case as she was. Not only was he a witness in his friend's death, he was also familiar with the crime boss.

Nate squeezed her against his side when she didn't answer right away. "Well?"

"Angelo Fiato was cooperating with our investigation."

He nodded, but quirked an eyebrow. "That can mean a thousand different things."

"He admitted to covering up financial crimes for Caselli. We confirmed money laundering and some tax fraud. Fiato wasn't his accountant, but worked closely with Caselli's money management team — two of whom were also recently murdered — and Fiato was involved in the exchanging of major funds — millions. Of course, he got a cut, which is how we caught him. We got him dead to rights, and he turned when confronted."

He frowned. "Oh, 'Lo." The sadness in his expression made it hard to breathe, but Lee restrained herself from touching him.

Case. Think about the case.

He needs to know.

"We're not the only division on this. White Collar has a few teams studying Caselli's financials, specifically. They're trying to reignite the RICO case that blew up a few years ago."

"RICO? Most of those cases don't hold any water. They're more a pain in the ass than anything else."

"Right. We keep him in court. Visible. Vulnerable. And spending that hard-earned *dirty* money. But if they do their homework like they're supposed to, we hope to actually have something on him. So it's not *all* red tape. There've been cases prosecuted — and won — under RICO."

"Guess it depends on the prosecutor."

Lee smirked and Nate grinned.

"Yeah, well, what we really need is to get back in on the inside. Since Lucas, it's been a no go."

"Well, if he's doing his own dirty work, there's a reason for it. So I doubt he'll let *anyone* in. Definitely not someone who shows up begging to be made."

She nodded. "If we can get him on RICO stuff, it buys time. Then the drugs and the girls can fall into the open. Hopefully. We're all working our asses off."

"Damn." He shook his head. "And Angelo was in on this. 'Lo, did I know you at all?"

When his eyes misted over, Lee couldn't take anymore. She straddled his lap and pressed her lips to his.

He took over, settling his hand at the back of her neck, tangling his fingers in her hair and deepening their kiss.

She kissed him harder, rocking in his lap until Nate's erection greeted her ass. She burned for him, from the inside out. Her sex ached, and she needed him inside her.

Now.

Lee undulated and he groaned.

"Don't you have to call your partner?" he whispered against her lips.

"Do you want me to do that right now?"

"No." He nipped her bottom lip, then his tongue flicked out in apology, caressing the spot.

A tremor shot down her spine. She reclined and ripped her T-shirt off. "Downs can wait." She wiggled in his lap, intentionally rubbing his hard dick beneath her. "This can't."

Nate moaned her name and grabbed her hips. He lifted up, rubbing her jeans-covered core.

It enflamed her even more.

He cupped her breasts through her bra.

It was her turn to whimper when he teased her nipples into hard peaks with his thumbs, through the fabric. Desire seared her whole body, making any place with a nerve ending ignite.

She needed his hands and mouth on her *everywhere*. They had too many clothes on.

"Damn good thing I was never very patient. But your partner... The guy seems to have patience in spades." He sounded strained, and his chest heaved as if talking was the *last* thing he wanted to do.

Lee grinned and kissed him.

Chapter Fourteen

Nate stroked her bare shoulders and Lee snuggled closer on the couch. He kissed her temple. "Are you cold?"

She shook her head and silence settled over them, but it was companionable.

"Angelo broke privilege," he remarked later.

His gut ached, and it had nothing to do with Lee's ambush. He couldn't get Angelo out of his head, but he *should*.

Concentrate on the naked woman in his arms who'd just pretty much had her way with him. Get himself ready for the inevitable round two.

He *wanted* that.

Her riding him on the couch had been sweet, hot and much too short. She obviously didn't want to see him upset, and even though she couldn't seem to say it, her showing him with her touch, her kiss, only made him love her more.

It didn't fix his disappointment in his old frat brother. Nate couldn't believe his friend—one of his *closest* friends—had not only been the lead attorney for a piece of shit like Caselli, but guilty of *crimes*. Crimes that should've sent him to prison for a long time.

Angelo had kept it all from him, but then again, the guy had known that Nate would *never* take part in anything like that. He would have also recognized that Nate would've urged him to turn himself in, if not called the FBI himself, for Angelo's own good.

Now his friend was dead.

It left him questioning everything about their friendship. He'd thought he could help Lee's investigation because he'd known 'Lo so well. Had he really known him at all?

She lifted her head and met his eyes. Her dark hair was loose, dancing around her shoulders. Her breasts pressed into him, their heavy weight comforting and arousing. Her bronze skin was supple and smooth from head to foot, and the contrast against his own just made him want her more.

God, she was beautiful.

Angelo wasn't worth wasting time on—as it'd turned out.

Lee *was*. All his time. For the rest of his life.

"That look on your face is killing me," she whispered.

Nate tried to smile. He cupped her cheeks. "I'll be fine, angel."

She scooted up his body and pressed her lips to his in a hard kiss that was much too fleeting. "I know it's gotta rock the foundation of what you thought you knew about him."

"Yeah." He nodded, holding her closer.

Lee settled on top of him, her breasts resting on his chest, her hips over his. Her legs were perfectly aligned between his.

He wrapped his arms around her.

"It's not like he wanted to talk. We didn't give him a choice on breaking privilege, as you say."

"Still doesn't excuse what he chose to do. For Caselli. *With* Caselli."

"I know…"

"I should've known something was wrong. He started calling more. We used to talk every few months, but… Then he started calling every week. Consistently. I mean, I should've realized asking me to come in early for our trip was a big deal. *Dammit.* Like he was calling for help, and I didn't see it." Nate clenched his jaw as emotions rolled over him. He was about to lose it.

"Bullshit." Lee's hard bark had his eyes snapping back to her face. Her kiss-swollen lips were a flat line, and her dark orbs flashed. "I'm not gonna let you do this to yourself, Nathaniel Dennis Crane."

"Do what?" He was torn between grief over 'Lo and amusement that she'd used his full name.

"I'm sorry your friend got in over his head and made the wrong choices. Broke the law. And I want to kick his ass for hurting you, but you're not going to take this out on yourself. This is *not* your fault."

Nate cupped her face and kissed her irritation away, swallowing her surprised yelp.

She got with the program fast, slanting her mouth into his and kissing him until his cock was hard and aching between them.

He chuckled as they parted, and she rested her forehead against his.

"What's funny?"

"I like when you take up for me, angel. I like the way it makes me feel."

I love you.

He couldn't say it. His stomach somersaulted.

A smile played at her lips, but Lee looked away, like she often did when their conversation skirted *feelings.* "I'm glad."

"So I guess you should call your partner."

She met his eyes again, relief evident in her expression.

Nate's gut ached. When would she really let him in? He needed more than her body.

"Probably." Lee slipped her hand between their bodies and started to stroke his cock. "But what about this?"

He groaned, hardening even more in her hand. His sac tingled with her attentions, and he sank his teeth into his bottom lip to keep him from crying out. The warming of his blood rolled into a slow boil. His pulse thundered in his ears.

What had they been talking about?

Did it fucking matter?

She scooted down his body, dragging her perfect breasts across his thighs and knees intentionally.

Nate's whole body shook, tremors starting in his spine and working their way through his limbs. He tightened his toes and clenched his fists, fighting the urge to thrust. "Leeeeeee." He couldn't contain her name when she dragged her tongue along the sensitive head of his dick, then sucked him into her mouth.

Coherent thought fled, and he buried his hands in her hair as she began to move up and down his length, using her tongue to tease his every inch.

Her fingertips skimmed his balls and he moaned,

throwing his head back and closing his eyes.

Lee wrapped her hand around him and began to pump as she sucked.

Nate panted and tugged her hair.

She caressed his thighs before slipping her hand under his ass, gripping him and holding on tight as she moved her mouth up and down.

Her long locks tickled his skin and heightened the sensations rolling over him.

His control started to wane and Nate tilted his hips, begging for more.

Lee responded, sucking him harder and caressing his balls, squeezing. Not hurting him, but the pressure made him burn.

He cried out, tumbling over the edge. His cock kicked in her mouth, in her hands. "Angel, I'm… I'm…" He tried to push her shoulders back, but she didn't stop.

She swirled her tongue around his tip as he started to come. Instead of pulling away, she buried his dick in the depths of her warm mouth, swallowing his release.

A shudder went through his whole body and he clamped his mouth shut to keep a declaration of love at bay.

Three words teetered on the tip of his tongue.

He wanted to drag her up and take her mouth, show her what he couldn't tell her, but his muscles wouldn't cooperate.

Lee stroked his thigh as the pleasure receded in waves, and Nate relaxed into the couch with a sigh.

"Angel, wow." He caressed her cheek and she

flashed a smile.

Damn, he wanted to tell her he loved her.

She moved up and snuggled into his chest. "What wow? You've done the same to me. Drives me wild."

"Good. I love to drive you wild."

Lee froze in his arms and he bit back a groan.

Shit.

He shouldn't have said that, in any context.

Nate couldn't read her expression. His heart dropped to his stomach, ruining the sated feeling in his limbs.

"As much as I want to lay here naked all day and do naughty things to you, I probably should call Downs." She dipped her head down and kissed his chest, but his gut burned.

She'd pull away from him now.

Your fault, idiot.

"Okay, angel." He made a go for her face, to taste her lips again, but she was off the couch in seconds.

With every garment Lee pulled on, the pain in Nate's chest sharpened.

Lee blew out a breath and gripped the phone tighter. She rested her hip against the large island in the kitchen and chatted with her partner.

Coward. You're a coward.

She'd run from him again.

Even though she'd kissed him before leaving him naked on the couch, it was pretty much the same damn thing.

The word *love* on Nate's lips had made her shake in her boots.

He didn't have to say he loved her. The look on his face every time they were together shouted it. It was only a matter of time before the unwanted phrase fell out of his mouth, if the intensity in those hazel orbs was any indication.

She couldn't handle it.

Love wasn't going to work.

Not after Russ.

Not even for Nate.

Lee needed to stop sleeping with him. Stop kissing him. Stop…tasting him. Definitely stop letting him into her body. She was already slipping deeper.

Losing control.

So, shit, yes, she really was a coward.

Even giving *him* pleasure had her whole body loose and wanting. Burning. Turned her on that she had the power to make him moan and beg. Her sex throbbed still. No doubt her panties were damp.

Lee wanted Nate again.

"Dammit," she whispered.

"Just keep Crane safe. We'll do the rest, partner," Downs' gravelly voice startled her and she rapped her knuckles on the counter.

Good thing he'd assumed she'd been expressing frustration about the case. "I know and I will." She cleared her throat.

"I know it'll kill you to sit it out, if that's what it comes to, but we're a team for a reason."

"I get it, I really do. But this is Caselli."

"Yup, and he'll look the same in metal bracelets the rest of them do."

"Squeeze 'em tight, Downs."

Her partner laughed.

"Want me to kick him for you, too?"

"A few times. In the balls."

"I'd laugh again, but I don't have a problem with that plan. And I know you're dead serious."

Lee grinned. "Damn straight."

"Hey, you haven't had any contact with Stewart, have you?" Her partner's humor was gone.

She frowned. "No, why?"

"He came in the other day with a pair of shiners and a limp."

"Oh yeah?"

"Someone beat the shit out of him, and he's not saying a damn thing."

"I don't talk to the guy, so I couldn't tell ya a thing about him."

"You don't talk to anyone, Dawson." His tone was dry.

She smirked even though he couldn't see her. "You think we have something to worry about?"

"I don't know. But I'm watching."

"Good. How's his partner?"

"No change. Coma after surgery because he was down so long, they think, but they repaired the damage in his heart. His lungs will be okay too, given time."

"It'd be nice if he'd wake up and tells us who shot him."

"No doubt." Downs paused. "Stewart's been

acting…odd…the last few days."

"Maybe he can't deal with Roberts' sitch."

"Hope it's just that."

Lee's heart skipped. "You think it's something else?"

"I don't know. I seem to be the only one that doesn't buy his appearance at the apartment hook, line and sinker."

She racked her brain to remember everything her fellow agent had said. His explanation hadn't made her flinch. She shook her head. She'd been too wrapped up in Nate that day. Making sure he was safe, getting the fuck out of there as soon as they could. Lee hadn't stopped to question anything Stewart had said.

And they had a rat.

"Clint…" His first name fell out, not something she said all that often.

"I know, Lee, I know. It's a big deal. A big *accusation*. Like I said, I'm just watching for now."

"Haven't said anything to Liv?"

"No. I need something solid before I open my mouth. Like I said, it could be nothing."

"Keep me posted." Lee bit back a few choice curses.

Right, nothing.

If Downs had spoken suspicion, even to her, he'd been thinking about it for a while.

"If he contacts you, just be wary. He's an FBI agent just like you and me, but cover your ass. And Crane's."

"You know I will."

"He might just be a guy who can't deal with grief."

He was calm, reasonable.

"Blaming himself for being with me instead of Evan?"

"Yeah, something like that."

"No harm in me keeping my eyes peeled, too."

"Good. I'll get you those pics you asked for," Downs said.

"Thanks."

"Take it easy. Just keep Crane safe. The quiet is probably killing you, but it's good for you to take a breather from the action once in a while, too."

"Geesh. Now you sound like Liv. I'm *fine*. Nate's fine. I'll keep it that way."

Her partner laughed. "Call me if you need anything."

"You know it. I'll respond to your email." Lee ended their call, but the conversation didn't sit right in her gut. She set the phone down on the counter and stared hard.

Never thought to question Stewart the day of the shooting.

He was FBI.

One of the good guys.

Right?

Chapter Fifteen

Jeremy scanned the hospital corridor. A bead of sweat rolled from his temple to his cheek and he swiped it away, turning the corner and throwing a nod to the nurse who glanced up when he passed the station.

You're just a guy visiting his injured partner in the hospital, nothing more, nothing less.

No one suspected he was supposed to kill Evan Roberts. Their whole team was concerned about them both.

Is Evan gonna be okay? Are you okay? How ya holding up? Don't worry, buddy, it's going to blow over. Evan will be back to work in no time.

The concern was killing him.

He'd only been back in the office for two days. At least the investigation of Michael Bellini's death had been wrapped up.

Jeremy was cleared. It'd been declared a good shoot.

Liv had told him he was to see the shrink weekly until she said otherwise. Other than that, he had no idea what the fucking doctor had reported from his first visit. On the surface, things had gone fine. The guy hadn't expressed concerns. Did Dr. Doran think he was nuts?

Yeah, well… You are crazy.

"Hey," Jeremy said.

Special Agent Bobby Smythe looked up from the crossword he was doing. His chair outside Evan's hospital room was propped against the wall, only two legs on the ground. He took one look at him and thumped all four to the linoleum floor.

"Jesus Christ. What the hell happened to you?"

Crap.

He'd almost forgotten about his face. "Nothing."

"Well, damn. Hope the other guy looks worse."

He chose not to answer. The dude he'd picked to beat the shit out of him had been a big SOB. Jeremy hadn't fought back at all. His ribs were sore and his leg still wasn't right.

But it'd felt good.

Only landing in the hospital would've made it better. Then again, he would've had too many questions to answer. Not to mention, he wouldn't have wanted the guy to get arrested for doing what he'd needed him to.

"I'm here to see Evan."

Smythe nodded. "Go for it. Maybe seeing you will make him wake up. Since you're here, I'm gonna hit the john."

He forced a nod back. He slipped into the hospital room, looking everywhere but at his partner in the bed. His gut was tight, making his ribs burn even more.

What the fuck was he going to do? Put a gun to Evan's head and pull the trigger?

Now would be the perfect time.

Protection detail gone.

But there'd be no getting away with it. A dozen

people had seen him come into the room. Bobby would ID him.

Did he give a shit if he got caught?

Once his partner was dead, Jeremy really had nothing left.

Wait.

He still had his family.

Beth and the girls were in danger and they didn't even know. His mom, too.

He surveyed the room again. A giant silver balloon shouting, '*Get Well Soon!*' floated in the corner, tied to a decorated basket with some sort of plant in it.

Colored stick figures drawn on a piece of poster board was taped to the wall next to the window. The little people were holding hands in front of a house. Green scribbles of grass beneath their feet.

'*I love you, Uncle Evan!*' was written in bright blue above the stick figures. It was signed, '*I miss you, too. Conor.*'

"Fuck. Me," Jeremy whispered.

Evan wasn't married—had no kids of his own— but he was extremely involved in his seven-year-old nephew's life. His sister had been widowed four years before.

He'd met the kid. He and his partner had taken Conor and Jeremy's own girls to the park on his weekend a few times. Zoe, Jeremy's younger daughter, was in Conor's class at school.

The beep from one of the monitors took his attention. Evan's heart beat steadily and he watched the little green lines move up and down with each beat. His stomach seized and he closed his eyes again.

"I can't do it." Jeremy's mind screamed over and over. Desperation clawed at his throat and he forced himself to breathe slowly. Clenched his fists at his sides. The gun at his waist scorched through his clothing, taunting him.

He stared at his partner's face. Evan's dark hair was plastered to his forehead. He was intubated, so a breathing mask obscured his face, but a beard covered his normally clean-shaven cheeks and chin.

I put him here.

It didn't matter that his friend could sit up and identify him at any moment.

Or not wake at all.

Finding out Evan was alive had been *good* news.

Jeremy hadn't killed him.

"You all right?" Smythe popped his head into the room.

"Fuck!" He jumped.

"Whoa. Sorry. Didn't mean to startle you." His fellow agent's eyes were wide and Smythe had his palms raised when he glanced over his shoulder.

"Nah. I'm good. Just didn't hear you coming."

"No worries." The guy smiled, shoving his hands into the pockets of his khakis. The Glock on his hip caught Jeremy's eye, but he tore his gaze away.

He shouted at himself to relax, loosening his shoulders and maintaining his teammate's concerned stare. "How's it going here?"

"Not bad. Liv wants at least one of us here twenty-four/seven. Docs won't tell us anything since we're not family, but I overheard that they want to take him off intubation in a day or two. The doctor thinks since his vitals are looking good after surgery he might be able to breathe on his own. His lungs should work. It would be a good sign. So, we wait." Smythe shrugged.

Jeremy swallowed. What he had to do threatened to cripple him. He couldn't finish Evan with the other agent here, anyway. He couldn't put Caselli off too much longer, either.

His partner was first, but Nate Crane had to be next.

"Have you heard from Dawson?"

Smythe shook his head. "Location remains undisclosed. Has to be that way, for now."

"Right. I get it. Just hope she and the witness are okay." It was too much to hope that Smythe knew the location. Or that he'd drop it into casual conversation.

Damn it.

"Dawson's tough, but I'm sure Downs still has her back, even from the office. They've had limited contact."

"Oh?"

"Yeah, I think she calls in. Pretty sure she has a burner phone or something."

"Good deal." Jeremy maintained his composure, but his heart sped up. "Smart." If he could dig discreetly, could he get the number?

Find out where Crane was?

You have to… But right now…normal. Be normal.

"Did you hear? Cole Lucas ID'd the shooter. Downs sent him the video."

"No. Who was it?"

"Tony, Jr."

"No shit. Caselli himself?" His whole body tightened and he fought the urge to fidget. Shoved his hands in his jeans and sucked in a breath, gluing his feet to the floor next to his partner's hospital bed.

What. The. Fuck?

Caselli *himself?*

Jeremy had missed unit briefing and hadn't had a chance to review the footage. "Can you send the video to my cell? Haven't seen it yet."

Why the hell had Caselli asked about witnesses if he'd killed Angelo Fiato himself? Was it some kind of fucked up test?

Bastard.

"Sure. I don't have it on mine, but I can shoot Dex an email." Smythe dug his phone out of his pocket. "He used facial recognition software to confirm it. The bone structure is right even though we didn't get a dead-on camera shot. He spent hours looking at all the photos we have of Junior. Sure as shit, it's our main man."

Jeremy's head spun, his fellow agent's voice fading in and out. The computer nerd on their team, Dexter Wayne, was a genius. If he was sure the shooter was Caselli, there was no doubt.

After a few blaring key tones, Smythe shoved his cell in his pocket and flashed a smile. "He'll get it to you shortly."

"Thanks. Hey, what time are you leaving here?"

"Not 'til seven. We're doing twelves, rotating."

"Who's your relief?"

"Kirk."

"Tell her not to bother."

Smythe's dark eyebrows shot up.

"He's my partner. I...should be here. At his side." The emotion made him cringe, but at least it wasn't faked. He refused to think of what he'd have to do when he and Evan were alone.

"You sure?"

"Yes. I... I'm so fucking sorry he ended up here."

The man's expression was sympathetic, and he nodded. "You got it. You need to be here? You do what you gotta do."

Jeremy winced.

That's what I'm afraid of.

Lee looked up from Nate's iPad when he called her name. He strode across the vast kitchen, disposable cell in hand. "Your partner's on the phone."

"Damn, I didn't even get through all his emails yet."

"Don't think it's about that," he said as she latched onto the phone.

"He's right."

Downs' affirmation made alarm bells go off in her head.

She sat straighter in the wooden chair. "Yeah? What's up?"

"I did some digging."

"Stewart?"

"Yeah. Not good. Not good at all."

"Damn. What is it?"

"First of all, we keep this quiet. You and me quiet. Haven't approached Barnes and I don't want to throw the guy who helped me peek into personnel files under the bus. Most of what I found out was off the record anyway."

"Of course."

Sad that he feels has to tell you that.

'Partner' should mean something. Lee ignored the guilt crashing down on her. She was done being a shitty partner. "We're partners, Clint."

"Right." He plowed on, but his tone said he'd recognized her apology in the simple statement.

His intuition was one of the things she liked about him most. Sometimes. He was a good guy. Wouldn't hold anything against her.

"Well, partner. History of gambling. In a big way."

"Shit." She shook her head.

He didn't have to say it. Jeremy Stewart owed Tony Caselli money.

"A whole *buncha* shit."

"How much?"

"It was a lot. Two hundred thousand dollars."

"*Was.* Son of a bitch."

Clint laughed, but there was no real humor in it. "You're sharp like always, Dawson."

Nate smirked, slipped into a chair and scooted close. She hadn't put her partner on speaker, but her lover was close enough to hear their conversation.

"Stewart is square with Caselli. Problem is, he's not broke. There's a shitload of money in a few accounts

I found. He's smart, so nothing obvious is in his name."

"This isn't concrete enough for Liv," Lee said. She met Nate's eyes.

His expression was thoughtful, fair head cocked to one side.

"Right. I want to talk to him," Clint said.

She shook her head. "No way. Not alone. When I can't back you."

"I don't have a choice, Lee."

"There's always a choice, *Clint*. Set up a meet and I'll come."

"No." He was firm. "If Stewart's involved in this, you *here* leaves Crane unprotected. Worse, if he's involved, and Crane comes with you, you're bringing him into the lion's den."

"Fuck!"

Clint laughed again and she could see him shaking his head in her mind. "Sorry, you won't get your way on this one. I'm touched you care. But I'll be fine."

She let his jibe slide. "Bring someone else in on this then."

"No way. If Lucas was still here, I wouldn't hesitate. There's no one else I trust like that besides you. Only Liv, and I can't open my mouth yet."

"If Stewart's involved, he killed two people, even if one was Caselli scum shooting at me and Nate. Shit."

"I know. I'll be careful."

"*Shit*," Lee repeated, the wheels turning in her head.

"What?" Clint asked.

Nate arched an eyebrow at her, echoing her

partner's inquiry.

"*If* Stewart killed Savannah Pressley, he shot Roberts. His own damn partner. Fuck. Me." She frowned and pressed into her lover's side when he threw his arm around her shoulders.

"I know. That's what pisses me off most," Clint spat. "They're close. More than partners. Good friends."

Lee wanted to wince. Did Clint Downs consider *her* a good friend?

She cleared her throat. "Are there any holes in the crime scene from the apartment?"

"No. I sent you the report. He knows what he's doing. If it was staged, it was seriously convincing. He thought about everything. Even the position of the shots. No prints, no blood. But it didn't look cleaned up, either."

"Dammit. I'll take a look. I didn't get through all your attachments. Been staring at Caselli's ugly mug for about two hours. I need to memorize his every angle."

"Oh, I got news about that, too. Dex did his fancy-schmancy computer shit. He doesn't doubt it was Caselli."

She pumped her fist and grinned at Nate. "Awesome. This…this is *good*. Let's get a fucking warrant."

"That's the goal."

Nate flashed two thumbs up.

"Something in my gut tells me there's more to all this." Now her partner was thoughtful and serious.

"Yeah, like why would Caselli do it himself?" Nate

asked.

Lee thumbed the speaker button on the cell.

"I wonder that too, Crane." Clint's answer didn't miss a beat.

"Other than the fact his minions can't get things right the first time, and this time, he did it himself and *did*," she said.

"I thought about that, but I'm not sure that's enough reason for the risk of exposure. He knows we're after him in a big way."

"No."

Nate's whisper caught her by surprise, his eyes wide, as if something had dawned on him. However, the denial dripped so much emotion, her heart tripped. Their gazes collided and held.

"No?" Clint asked.

"This was personal. Caselli wanted 'Lo to look him in the eyes when he pulled the trigger. And he did. I'll never forget the look on his face. Besides, Caselli is an arrogant bastard. He'd never even consider being identified or getting caught. Cameras or not. He has one on the inside, even if Downs is wrong about *who*. The asshole's history tells us he always cleans up after himself. So maybe there's no overall secret plot. He just wanted my friend dead and did it himself."

Lee fought against his pain seizing her gut. She moved closer, squeezing her arms around him and wishing the phone call was over and done with.

So she could be alone with Nate again. So she could kiss him. So she could make him forget.

Protective custody had an upside. Them, up close

and personal, the rest of the world in the background. Like they'd started over.

She'd got to know him like never before. Living with him. Eating, bathing, sleeping. Talking, laughing. Even watching TV was fun. *Together.*

For the first time in…longer than she could remember, she was living for something *other* than the FBI.

"Angel," Nate breathed against her temple.

She shot a look at the phone and prayed her partner hadn't heard. The man wasn't stupid, but Lee wasn't quite ready for her and Nate to be out in the open, despite her craving to be locked away with him.

Her and Nate.

Like an item, a thing. A couple.

A…relationship?

More than fucking. Nate's words teased and she shuddered.

No.

It wasn't going to last. It couldn't. So why tell anyone about it?

He squeezed her against his chest as if he could read her mind and Lee swallowed. Couldn't look at him.

She teetered between her yearning for him and reality.

Reality swallowed her whole and began to chew, agony splintering her body as she averted her gaze from what couldn't be forever.

"Not a bad theory, Counselor. Guess time will tell." Clint's voice jolted and she made herself sit still.

Forced herself not to pull away from her lover. She didn't want Nate to sense her turmoil.

"Lee, read the report. Let me know what you think. I'll let you know when I can get Stewart alone."

"I still don't like this," she complained.

"It's not a party for me, either. But I think the guy deserves a chance to defend himself. Rather it be me and not Barnes."

"Defend himself? How often are you wrong, Clint Downs?" she made a fist.

Nate grabbed her hand and kissed her knuckles.

Her partner blew out a breath that whistled into the air over the phone. "Not very damn often. Hope to hell I am this time."

"Put him in cuffs if there's any doubt."

"If I can cover your ass, I can cover my own."

Lee had to give in to her smile. "Yeah, yeah."

Clint chuckled.

"You know how I always say you're too damn careful?" she asked.

"Yeah."

She could hear the smile in his acknowledgment.

"Show me how wrong I am about the *'too damn'* part."

"You got it. Keep that phone on."

"You got it."

When the line went dead, Nate tightened his arms around her. "He'll be fine."

"Hope so." Lee burrowed into his chest.

God, please let this work out.

Was she talking about Stewart and Clint or Nate?

"What do we do now, angel?"
"I wish I fucking knew."

Chapter Sixteen

Jeremy stared at Evan's still form. His partner appeared to be simply asleep. Breathing machine gone. Doctors had pulled out his intubation the night before. He was breathing on his own, but hadn't even stirred.

No surprise wake-up.

So there he lay, coma still embracing him.

Peaceful.

Too silent.

His partner wore a full beard, making him look more mountain lumberjack than FBI agent.

Jeremy was on a nightly vigil—this was his third twelve-hour watch in a row. The last two mornings he hadn't wanted to leave, but staying was killing him.

Still hadn't been able to fulfil Caselli's orders.

None of the accusation he felt actually stared back at him when he studied the strong lines of Evan's face.

Gazing at his buddy did nothing but knot his stomach and taunt him with what he had to do.

"Jesus, maybe you have gone nuts." He shook his head, cursing himself to hell. Couldn't bear the whole saying—*to hell and back*—because he didn't deserve to come back. Needed to go there. Stay there.

Wait. Aren't you already there?

He imagined deep blue eyes popping open. Evan would sit up—shout for help and frantically look for the weapon that wasn't at his side.

To shoot your ass. Like he should've at the apartment.

Jeremy's body shook and he grabbed the arms of the bedside chair until his knuckles whitened. He squeezed harder. The leatherette padding tacked to the wood creaked. White-hot pain shot over his joints, rushing toward his wrists, but he didn't give a shit. Maybe he'd rip his nails off. Bleeding wouldn't fix things, but it would relieve some of the pressure in his head.

Sweat rolled down his cheek but he didn't release his grip to wipe it away. The moisture on his forehead would likely make its way into his eyes. It'd make his contacts burn. Or was that just the tears threatening?

"Fuck you, Caselli." The soft whisper from his own lips only made him wince. The statement had no impact on the bastard.

The man had laughed long and hard when he'd called him to discuss the video. Confronted him about not sharing that he'd killed the lawyer himself. Caselli had ordered him to mind his own fucking business. Reminded Jeremy he was on a *need-to-know-basis*, and who'd killed Angelo Fiato mattered little.

His words had sounded like a light admonition regarding his unfinished tasks, but Jeremy wasn't stupid. Threat—no, dark promise—interlaced the asshole's every statement.

Handle your partner.

As for Nate Crane, the crime boss' patience was wearing thin. The location was to be disclosed immediately.

Jeremy had twenty-four hours. If he failed to

contact Tony Jr. with *good* news, he was to pick between his mother and his ex-wife.

"Choose who dies," Caselli had barked.

If he killed Evan tonight, they both would live another day.

The bastard had dared him to fail. Said he already had two *'caretakers'* chosen for each of Jeremy's daughters. Boasted he'd enjoy *raising* the girls.

A tremor shot down his spine and his leg jumped of its own accord. Didn't stop bouncing. The *tap tap* of his boot on the linoleum burned his ears.

He pushed to his feet.

Just do it.

Jeremy dragged his boots as he strode to the threshold and shut the door to the private room. No lock, but that only ensured he'd have to hurry.

Evan's heart monitor was like blaring sirens when he closed in on the side of the bed. Like it was goading him to silence it.

Just do it.

He looked down at his best friend. Made tight fists and glued them to his sides. His heart sped into overdrive, making a headlong dive. His stomach plummeted like a car going over a bridge, threatening to eject the McDonald's he'd crammed down about an hour before.

One of his teammates, Special Agent Delina Kirk, had come with food in hand, wanting to switch out with him. He'd taken the burger and fries and sent her on her way. Told her he wasn't leaving Evan's side.

Devoted partner, right?

He snorted.

Just do it.

Suicide was going to be a gift after this. Jeremy would never get over killing Evan. As soon as his mom, Beth and the girls were safe from Caselli, he was out. Refused to let guilt eat him up from the inside out.

Beth would just have to forgive him for being a coward like her father.

He hadn't known Savannah Pressley, but she was currently starring in every dream—nightmare—that slammed down every time he managed rest. Sleep was fleeting anyway, but dripping blood and stained blonde hair made it even worse.

Nothing was worse than the special feature of last night's visit. Evan's blue eyes. Shocked expression as he'd fallen. The *thud* as he'd hit the hardwood floor.

Quit stalling, you fucking coward.

Just. Do. It.

Jeremy ignored the tear making its way down his cheek. He inched the pillow out from under Evan's head, but slipped his hand to the back of his partner's neck. Gently returned him to his peaceful position.

He stared for a full minute, the silence of the room broken only by the heart monitor. Daggers sliced into his chest with every forced breath. Shouting at him for what he was about to take away from Evan Roberts.

Jeremy sucked in a deep, painful breath, but it didn't help the ache.

He dropped the pillow over his partner's face and bent at the waist. Gripped the edges of the white linen pillowcase and shut it all out. Couldn't watch what he was about to do.

Maybe it would make it less real.

Nothing will make you less of a murderer.

A cellphone roared. His whole body jolted and he couldn't bite back his shout. "Fuck!" It took Jeremy a second to recognize the default ringtone. He hadn't personalized the device after wheedling it out of IT at the office.

He let go of the pillow and it slipped to the floor. Unassuming. Looking nothing like the murder weapon it had almost been.

Jeremy made a go for his phone. His hand shook so bad it was a wonder he'd found his damn jacket pocket. "Stewart," he barked.

"This is Downs. You all right?"

He cleared his throat and nodded, called himself an idiot. The other agent couldn't see him — thank God. "I'm good."

"Where are you?"

Why the fuck does Downs want to know where I am?

He tilted his phone back to glance at the time. Almost nine p.m. "Hospital."

"Ah. With Roberts."

"Yes."

"When you get off detail in the morning, me and you need to talk."

Icicles shot down Jeremy's spine.

The whir of the treadmill and clop of his sneakers rang in his ears, and Nate adjusted his gait. After running hard for two miles, he slowed to a four-and-a-half mile-an-hour walk. He wanted to put in two more miles, then shower.

Then…

Well, they'd been in the house a week. Had a lot of sex. He couldn't get enough of her. Had already been inside her that morning.

After the call from Downs the day before, and the results of the off record mini-investigation of Special Agent Jeremy Stewart, Nate couldn't reach Lee. Not really.

She was distracted. Obsessed with her email. Nothing but electronic case files filled the screen of his iPad.

Last night, she'd called her partner back and begged for more reports. Had even started looking into Stewart's partner, Evan Roberts, but after only two reports and another call to Downs, they'd both discounted the chance of the injured agent being involved in anything illegal.

Of course, on paper Stewart looked clean too. The more they talked — the more Nate overheard — the more they believed he was tangled with Caselli. Had taken money from the bastard. Shot his own partner.

Lee had let him read some of the reports detailing Angelo's crimes.

Nate winced, gripping both handles on the treadmill as he moved his feet. His gut still ached when he thought about his friend and the choices he'd made.

What'd driven Angelo to cross the line?

Was it the money?

Angelo's parents, both passed now, hadn't been rich, but he'd never suffered as a boy. His mother had been a legal secretary, then, later, a paralegal. She'd sparked Angelo's love of the law.

His father had been a cop, like Nate's dad. Instead of moving up the chain, like Dennis Crane had, Angelo's dad had spent his career as a beat cop. Been happy doing it, too. His neighborhoods had loved him.

Nate could remember how the man who called him, '*the Texas boy*' had boasted any time he'd visited their apartment in the city, about how 'Lo had been raised there; he was a genuine local.

If he closed his eyes, he could see Angelo's grin. Hear his laugh. The New York accent and the dark gaze women couldn't resist. He remembered all the times they'd bar hopped in college. Picked up women. Declared they were attorneys when they weren't—yet.

He chuckled and shook his head. Sweat trickled in between his shoulder blades on its way to the small of his back. He twisted his waist as it tickled. Nate grabbed a towel from the side of the treadmill without missing a step. He wiped his face and draped the white terry cloth back on the arm. His back would have to wait. He couldn't reach the spot, and he wasn't ready to wrap up his workout.

He scanned the well-equipped exercise room and considered hitting the elliptical next, or using the Bowflex.

No… Lifting weights would be better. No need for the elliptical after the long run and even longer walk.

Not like his heart needed the cardio, from all the

bedroom exercises he and Lee were putting in, but Nate needed to focus on something other than sex.

Damn, he wished there was an indoor pool. Swimming always cleared his head.

He glanced out the window and suppressed a shiver. Fat snowflakes drifted down without care. Some clung to the window, showcasing an intricate design he was too far away to study. Beautiful no doubt, but too cold for his tastes.

Below in the driveway, he couldn't see the whole car from his position, but the trunk had at least two inches covering it. So did the front yard.

Real winter was a college memory. The North Texas version was much abbreviated.

"And you want to move to New York?" he whispered.

It was the first time he'd admitted that his plan— his aim to win her back—would have to include relocation.

Yes.

He'd move to Siberia if it was for Lee.

Too damn bad she didn't feel the same.

You just have to convince her.

Nate's heart flipped and it had nothing to do with his vigorous walk. He needed to tell her he knew about her past and didn't give a shit. Needed to open up to her, so maybe she'd open up to him.

Help her heal?

One look at the *real* Lee, and it was obvious his woman had a long way to go before she was fine. He was dying to ask her if she still went to meetings. Was being here keeping her from something she needed?

There was no alcohol at the house. Did she want some?

The owner of the place had stocked it with all the groceries they'd need for a month, so they hadn't gone out. They shouldn't leave, of course, but Mr. Mullins had prevented the need. Nate's buddies would have brought all the beer and wine if they'd had a chance to arrive.

Being here...at the house. As well as at the apartment before. It was like really living with her. Glorious.

A real...relationship?

They ate together, played together. Made love. Slept in each other's arms. Even worked together. He didn't want to let her go.

The Dallas office of the FBI wouldn't have Lee back. Although it hadn't been spelled out in the reports he'd read, it was implied. So, New York it would be.

The FBI was her life.

But can I be her life, too?

He left the question dangling, even in his own head.

Before leaving Texas, Nate had inquired discreetly about contacts in New York of his boss and mentor, the District Attorney, Dean Foreman. As much as Dean would hate to see him go, there was no doubt in his mind his boss would recommend him to the county District Attorney here. Just so happened the man, Mario Malcuri, had gone to law school with Dean.

A few phone calls. Glowing letter of

recommendation.

He could have a new life.

No. You will have a new life.

What would his FBI agent's role be in it?

"Hey, Nate."

He jumped, then cursed when she arched an eyebrow at him. Her arm was bent at the elbow and resting on one shapely hip, hand splayed, two fingers in her jeans pocket.

Lee's small frame didn't fill the doorway. Amusement flickered across her face and she smiled. "You okay?"

Nate nodded, pressing the treadmill's *stop* button and hopping off. His heart raced, and it had little to do with his workout. His hands itched to touch her. His lips burned to kiss the curve of her mouth. He wanted to hold her close.

Tell her how he felt about her.

Tell her he was moving to New York.

"I feel great."

"Good. Maybe I'll hit the elliptical later. I could use a break from reading reports. Gettin' kinda stiff." Lee rolled her shoulders. "The iPad is portable, but I wish the screen was bigger. My monitor at the office is twice the size."

He didn't tease her about her aversion to modern technology. "C'mere."

She crossed the room and he turned her back to him. Nate rubbed her shoulders and the back of her neck until she moaned.

"You're going to make me forget why I came in

here."

He chuckled. "Is that a bad thing?" He laid a row of wet kisses down her neck, stopping to nibble her earlobe.

She shivered, and whirled around. Scrunched up her nose. "You smell like a sweaty boy. Or a locker room." Her eyes grazed his bare chest, belying her jibe. Her lips parted, tongue darting out to moisten the plump bottom one.

His mouth went dry and he chided himself to focus. Blood was already headed south, making his cock twitch.

Her gaze continued downward. She smirked at his crotch. "You do look super-hot when you're all worked up."

Nate tried to laugh, but lust clouded his brain. "I…better…get a shower."

"Damn straight, I'm not going to bed with a sweaty man unless I made him that way."

He laughed. "Is that a challenge?"

She winked and giggled.

Actually giggled.

It made him burn for her.

"You decide, Counselor."

"I never could turn down a challenge." Nate brushed his mouth against hers, but Lee pulled away.

She darted out of the room and down the hallway toward the bedroom they'd been sharing since the first night.

Shedding her clothing as she went.

He growled and gave chase.

Chapter Seventeen

e was rubbing her back. Long, soothing circles that made her thoughts scatter and determination to leave his bed dissipate.

Yeah, like you were serious anyway.

Lee said the same thing in her head every night she climbed into bed with him.

Go to a different room.

And every night, she pulled the covers up, ignoring the command. Let him pull her into his arms and kiss her.

Touch her.

Make love to her.

Those two words made her bite the inside of her cheek to stave off a groan, but no matter how many times her mind shouted the denial, she couldn't convince herself it wasn't true.

The tenderness in his eyes. The meaning in his kiss. His every caress shouted how he felt about her, but he said nothing. Which was fine as far as Lee was concerned. She couldn't reciprocate.

She cared about him.

Nothing more.

They made each other feel good.

Nothing more.

When the warrant for Caselli came through, she didn't know the details of the time—it could even be first thing tomorrow morning. Her team would go arrest him.

Finally.

Nate would probably be free to go home until the trial. Get back to his life.

Without you.

When his hand slipped under her arm and his fingertips brushed the underside of her breast, her sex throbbed.

Lee made herself lie still, sinking into his touch, the warmth of his caresses. She sighed. There was nothing sexual about his roving hands. He was lulling, comforting. But she was on fire for him.

Moisture flooded her core. Her body wept for him. Begged for him. She wouldn't tell him to hurry. The torture was exquisite.

Finally, *finally* he rested his hand on her lower belly and tugged backwards.

Lee's shoulders hit his chest, and her ass, his thighs. The coarse hair on his legs and chest didn't abrade—it made her want him more.

Nate pressed warm, wet kisses to the back of her neck and she wiggled against the erection pushing into her bottom.

Now she pulsed.

He groaned into her overheated skin, following the curve of her hip with teasing fingertips. When his large palm claimed the front of her thigh, urging her to open, she moaned.

"Angel…you're killing me."

She wanted to say '*Me?*' but it refused to breach her lips.

Instead of sliding into her from behind, he pulled back, spreading her legs, rolling her over and settling on top of her. His hot mouth took hers, and Lee didn't hesitate to twine her tongue around his. She pressed harder into his kiss, slipping her hands onto his shoulders, exploring his back like he had hers.

Nate made a noise in his throat, but broke their kiss only to leave a heat down her neck and collarbone.

Lee arched when his tongue swirled around her nipple, and she buried her hands in his hair. She tugged, but he moved into her touch instead of away.

His teeth skimmed the hard peak and his name fell from her lips. Then he licked the spot, flicking his tongue and blowing a puff of air that hardened the tender skin to the point of pain. He was killing her, but she could die happily at the moment.

After lavishing the same attention to her other breast, he moved on, licking, nibbling and kissing his way down her belly. Nate was mindful of her stitches since she'd done away with the bandage, but she didn't give a shit about her side. Didn't even hurt anymore. Certainly didn't hurt right now.

His rough stubble nuzzled her oversensitive inner thighs and she pulled his hair. He laughed and did it again. Blew lightly on her swollen, aching clit. Then he licked her. It was fleeting, a tease.

"Oh, God."

Nate laughed again, but didn't make her wait. He grabbed her ass with both hands, tilted her hips and sucked her into his mouth.

Lee screamed.

Orgasm refused to be held at bay. He had her so revved up there was no chance of drawing it out. Pleasure crashed into her like a tidal wave, stealing her breath and her thoughts. She pushed her pelvis into his mouth, rocking and panting his name.

He lapped at her clit and her entrance, his mouth relentless as she rode out the climax.

Then he was behind her, holding her through the shivers racking her frame, coaxing her muscles to let go and relax into him. He nestled her into his chest, kissing the crown of her head.

Tender.

Expecting nothing in return, despite the erection scorching her hip. If she wanted to go to sleep right now, without even touching him, it would be fine with Nate. Because he'd given her pleasure.

Just who he is.

Damn good thing she was selfish.

Lee closed her eyes and lifted her mouth. He didn't hesitate, pressing his lips to hers and forcing her to open. Their tongues danced and dueled, her essence lacing the kiss and making her burn for him even more.

Foreplay, kisses, touches.

Only with Nate.

She snaked her arms around his neck and tugged him over her. The bedding was already warm and damp from her body heat and their sweat, but she didn't care. The cotton was as welcome under her shoulders as his weight covering her.

"Angel…" he whispered against her lips.

"Get inside me. I'm far from done with you."

Their gazes collided and Lee gasped at the undisguised emotions there.

She bit her bottom lip and ignored the flip of her stomach.

Just be with him, Lee. Shut the rest out.

Nate's heart galloped at the look on her face.

Lee was always intense, but only in bed was her body more honest with him than words ever could be. Heat, passion and her response, even her touch, spoke to him.

He wanted more. She felt *something* for him other than lust. *She* sure as hell wouldn't tell him. His gut shouted as much, even if it caused his heart to cry out.

So he'd take what he could get. He loved her. If he couldn't tell her, he sure as hell could show her.

The tender moment passed, and Lee tilted her face to meet his mouth again.

He kissed her, twining their tongues and rocking his pelvis into hers. They fell into a rhythm that was more torture than pleasure because it wasn't nearly enough.

After her demand, he was shocked she was letting him tease her.

She moved with him, her dark eyes heavy, gorgeous face flushed.

Their sexes touched, brushed and rubbed, but never merged.

His blood boiled.

"Tease," Lee moaned.

"Me?" Nate's amusement didn't come across in his grunt.

She grabbed his ass and yanked him forward.

The tip of his cock parted her folds, but the angle was wrong for entry.

They both moaned.

"Let me help," he groaned. He gripped his erection, positioned himself and slid into her to the hilt.

God, she was tight, and so wet.

So hot.

Nate circled his hips and her sex clenched around him as she climaxed again. He sucked in a breath and stilled. He had to, or it would have been over for him, too.

"Oh, my God," Lee breathed.

Her nails sank into his forearms and she whimpered, but he didn't care if she made him bleed.

"Angel...damn...I didn't even move yet."

She writhed and her breasts lifted as she panted, the tight buds of her nipples catching his gaze. The brown color of her areolas was darker than the bronze skin of the rest of her gorgeous body.

Nate wanted to lick her there, suck on her again. He lowered his head, hovering over her mouth. "Did I get you that hot and bothered?" His dick pulsed inside her, threatening to blow.

"You're still a tease," she said against his lips. Lee crushed her mouth into his, burying her tongue deep and cutting off his ability to give in to a laugh. At the same time, she tightened her legs around his waist and shoved her hips up.

He met her second thrust. Their bodies took over, carrying them higher. He propelled forward again and again, lost in her. Her skin, her scent, the slant of her lips moving under his. Every inch of her supple form touching his, heating him, driving him.

Lee had claimed him, even if she couldn't say so.

Branded him.

One more powerful lunge forward and he was a goner. His spine tingled and his balls jerked. Then Nate's release shot deep inside her.

She joined him in orgasm again, a gasp breaking the seal of their mouths as her whole body contracted beneath his.

They held each other tight, her arms and legs wrapped around him as he pinned her to his chest. He stroked her thigh and hip as Lee made lazy circles on his sweaty back. Tremors shook his frame and Nate buried his face against the damp, overheated skin of her neck.

Muscles lax and heavy, he collapsed on the bed. Tried to roll to his side so he wouldn't crush her, but she held onto him as if for dear life.

Their hearts beat in tandem, and he couldn't form a coherent thought, let alone anything intelligent to say, but he wanted to tell her something.

Anything.

Too bad every phrase contained the L-word.

She never clung to him like this, not even after all the times they'd been together.

"Angel?" He lifted his face and met her eyes.

Lee smiled. "I like when you call me *angel*."

Emotion threatened to bowl him over. Nate swallowed. He pressed a gentle kiss to her mouth that melted into a slow dance for their tongues. Heated and meaningful, it made him wish his cock was ready to go again, despite the satiation in his bones. He slipped from her body against his will, but pulled her closer.

She nestled into him.

"Thank you."

Lee didn't answer, but she didn't have to.

Nate kissed her temple and ran his fingers through her long, hair.

Silence settled over them and he started to drift off.

"Don't leave me," she whispered. Her voice was thick, her cheek plastered to his right pec.

He stilled, palm against her hair. "Lee?"

Her dark orbs locked onto his. "Don't leave me."

Not as good as *'I love you'*, but he'd take it. Nate cupped her cheeks and kissed her softly. "You couldn't make me leave you, angel."

A ghost of a smile played at her lips and kicked his heartbeat up a notch.

She nodded and moved closer, resting her leg, bent at the knee, between his. Lee pressed a kiss to his chest before putting her head back down. Next to her cheek, her fingertips teased his sparse golden curls and he shivered.

"Cold?" Her warm breath danced across his skin.

Nate's nipple tingled, started to harden.

Lee noticed, rubbing the blunt peak with her thumb.

"Not cold. Hey, now. That tickles."

She scooted up, entwining her fingers on his chest and propping her chin on top. He flashed a lopsided grin that made his stomach flip. "Yeah?"

He chuckled and caressed her cheek. "Yeah."

She sighed. "Too damn bad, 'cause I like touching you even if it tickles. Tasting you. Being with you like this."

"Oh?"

Her expression slipped into sheepish, and she averted her gaze.

"What's wrong?" he whispered, tugging on her earlobe so she'd look at him.

"Nothing's wrong." Lee paused, but her breasts rose and fell against him as if she'd taken a deep breath. "It's better than fucking."

Nate froze and his heart skipped.

First *'Don't leave me'*, then a confession?

Was he finally getting through to her? Would Lee admit she felt something for him?

He needed to temper his answer. The last thing he wanted was to freak her out and have her pull away. Shut him out.

Normal. Be normal.

She wasn't ready for him to bare his heart. His instinct yelled it.

He ignored the need for a fortifying breath and prayed she couldn't see right through him. Nate tweaked her nose and flashed a grin. "Told you so."

Lee hovered over his body and kissed him.

He pulled her closer and kissed her back.

Chapter Eighteen

T he clip-clop of heels jolted Jeremy awake. He opened his eyes and blinked to orient, looking around.

A tall brunette wearing a business suit and carrying a briefcase passed him without so much as a nod. Her shoes were even louder, reverberating in his ears.

A clean, astringent scent tickled his nose.

Ah, got it.

Hospital corridor. Outside Evan's room.

He made it to his feet and stretched out his back, swallowing a yawn.

Shit. Must've drifted off.

Not like Evan was in danger from anyone but Jeremy, so the nap hadn't hurt anything. Caselli still trusted him to carry out his orders to kill his partner.

For now. Today's my last day…

"Morning, Stewart."

He whipped his head around and met a pair of deep blue eyes.

Petite and blonde, Special Agent Delina Kirk held out a huge cup from Starbucks and smiled. She was dressed casually in jeans and a black, long-sleeved button-down.

Forcing himself to be polite, he thanked her for the coffee and took a sip. "Morning."

"Have a good night?" Her smile widened. His

teammate was in a good mood.

"It was quiet."

"Good. How's Roberts?" Kirk glanced into the hospital room he'd given up on being *inside* at about midnight.

Jeremy hadn't been able to endure sitting there, five feet from his best friend.

Evan was too silent, too still.

Every glance at the beard on his face, his hands lying helpless beside him, the slow rise and fall of his chest. The blanket cocooned his torso and legs. Not even his feet shifted. As if he was already in a coffin, instead of simply asleep. The peace Evan seemed to exude was a lie.

All of it made guilt twist his gut.

Lights and noises from the monitors had made him jittery. In the chair, his leg had started to shake, then his hands and arms had twitched until he'd hopped up. He'd dragged the seat into the hallway, sitting where Smythe had the other day.

His partner was supposed to be dead right now.

He'd almost done it.

Downs had interrupted him — saved him from it.

Temporarily.

Jeremy's thoughts swirled. Chaos he couldn't make much sense of.

What did Downs want?

Did he know something that would fuck Jeremy even more?

A tremor threatened to bowl him over and he swallowed hard.

No.

He'd tidied up his gambling problem. His debts were paid, and no one in the FBI was any the wiser. At the scene of the apartment, he'd staged it like the pro he was. Not one little red flag. Jeremy had read the report. He was free and clear. Evan's missing cellphone hadn't even come to light.

Downs knew nothing. He couldn't.

"Stewart?"

He cleared his throat. "Yeah?"

"How's Roberts?"

Shit.

The repeated phrase made him remember she'd asked already. He'd left her hanging. "No change."

Kirk nodded. Her gaze was sympathetic, but her expression, her whole body, was still upbeat. She was stoked about something.

Her mood was too good for someone doing nothing but standing guard over an injured teammate for the next twelve hours.

"Something's up," Jeremy said.

"You're right." She beamed, showing every tooth in her damn head.

"Spill it."

"Let's step inside." The other agent thumbed toward Evan's room. She closed the door and whirled around. "We got a warrant."

Chills raced up and down his spine.

She didn't need to tell him more.

Caselli.

A warrant to arrest Antonio Rodolfo Aldo Caselli,

Junior.

For murder.

Kirk stared, her smile falling off a bit when Jeremy didn't react. "You okay? You paled out."

"I did? Sorry." He blew out a breath and dragged his hand down his face. Stubble grazed his palm. "Just…shocked. After all this time. We finally got him."

"I know! It's awesome!"

"It's great. Hard work paid off."

She nodded, but her gaze was keen. Like she could see right through him.

"Look, I gotta go." He strode past her without waiting for an answer. Ignored the look on her face that shouted she thought he was nuts. He rushed down the hallway, ditching the full coffee cup in the nearest trashcan. His thighs shook when he paused at the elevator and punched the down arrow, so he rubbed sweaty palms dry and licked his lips.

What the fuck am I supposed to do now?

"Just get outta here." Jeremy tried not to bounce in place as he waited for the damn elevator.

Where is it? Where is it?

An elderly couple stood arm in arm next to him, also waiting. The man kept throwing him furtive glances.

Rather than smile to reassure the geezer when he protectively pulled the old lady closer, under his thin arm, he ignored the couple. Only manners long instilled by his mom made him allow them to get on first when the stainless steel doors finally opened. He couldn't keep his knuckles from rapping the handicapped rail, which only made the blue-haired woman glare.

Jeremy dashed into the basement level of the parking garage in no time, but the tremors in his body refused to subside. Fingers fumbling, he dug his cell from his pocket. He paced, phone plastered to his ear as soon as he was in sight of his parking spot.

Damn good thing his phone had a signal by the glass double doors leading into the hospital. He'd still have to keep his voice low. There was no one around, but the area was far from secluded.

His first call went unanswered.

So did the second.

He could hear the sound of the girders above him clunk and shift as cars drove over them. Bitter wind whistled by, burning his ears, and he shivered, forcing his boots in a straight line.

Jeremy whirled, going back toward the hospital doors. He stopped short of returning inside, falling back into the pacing.

"Think. Think. *Now*."

Need to go. Need to go.

He chanted, but he had to make a decision first.

Shit.

"They've—we've—really done it. A warrant." His own shock made him shake his head as the winter cold formed tears at the corners of his eyes. The wind tore through the garage again. Pacing wasn't keeping him warm.

The crime boss they'd been investigating for *years* was going to go down because he couldn't bear to let someone else kill his attorney. Because it was *personal*, obviously.

Whether or not Caselli wanted to admit it, there was no other logical conclusion. The idiot was conceited enough to not have even considered getting caught. Although, normally Caselli was smarter than such reckless behavior. He'd risked a great deal being out in the open like that. Doing something himself was new.

For years, that'd been the only reason the man was free to run his empire. They hadn't been able to get him with blood on his hands.

Sure, the RICO stuff had kept him in court from time to time. But it was red tape, technicality stuff. With endless income and a fantastic legal team — led by Fiato, of course — Caselli had never seen the inside of a jail cell.

This… The FBI had *video*. Actual evidence. Proof.

Caselli couldn't have an out.

Now the bastard wasn't answering the phone. He'd never missed a call from Jeremy before. No matter the hour. And half past seven wasn't all that early.

"Fuck."

Jeremy ended the fourth call — or was it the fifth?

The generic, robotic voice started to state the number he'd called, but he slammed his thumb on the red *'end'* icon on his touch screen. No message.

Why bother?

Could Caselli already know about the warrant? Had the man disappeared upstate? Out of state? Maybe out of the country?

He owned several yachts and two Learjets.

"No way. How could he know?" He tightened his grip on the cell.

Why do you care?

Wouldn't Caselli's arrest fix his sitch?

"No."

It really wouldn't. Even if the bastard went quietly—yeah, like that would happen—he'd blame Jeremy. Accuse him of helping the FBI—his team.

Have him killed.

Orders could be carried out even if the boss was in prison.

The clock on his phone's screen taunted him. He was going to be late to meet with Downs.

Jeremy didn't know what Clint Downs wanted, but not showing would lend suspicion. The other agent would think he'd run.

Could he know why?

He'd convinced himself Downs knew nothing.

But...

Maybe the guy knew when the team was going to serve the warrant. Insider info. Why the fuck hadn't he just asked Kirk? He couldn't go back inside now to find out—she already thought he was crazy.

Jeremy tripped over his feet as he paced but managed not to fall on his face. Gnawed on his thumbnail until one tug too many shot pain up into his joint.

What the fuck am I going to do?

He glanced at the black Dodge Charger parked up against the retaining wall about ten feet away. His duty car was FBI standard issue. Government plates. Could spot the damn thing from a mile away.

His cell told him three minutes had passed.

"Wasting time. Wasting time." He sounded frantic to his own ears. Jeremy shoved his phone in his pocket and surveyed the garage. Still no one in sight.

He hit the street, slipping his sunglasses on to block out the bright winter morning. The sunshine belied the bitter temperature and he hunkered down in his jacket.

People rushed by on foot so he tried to stick to one side of the sidewalk.

When he got to the corner, he hailed a cab.

Had two choices…

Caselli or Downs.

Which one would fuck him more?

"I can't get a hold of Downs." Her eyes were wide. Lee's body jerked as she moved across the kitchen. She was fighting tremors.

Nate's instinct was to calm her, but she'd pull away if he put his hands on her. Although her panic was contained, he could see it, sense it. "Voicemail?"

"I left *three*. Cell and direct line at the office. Then I called the receptionist. Nothin'. Talked to Smythe, too. No one has seen my partner this morning."

"What about Special Agent Barnes?"

"I don't want Liv to know something's up, so no. Not calling her."

"You don't know something *is* up, angel."

She shook her head. "Clint always answers his

cell."

"What about being off grid?"

"When I leave him a message at night, he always gets back to me first thing in the morning. Actually, it's usually the ass crack of dawn. He gets up at five to run."

Nate laid the iPad flat and rose from the table. Reached for her hand.

Lee came to him, entwined their fingers, but she shook her head again. "No. Something's *wrong*. I can feel it. I don't like this."

"Stewart?"

She sucked in a breath and stepped closer. "The meet was this morning. That's all I know."

"Your partner knows what he's doing, angel."

She made a fist with her free hand and rapped his chest. "Dammit, Downs." Her voice was low, thick with emotion.

His stomach fluttered. He drew her into an embrace. Even though she didn't fight him, she didn't wrap her arms around him, either.

"I need to go."

The whisper was so slight he'd almost missed it. Nate froze.

When their gazes locked, her midnight orbs begged him.

"I'm going with you." The sentence tumbled out without thought. Or pause. He'd stay by Lee's side no matter what.

She didn't argue, but she was silent—too silent. Unnamed emotions flickered across her face, danced through those eyes. "I *can't* go. I *have* to go." Lee chewed her bottom lip.

She was weighing things aloud, but had she even realized what she'd said?

Lee looked lost, distant.

Un-Lee-like.

"Fuck."

Nate cupped her face. "I understand. He's your partner."

"You're my—" Her mouth snapped shut, as if the words hadn't the permission to exit. She'd caught herself.

From saying *what?*

His heart stopped. "Your what?"

God, please don't say 'witness'.

"Lover." She shivered in his arms.

Lover.

He could deal with that. Wished she'd ditch the *r*, but considering Lee's nature, her choice was an accomplishment.

Was he disappointed?

"This is a life or death situation. I really do understand."

"I know you do." She nodded. Didn't pull away from his hands surrounding her cheeks. "But *yours* is life or death, too. You and Clint could both be in danger."

"I'm going with you." Nate's repeated statement made the love of his life look even more torn.

"If I leave you here, you're in danger unprotected. If I bring you with me, I'm bringing you *to* the danger."

He chuckled. "Fucked, huh?"

One corner of her mouth inched up and he wanted to lick her there. "Not the way I'd like to be."

He laughed. Kissed her hard and fast. "Say the word and I think I can arrange something."

Lee let a genuine smile curve her lips, but the turmoil hadn't left her gorgeous face.

"Listen to me, Selena Dawson. Your partner is the one in more immediate danger. I have you to cover *my* ass. He needs you to cover *his* now. I'm okay with that. Let's go. Better yet, gimme a damn gun."

"Nate—"

"I promise I understand. It's fine. We *need* to go."

Her breasts heaved and Nate made himself look at her face instead of staring there.

Banished the memories of how her nipples tasted.

"I can't give you a gun."

"Okay…" He studied her. That was the last thing he'd expected her to say.

"Downs is going to chew my ass out for bringing you into the city if I'm overreacting. If this is nothing. If his cell is in the car, or on silent. Or, hell, even off. But my gut says—"

"Hey." Nate slipped his hands to her shoulders. Squeezed and shook her so she'd look at him again. "There's nothing more I'd like to see than Clint Downs *try* to kick your ass."

Both her eyebrows shot up and her mouth twitched as she fought a smile.

"But we have to find him first," they said at the same time.

Chapter Nineteen

She was jittery. Body jerky, and mind racing in an endless loop of havoc.

Worse than the day she'd had to whisk Nate away from the FBI-owned apartment.

This was *different*.

They'd been fleeing danger that day.

Now they were running toward it. *She* could handle it. But she wasn't alone. Dragging a witness *into* danger was a first.

Nate wasn't just any witness.

Lee gripped the wheel of his rented Honda Accord even tighter. Her fingers couldn't tingle. They were squeezed free of blood. White didn't look like it belonged on her normally dark skin.

"Relax, angel. Just drive."

In lieu of blowing out a breath, she forced a nod and sank her teeth into her bottom lip until the pain bit back.

She flexed her fingers. Blood rushed to the digits, making them throb and burn. It helped — more pain she could use to focus.

"Lee, you're going to make your mouth bleed."

She jumped in the driver's seat and ordered herself to sit still. Cleared her throat. "I'm fine."

Nate smirked. "Right." He relaxed into the passenger seat, no longer causing his seatbelt to strain. He wasn't looking her way; staring ahead, out the windshield.

Silence fell, disturbed only by the *whoosh* of the wiper blades. Thick, wet snow fell, making the bright day even more so. Radiant and white. A false sense of peace, if Lee had ever seen one.

"You know I trust you, right?" He was even and calm.

Her heart skipped. Nate Crane was a control freak like her. Drove her crazy sometimes, but lately, seeing him—hearing him—be the one *in charge* stoked her libido from cold to smoldering in about two seconds flat.

Yeah, like now's the time.

The look on his face at the moment, fitting right along with his smooth tone, made her throb between the legs. Couldn't help it.

"Lee?"

Her name on his lips, in that same placid hum made her stomach flip.

"Yeah… I mean yes, I know you trust me. I trust you, too."

"Then we're gonna be fine." Nate spared her a glance, one corner of his mouth up. "Even if you won't give me a gun."

She snorted, fighting a smile. "I like my job, babe."

He paused. "'Cause you've never broken any rules before."

"'*Rules*' are quite a bit different than '*laws*'."

"Touché." He smiled.

Lee sighed, ordering her shoulders to loosen. Bantering with him helped, but it didn't get her mind off her partner. Even though Nate's smile made her insides mush. "Clint is…reliable."

"I don't know the guy like you do, but I'd agree."

"So that's why I'm freaked the fuck out. Not being able to get a hold of him is foreign. Doesn't sit right in my gut."

He nodded. Reached to squeeze her forearm.

She would've preferred he held her hand. Too bad she needed both on the wheel to navigate winter-coated roads safely. She couldn't feel the heat of his palm through the leather of her jacket, either. His touch always calmed her. Lee wouldn't ask for more. Not now.

"We'll get to him, angel. And it'll be okay. If he's not at the office, where could he be? You think he's home?"

"No. Besides, I'm not going to call Robin to ask. She's a stay-at-home wife and mom. Actually, she home-schools their youngest daughter. Kid's autistic or something. I don't want to scare her. He's not only reliable to me, he's reliable to her. If I let on *I* can't find him, she'll worry. I'm not doing that."

"All right. I get it. What next?"

"Shit," she growled. "I'm gonna have to call in."

"Your boss?"

"Not that bad. I'll just have to swear Dex to secrecy."

"Ah. The computer analyst guy?"

"Yeah. If Clint's phone is on, he can track it through GPS."

"Right. Good thinking."

Nate dug her cell out of her bomber jacket's pocket and dialed the number for her. It only rang once.

"Wayne."

"Hey, Dex. It's Dawson. I need a favor."

"Sure. 'Sup?"

"You in your office?" Lee pictured the easy-going analyst at his desk, kicked back in his chair with his feet propped up.

Fair-haired and good-looking, Dex wasn't exactly a normal computer nerd. He liked the ladies and wasn't shy. He'd hit on her when she'd joined the unit, but she hadn't taken him up on his overt offer.

They worked together. Besides, they were too much alike.

"You bet."

She heard a door close. "You alone?" She cleared her throat.

"Yes." Dex paused. "Everything all right?"

"Can you do your thing and get me an address from a cell phone's GPS?"

"Of course." The *tap tap* of the keyboard told Lee he was about ready. "Go for it."

"I need to know where Downs is."

"Okay." He didn't ask why, and for that she was grateful.

She probably didn't need to ask him to keep her call on the down-low, but she did anyway. "Don't mention I asked, please."

"You got it," he said without missing a beat.

She swallowed the sigh of relief. "Thanks."

"No problem. I got your location."

Lee repeated the address aloud, and Nate jotted it down. She thanked Dex, her thumb hovering over the *'end'* icon.

"Hey, Dawson, wait a sec."

"Yeah?"

"I wanna check something. That address looks really familiar, but I'm drawing a blank. Let me look it up in the database."

"All right."

"Son of a bitch." Dex's voice was a hard bark.

Alarm bells roared in her head, Lee's heart stuttered.

Fuck.

She knew what he was going to say before the computer guy confirm.

"That's the address to Caselli's mansion."

"You better step off. I got no issue poppin' you."

Jeremy wanted to roll his eyes, but it wouldn't do him any good. He needed to get past this asshole, to go *into* Caselli's place. "I think your boss would be kinda pissed if you *'popped'* me."

"Doubtful, since you killed Mikey. I know who you are, FBI man. Boss thinks you changed teams."

He made a fist, then shook his hand out. His palm itched to grab his Glock. "I'm gonna add you to my body count if you don't move the fuck outta my way. I need to talk to Caselli. *Now.*"

"Watch your mouth." An oversized thug came out the gatehouse door, aiming an assault rifle at the middle of Jeremy's chest.

Nice. Make that two assholes.

His gut clenched and he let out a breath slowly, silently. Needed to stay cool, stay in control of himself so he could one-up Caselli's guys. Basically, lie his ass off about being calm, because truth was, he was a total head fuck.

It was either fake it or kill them—which actually had more appeal.

Revenge on the fucker that held his family's safety over his head. The higher the body count on Caselli's thugs—*his* family—the better.

The one in front of him was short and stocky, but the other was bigger, probably about six-two and packed with muscle. Both had the requisite dark hair and Italian looks, but Jeremy didn't know either of them.

Could he take them both and not get his ass shot?

"I'm not gonna play this game with you," he barked.

"Not like you got a choice, FBI-guy." Guido Number One crossed his arms over his chest. He didn't have a gun visible, but no doubt he had one—or more—on him.

Guido Number Two narrowed his gaze and flexed his hand on the stock of the AK-47.

Jeremy's pulse roared in his ears as his blood boiled.

Calm down. Calm down.

He rolled his shoulders and made a tighter fist.

Guido One took a step back.

Fuck it.

Rushing forward, he clocked the shorter man with one fist, shoved his chest with the other. The guy stumbled, hitting his head on the doorframe of the gatehouse.

Jeremy didn't pause. He slammed into the bigger thug then grabbed the assault rifle and rammed the stock in the guy's face.

His nose broke with a sickening crack, blood spurted and he hollered as he made a grab for his face. The man whined and threw one hand up, but it was too late for begging.

Jeremy flipped the AK around and pulled the trigger. Held it down. The spray of the fully automatic weapon's bullets tore through Guido Two's massive chest.

His arms flew straight and his body jerked in a morbid dance. Muscles jolted and lurched until he finally crumpled, landing in a pile of blood and holes.

A groan took his attention and Jeremy turned to see Guido One rubbing his head.

Blood trickled down his forehead. The ass took one look at his buddy's body and his palms hovered high and flat. "Don't kill me."

"Why?" he growled. "I told you I wasn't fucking around."

"I'll take you to the boss."

Jeremy snorted. "Don't need a tagalong."

"Fine. Forty-five, then eighty-seven. Then hit the pound key and hold it down until you hear the beep."

"What the fuck does that mean?"

"It's the code to get into the kitchen back door. Only way in without a key—the front door is barred at night. Boss had a huge party last night to celebrate his favorite girl's birthday, so they're probably all passed out."

"Who's inside?" He narrowed his eyes.

Guido One hesitated. "Just the inner-circle. Guests are gone. The boss doesn't like sleepovers. He's a private guy and all."

"How many?" Jeremy made sure the thug saw his finger hovering over the trigger.

"Uh…"

"How. Many."

"Five. *Five.* They all have their own suites. Different wing than Caselli's private one."

The bastard didn't have to name Caselli's inner circle. Jeremy was familiar with the whole cast of characters. Party or not, the crime boss always had bodyguards. "So he's alone."

"He's never alone."

"Who's his private guard these days?"

"I don't know."

He kicked Guido One in the gut.

"Last night he told everyone to take a hike. When I got out here, he was on his own. Only—"

"You're talking too slow." Jeremy kicked him again.

"Females! He probably has a few in his bed! That's all I was trying to say, man." The guy coughed and grabbed his middle, doubling over on his knees.

"Don't bother getting up." He raised the rifle.

The man's eyes went wide and he shook his head, waving his hands. "No. Don't. Ple—"

He shot him in the head.

One and done.

Jeremy jumped over the body, ignoring the brain matter and blood spatter; dashing into the gatehouse. He grabbed two full magazines for the AK. They were laid out on the counter, already loaded. A box of ammo stood open beside them. "Thanks for having these ready for me."

After slipping the mags in his pocket, he surveyed the small station.

The gates to the vast property were still open, but he didn't bother closing them.

He watched the scrolling images on the huge flat-screen monitor on the desk.

"Gee, Tony. Black and white?"

The cameras were high quality, though.

He made a mental note of the property layout. Seeing photos from case files was different from being here.

Jeremy studied the multiple camera views until he was satisfied he could remember everything. There were no others in sight outside.

When he breached the inside of the mansion, he'd have to find out where Caselli had his indoor camera monitoring system set up. The mobster's paranoia was equaled by his professionalism, so he probably had an actual security office.

Then what?

The question bounced around in his head.

Go to Caselli's suite. Kill him in his bed? Or tell him about the warrant, get some money as a reward and help him get out of town?

He could go with him. Get away from all this. Jeremy was fucked anyway. He'd just killed two more people.

Or...

Could he arrest Caselli himself?

Be a hero?

He could worry about the logistics of why he hadn't waited for his team, why he didn't have the paperwork in hand, later.

It won't make Evan wake up.

And it wouldn't save his family. Caselli could have them killed from prison just as easily as he could order Jeremy dead.

"There's no real way out of this." It'd gone too far. He ignored the tremors in his sentence. The tingles in his spine as reality smacked him in the forehead.

Taking Caselli down wouldn't fix where he was going—hell or prison—but it *might* make him feel better.

He made a fist, then cursed long and hard. He swiped the sweat from his brow. With the frigid temp outside, it didn't belong on his forehead anyway.

Holding the AK-47 against his side, Jeremy slipped from the gatehouse and jogged toward the mansion. The place was huge.

He needed to get in, stay silent and unseen until he was ready to reveal himself.

Preferably at the end of Caselli's bed, the assault

rifle pointed at his head.

The hairs on the back of his neck stood on end and his heart kicked up faster than required for the energy he was exerting. He glanced over his shoulder, pausing his step.

Nothing.

Bright winter sun shone over the blanket of white covering Caselli's grounds. Wind blew, frosting cold kisses onto his cheeks, but Jeremy saw nothing.

He scanned the giant fountain in front of the house. It was made up of naked goddesses or some shit, and of course was off, being the dead of a northern winter.

Large enough to be cover for someone trying to shoot him, but there was no one there.

Stop being paranoid.

He resumed his run, boots crunching through fresh snow. He tightened his grip on the gun

Big. Strong. Real.

The rifle would help him accomplish his task.

He rounded the side of the house, making it to the back door of the kitchen in minutes.

A garage that was more warehouse-sized loomed from across the back driveway. A black Mercedes sat closest to the residence, covered with snow and ice.

The line of Escalades behind it varied in color, but four were dark to the last silver one. They too, were covered with fresh snow.

So Guido One was right.

The house was still asleep.

Jeremy studied the door in front of him. Far from a standard house door, it was stainless steel, no doubt reinforced. Bulletproof.

The keypad above the handle looked like it belonged on a bank vault more than an entrance to someone's home.

He pressed the four and jolted. The *beep* it screamed was loud enough to wake the dead. He shook himself and pressed the five.

"Stewart, stop!"

Jeremy whirled, swinging the assault rifle high. He met the wide, crystal blue eyes of Special Agent Clint Downs.

Chapter Twenty

"What the fuck are you doing here, Downs?" The other man's Adam's apple bobbed as he swallowed, but the Glock didn't move from where it was aimed at Jeremy's center mass. "I could ask you the same damn thing."

He laughed. The maniacal edge to it shot a tremor down his spine. It was almost as if he was outside his own body. "I'm gonna get Caselli."

"We got a warrant."

"I heard."

"Right. Good." The agent nodded, but the forty didn't waver. "But not this way, Stewart. No vest. No backup."

"This is the *only* way." Jeremy heard the desperation in his statement. His hands shook. The AK rattled in his hold, but he didn't lower it from his teammate's torso.

Flashbacks of Evan in the duplex safe house crossed his vision. His partner begging him to lower his weapon. Telling him there was another way.

"There's no other way." The words fell out in little more than a whisper. All he could see were Evan's eyes.

"There *is* another way," Downs said. "Protocol. Procedures we have in place to keep everyone safe. That's why we're a team."

The guy's calm, even tone gripped him as surely as if he'd rested his hands on Jeremy's shoulders.

He stared into the tall man's face.

Neither moved their weapon.

"No. This is the only way. I… I'm fucked."

"Why?" Downs sounded normal, like he was asking about the weather.

"'*Why*' is a good question. As in, *why* did you want to meet with me?"

"Why do you think?"

"No. Not doing this. Tell me what you know."

"Let's flip that around. Tell me what *you* know, Stewart. Who shot your partner?"

Jeremy shook his head. "You want some sort of confession?" He laughed again.

"Confession? What do you have to confess?" His teammate slipped closer.

"Stop right there. I don't want to shoot you." He tightened his grip on the AK.

Downs paused. His Glock still didn't move away. "Okay. I'll stop. Put the gun down, Stewart. *We're* FBI. This isn't the way we do things. I'll call in and the cavalry will come. We weren't serving the warrant until tonight, but we're here… You and I. Let's get some cover, and we'll get this bastard. The right way."

"Then what?"

"Let's talk. Just you and me."

"No. No." He shook his head again. His chest ached with the effort to breathe normally. Jeremy barely contained his urge to pant. "There's nothing to talk about." He paced. His thighs burned as his boots sliced the wet snow. Nothing but the sloshing of his frantic movements cut through the silence.

"Stewart." Downs threw his palm up and raised his Glock, taking it off him for the first time. "What if I put my gun down?"

His eyes shot to the man's. "That would be fucking stupid." Jeremy froze, training the AK-47 on his fellow agent's broad chest.

Downs dropped his stance, and they were at stand-off position. One second flat and that Glock was pointed at him.

If the guy pulled the trigger, so would Jeremy.

His gut told him neither would hesitate.

Who would *win*?

"Want to hear what I think?" his fellow agent asked, once again casually, as if they were discussing sports.

"Not really," he growled.

"Well, I'll share with the class anyway." Downs took a breath, his gaze shrewd. "I think Caselli paid off your gambling debts. I also think you've been helping him out. He's been paying you. You shot your partner and killed Savannah Pressley. I haven't put my finger on the extent of your involvement in the attempt on Nate Crane at the apartment, but I think *you're* the info leak. Am I right?"

Jeremy's heart skipped and his stomach threatened to eject the coffee Kirk had bought him, even though he'd only had a few sips. A cold winter breeze shifted his hair. It tickled the back of his neck, and a shudder racked his frame. "I don't want to kill you."

"Ditto. So drop the rifle. Come with me back to the office."

"I can't." The denial flew out an anguished moan. "He'll kill my family."

"No, he won't. He can't. We're taking him down."

Jeremy threw his head back and laughed. "Are you fucking stupid? Unless he's dead, he won't stop. Prison won't contain his orders. I need to fucking kill him."

The big FBI agent shook his head. "No, Stewart. That's not the way. Put the rifle down." This time the order was clear. A harsh bark. His teammate's patience was waning.

"I have to do what I have to do."

"So do I."

"Okay then." He sucked in a breath and rushed Downs. The man had height and muscle on him, but Jeremy was younger. Faster.

Downs hollered and pulled the trigger of his weapon, but Jeremy dropped his body, heaved the man's arm high just in time for the bullet to soar over his shoulder.

He shoved the butt of the rifle into Downs' gut. The man doubled over, and when he hit the driveway, Jeremy brought the stock of the AK down on his head.

Blood trickled from the other agent's forehead, but he was alive. Lying on his back, one arm flung across his torso and one knee bent. He'd be wet and cold as fuck when he awoke in the snow, but at least Jeremy didn't have an FBI death on his hands.

Evan's blood is enough.

"Fucker. You couldn't *fucking* listen to me." He cursed some more and bent to retrieve Downs' Glock from the snowy cement of the driveway. He wiped the moisture from the weapon and tucked it into his waistband.

He turned back to the kitchen's steel door and punched in the code. Unless Caselli's home sported soundproof bedrooms, someone had probably heard that gunshot. Not to mention the previous shots when he'd killed the Guidos.

Jeremy didn't have much time.

"No way. No fucking way, Dex. I'm closest and I'm not waiting for over an hour for the team to arrive. Downs isn't answering his phone." Lee ignored the glare Nate threw her way.

He obviously agreed with the stupid analyst on the other end of her call—AKA shouting match.

She'd pulled off the freeway and headed back north about two seconds after Dex had told her where Clint was.

"I'll get Liv to mobilize the guys."

"You do that."

"You need to wait for back-up."

"Do me a favor. Check the GPS on Stewart's phone," she barked. She didn't bother contradicting his declaration, because she wasn't waiting. She was going to get to Caselli's, find her partner and hope to God she didn't have to shoot Jeremy Stewart.

The look on her lover's face suggested he'd already done the math regarding the other agent.

"Stewart?"

"Yeah."

To his credit, Dex didn't ask why. When his answer was a string of curses, Lee responded with a few of her own.

"Definitely not waiting for backup."

"What the hell is going on?" the analyst demanded.

"Not sure yet. Let you know when I get there." She ended the call and pitched her phone across the car.

Nate caught it and set it in the cup holder. "Take a breather."

"Hell no. How can I? Clint was right. Stewart's dirty. He probably has my partner hostage or something. Brought him right to Caselli. Fuck." She shook him off when he patted her arm. Her gut churned.

"I hate to agree with the analyst, but you don't even have a vest."

"I don't care. Stewart shot his partner. What makes you think he won't kill *mine*?" Lee shivered and shifted in the seat.

Clint had looked into Stewart on his own. It didn't matter that she couldn't have been there for him — *with* him — if she'd wanted to. She had to protect Nate.

Now she was forced to take her witness to Caselli's mansion. Take him right *to* the man who wanted him dead.

"*I* care. I don't want you hurt."

Lee shook her head. "I won't get hurt. Neither will you."

"Not worried about me."

She glanced at him. "I am."

He chuckled and shook his head. "Wow. We're sitting here worrying about each other."

"Right." She couldn't even crack a smile. "And I'm worried about Downs."

"It'll be okay."

Nate had said that a dozen times.

No amount of *faith* was going to fix this.

She wanted to close her eyes, but resisted since she was driving. Wanted to hit something. Or shoot something. Or cry. "Dammit," she muttered instead.

"Just get us there. We'll assess the situation and then act. Only if it's safe."

"Safe? That's hilarious. Nothing about this will be *safe*. Besides, there's no *we* here. You're staying in the car."

"While you go in alone? With no protection against flying bullets."

"That about sums it up. AKA, my job."

"Fuck. That."

Lee growled. "Not arguing about this, Counselor. Caselli wants you dead. We're going *to* his home. It's like serving you up on a platter. You'll stay in the car. Out of sight."

He harrumphed and crossed his arms over his broad chest. Nate said nothing, but she wasn't stupid.

No way would her lover drop it that easily. Not to mention his tendency to require the last word.

"Just get us there."

She narrowed her eyes. "Workin' on it."

They didn't speak. Neither made an attempt to fill the silence.

She'd never been out to Caselli's vast property, but had seen aerial pictures, blueprints and even the lot layouts from the county tax office. Luckily for them, the mob boss had only built the mansion a few years ago. All the data they'd needed was easily accessible. And public.

The place was huge. No doubt laid out with all sorts of custom things. Fancy furniture and top of the line *everything*. Dirty money bought whatever the hell you wanted. Besides, the bastard was known for his expensive taste.

"You know where we're going?" Nate asked as she exited the highway.

"Yes."

They continued on, until the terrain became rougher, and there was nothing but snow-covered fields and big red barns. Farmhouses were farther and farther from each other. Then sleeping woods lined both sides of the roads.

Caselli had no love for neighbors. He'd purchased all the rest of the land surrounding his property, so his mansion was remote. No witnesses, no place to run.

There was one thing in their favor — only one road in and out.

The arrogant asshole had named the private drive '*Caselli Way*'.

"Damn, there's nothing out here," her lover whispered as he looked around. "Acres and acres of snow."

"And he'll see us coming." Lee pointed to the telephone pole at the end of the long driveway of

Caselli Way.

A panning camera surveyed the area, probably catching the public roadway as well as the private drive. The asshole had spared no expense—the pathway toward his house was paved and in better shape than the county country road.

"It's probably fortified."

"Yeah, gets better and better." She slowed the Accord and yanked her Glock from its holster, controlling the wheel with one hand.

Nate said nothing, but his gaze was sharp as he surveyed.

"The place is surrounded by twenty foot high iron fencing—old school haunted mansion style. There's a gatehouse at the end of the driveway. Get down and stay down when we get there."

A curt nod was all the answer he gave her, but that was okay with her.

"The gate's open."

She didn't respond, but she'd spotted what he had as well.

He then ducked low in the seat.

Good.

He planned on listening to her.

Lee inched the car closer. Ready for anything. She screamed at herself to focus on what was in front of her. Tried to ignore her worry for the man *in* the car with her.

More than her witness.

More than just her lover.

She banished dangerous thoughts and stared

ahead, then scanned the gatehouse. "Son of a bitch!"

"What?"

"Bodies. Two. Just stay down."

Blood spatter dotted the snow and the side of the building.

She pulled past the gatehouse slowly, observing as much as she could without stopping.

One guy was up against the side of the building, slumped over, the back of his head gone. The other lay about five feet away, his chest—no, whole body—riddled with wounds.

"No way that was just a handgun," Lee murmured.

Nate's palm settled on her thigh and squeezed. "Be careful."

"I am." She continued to look around as she drove farther onto Caselli's property. "Clint's car." Her partner's Dodge Charger was parked by a large fountain.

"You see him?"

"No. I don't see anyone. But if there's a camera on the driveway, there're more."

"But who's seen *us*?" Nate breathed.

"Right." Lee stopped the Accord on the right side of the FBI Charger. "I see tracks in the snow. Two sets. I'm gonna follow."

"On foot?"

"Yes."

"Lee—"

She made a cutting gesture with her free hand. "Nate. Don't start."

He glared up at her, his tall, lean frame cramped low in the passenger seat.

"There's nothing for you to worry about. You need to stay here. Out of sight."

"A sitting duck?"

Lee sighed. "You're right. I'll leave you my backup. It's a forty. Use it if you need to." She unhooked her seatbelt and hit the driver seat release. The chair slid all the way back with a resounding *click*.

She bent to tug her Glock-27 out of her ankle holster. Held it out to her lover.

He took the gun, a scowl marring his handsome face. "You're not going alone."

"Dex mobilized my unit."

"Like you said, they won't be here for an hour."

She frowned. "If something happens to you, there's no case. No justice for Angelo."

Nate shot upright and yanked her close. "If anything happens to *you*, I'll never be okay again."

Her heart stuttered and Lee crashed her lips into his.

He deepened the kiss without hesitation, plunging his tongue into her mouth.

She slanted her mouth under his as their tongues dueled, kissing him back with all her might. She scooted as close as she could get with the shifter between them, wrapping one arm around his neck. Lee slid her other hand behind her back, moaning into Nate's kiss to cover the *snap* as she opened the handcuff case on her left side.

When she closed her fingertips on the metal rings,

she pulled as gently as she could. Didn't want to jar either herself or her lover, let alone give him a clue to what she was planning. The stainless steel was warm from her body heat and caused a shiver.

He was going to be *pissed*.

She'd have to be quick.

Lee slipped her hand inside Nate's jacket sleeve under the guise of a caress, but her man didn't react as he continued to kiss her. She nipped his bottom lip and he groaned. She licked the spot and kissed him again, more vigorously. Needed him even more distracted so she could get the handcuff on him without getting caught.

He responded, settling his hand at the back of her neck and kissing her harder, deeper.

She needed to do this now, before desire clouded her brain completely. Her body was already on fire for him. She wanted to get lost in him, but she had a job to do.

Lee had to keep him safe.

With a deft snap, she closed one side of the handcuff around his left wrist, tugging him forward and clipping the other on the steering wheel. She made sure they were locked before letting go.

Wide, frantic hazel orbs met her gaze. "What the he—"

"Sorry, babe, I can't risk you getting hurt." She pressed her mouth to his in a fast, firm kiss then slipped out of the Accord.

Chapter Twenty-One

Jeremy made his way through a kitchen that would make any five-star chef jealous as hell. Stainless steel and top-of-the-line *everything* surrounded him. He held the AK-47 high and tight, ready to pull the trigger at any moment.

Moved at a jog, but as quietly as he could. Still encountered no one even as he passed by two side-by-side walk-in freezers.

He smirked, but didn't stop to look in the little window on either one.

On-sight body storage if you piss him off. Nice.

Maybe he could leave Caselli hanging in his own freezer.

If he told the man about the warrant, would it get him a ticket to safety? Anonymity?

Then he'd be on the run like any other criminal. Out of the FBI forever, but that was his fate anyway.

Never to see Beth and the girls again. Or his mom.

Could he do it?

Work for the man he despised. Sell drugs and little girls. Continue his killing spree and get paid for it?

Be a Caselli enforcer.

No.

Jeremy was going to put a bullet in the bastard. Scratch that—a lot of bullets. Swiss cheese anyone else who stood in his way of doing so. He wasn't stupid enough to believe Caselli would leave his family alone permanently.

If the mobster offered him a deal that was too good to be true to save his own ass, it would be just that.

Lies.

An AK-47 in one's face tended to elicit promises. But in Caselli's case, *'promises'* would still belong at the shallow end of the pool.

Jeremy exited the vast kitchen and passed through a set of double doors that spilled into a formal dining room, complete with an extremely long table.

Chairs lined both sides—there had to be thirty seats, if not more. Royalty style. Ornate, carved dark wood. Huge marble fireplace at the far end of the room. The place was like the great hall of a medieval castle.

"Hmmm, maybe burning him would be better than freezing his balls off." His voice echoed and jarred him. He shook his head and kept going.

The sprawling foyer was next. Full of red and black velvet tapestries, iron and white marble sculptures. Framed art hung on every wall.

There were two stairwells, rounded and curving inward. Like arms spread wide, giving off the illusion of welcome—a call into a warm embrace.

Jeremy snorted. Caselli should have a sign that announced the place to be the den of the devil it was.

An open balcony rested at the top of the stairs. The bastard probably stood up there, hands on the decorative rail, watching over his kingdom.

Behind it, even more stairs led up to the innards of the mansion. All the steps were covered with a deep red carpet—hell, it looked as soft as velvet, too.

He tried to ignore the opulence around him, but the Italian marble floor beneath his feet pissed him off. Made his blood boil. He wanted to stomp it. Crush it, or shoot it up. Jeremy growled and surveyed the large space, cataloguing everything.

There were four closed doors off the main room.

Corridors behind the stairs on the ground level led to hell knew where, but the security office couldn't be far. It made sense for it to be central to the front doors, but hidden from obvious view.

He had to locate it. Find out where Caselli's suite — wing or whatever, according to Guido One — was.

The house was too big to search every hallway, every room. He needed to learn *where* he needed to go.

Place was silent. No one in sight.

It looked more like a museum than a house where people actually lived.

Guess it's tough living the life of a high-dollar trafficker.

Jeremy's entrance has been easy.

Had Caselli become careless or was he really running a skeleton crew because of some wild party?

He moved forward, studying the stairwells and the support wall that gave way into the hallway entrance behind them.

Which way, which way?

His gut screamed right, so he hurried into the dim corridor. An unmarked door beckoned.

He slipped the strap on the assault rifle over his torso and reached for the handle, but tightened his grip on the gun so he could pull the trigger with his right hand alone if he had to.

Jeremy's arm shook when he reached for the handle.

Not locked.

He dropped back and raised his weapon, pushing the door open with his foot.

The hum and whir of electronic equipment teased his ears.

Pay dirt. Security room on the first try.

A large man sat slumped in a chair at a desk in front of the wall-to-wall monitors. Snoring loudly.

Jeremy froze.

The oversized Italian didn't stir, even with the soft creak of protest as the door inched open.

Two choices stared him down. Kill the bastard while he slept, and risk rousing the whole house. Or wake him and demand Caselli's location.

Wait.

He could study the cameras himself. Didn't want to hazard a welcoming party.

Jeremy slipped behind the guy and raised the AK. Slammed the stock down on the man's head. A sickening crack made him wince.

The rotund man rolled more than fell out of the chair, landing with a *thud*. Blood leaked from the top of his head, but he still didn't move.

He rolled him over with a damp boot, looking down into his face.

The man wasn't dead. His massive chest rose and fell, one arm across his body and the other beneath him. The position couldn't be comfortable.

"You're gonna wish you'd died. Caselli probably

doesn't appreciate guys falling asleep on the job. Then again, you can just thank me for saving your ass after I kill him."

Not even a grunt.

After a kick to the guy's hip—for good measure, of course—Jeremy stared up at the monitors, darting from screen to screen.

It only took him a few minutes to discover the location of Caselli's private rooms. All the corridors looked the same—except one. Unlike the cameras outside in the gatehouse, these were high definition and full color.

The gold-leafed frames on the wall-art were his first clue. From what he could tell, every painting was of a naked woman. The walls of the hallway were blood red, contrary to the rest of the house's corridors, which sported a beige color.

"So *where* are you, Caselli?"

He stared at each monitor for a few moments before moving on, mentally walking through the house as he went.

Caselli would want the utmost privacy for his quarters.

'Wing' was what Guido One had called it.

Winter sun shone through the window, making a bright white spot on the camera view. Blotting out the painting on the wall beside it.

"Ah-ha!"

East.

It was morning and the light bathing the hallway was bright.

The mobster had to be in the east wing, facing the outside of the house, since there were several windows in the red-walled corridor.

Jeremy would have to figure out what floor by trial and error, but knowing Caselli, he'd be high and as far away from the front entrance as possible.

The place had five floors. He'd start at the top.

He left the security office at a jog. Instead of heading back around to the front of the stairs, he slipped farther down the dark hallway.

There was an elevator at the back.

He hit the up arrow, tapping his foot and flexing his fingers on the assault rifle. Stairs might be faster, but he was less likely to run into anyone else if he could hit each floor via the elevator.

There hadn't been any movement on any of the cameras. The guy he'd knocked out had been the only other soul he'd seen, except for the Guidos at the gate.

"Where the fuck is everyone?" His inquiry shook even as the elevator dinged. Jeremy jumped, but scrambled inside.

Anyone could pop up at any time, and he wouldn't see it. Wouldn't be able to see where they might come at him from.

That made him twitchy as hell.

Unknowns had never been his cuppa.

He tapped the button for the fifth floor — his best guess for the red-walled corridor.

The doors opened several minutes past his comfort level. Everything was taking too damn long.

When Downs woke up, he'd call the team in.

Jeremy needed to be long gone by then. Leaving a dead Caselli in his bed.

He stepped off the elevator. "Fuck yes."

The walls were red. He'd been correct the first time out the gate.

He headed down the carpeted hallway without a sound.

"What the hell? Who the fuck are you?"

Jeremy bit back the shout on the tip of his tongue and whipped around.

A tall dark-haired man stood at the top of the stairs, one hand on the rail. He was dressed in black silk pajamas and had a steaming mug in the other hand.

He was too far from Jeremy to simply knock out like the sleeping camera babysitter. Besides, he wasn't far from Caselli's private rooms—could feel it in his gut.

All or nothing time.

Raising the AK, Jeremy flashed a feral smile. "Don't worry about it."

Then he pulled the trigger.

Lee squeezed her eyes shut as she rounded the corner and pushed her shoulders into the side of Caselli's house. She flexed her fingers on the grip of her Glock. Her arms shook.

Get it together. Breathe.

"Just breathe." Her whisper fell out at the same time a frigid breeze burned her cheeks, but the cold cleared her head.

Like a good smack.

Handcuffing Nate so he *couldn't* leave the car had been the right thing to do.

Right?

Her pulse thundered in her ears, sounding more like a tidal wave than her heart.

"Fuck."

The backup weapon was right there. In his reach. He knew how to shoot. He'd be fine.

He has to be.

She sucked in cold air and let it out slowly. Did it again until her head stopped spinning.

Had Stewart killed the guys at the gatehouse? Or had Clint shot his way in?

"And why's it so quiet around here?" Lee pushed off the house and squared her shoulders. She studied her surroundings, then glanced down at the tracks she'd first spotted by her partner's car.

She followed the boot prints. Two sets, larger than her own and similar in patterns.

Lee would bet money they belonged to her partner and Stewart. If that was the case, why only two?

If the dirty FBI ass was turning Clint in to Caselli after a negative confrontation, wouldn't he have backup, thug-style?

Downs could take a skinny little bastard like Stewart in his sleep.

She stuck close to the side of the mansion, crouching low as she went, and searching for any movement. Held her Glock at the ready and prayed she wouldn't be ambushed; there was no cover in sight.

Lee spotted what had to be a garage looming from across a stretch of snow-covered cement. She glanced over her shoulder, observing that the driveway curved around the whole place.

She and Nate could have followed it around if they'd gone to the right instead of parking next to the Charger.

There were seven closed bay doors on the huge building as she came to the end of the house. "Damn. It's like a warehouse." The wind whipped her words from her lips and she shivered.

Shit, it's cold.

Her glanced over a long line of vehicles. A black Mercedes sedan and four—no, five—Cadillac Escalades. They were parked in a row, one behind the other. Close together. All covered with winter's gift of white blankets from the night before.

She looked up into the sky. It was bright blue, but the fat fluffy clouds promised more snow. It'd let up for now, but Lee wanted to get this crap over and done with.

With her luck, a fricking blizzard would trap them at Caselli's place and keep the team from arriving any time soon.

Hopefully the guys had wasted no time after she'd hung up on Dex. Liv was going to be pissed about being in the dark about Stewart, but her boss would have to be placated later. She needed to find her partner and the dirty agent.

To her immediate right was the back of the house.

Has to have an entrance somewhere.

Lee scanned, looking for a —

"Shit! Clint!" She saw her partner's boots first.

He was lying about ten feet from the house.

She dashed to his side and hit her knees hard on the pavement. Winced at the sting from impact as well as the wet snow leaking through her jeans. She visually swept the area before she took the risk of holstering her Glock. Needed both hands to check Clint.

Blood trickled down his forehead, but a cursory glance didn't notice any other damage.

No holes.

"Thank God." She shook his shoulder. "Downs."

Nothing.

Her heart skipped and Lee ran her hands through his short dark hair. Besides the lump above the cut on his forehead, she couldn't feel or see any other injury. "Clint. C'mon, partner. Wake up." She slapped his chest, calling his name again.

Clint groaned. Opened his mouth, making his moustache twitch.

But his eyes stayed sealed shut.

"Downs. It's me, Lee. Buddy, please wake up."

"Lee." Her name exited his mouth on a breathless moan.

"Yeah, Lee." She grabbed his wrist and tugged.

Finally pale blue eyes met hers, but he cradled his head.

Clint squinted. "Bright."

"Right. I need you to get up, partner. Can you do that? We're totally out in the open."

"My ass is wet."

Lee grinned and helped him to his feet. "You're gonna be fine, thank God."

"My head is pounding." He wiped the blood from his forehead and looked around, eyes going wide as he orientated. Probably remembered where the hell he was. "Shit."

"Right again. We need to move. Now." She pulled him behind a wide pillar under a cement overhang protruding from the back of the house. It reminded her more of a fancy hotel valet entrance than something at a residence.

A massive steel door on the back of the house was ajar.

She slid around her partner, making sure they were both out of view. It wouldn't buy them much cover if someone came out that door shooting.

Lee drew her Glock, glancing at her partner.

He rubbed his face and groaned, but didn't miss her searching gaze. "Stewart?"

"I haven't seen him. Where's your gun?"

Clint peered around the pillar, scanning the ground where he'd lain. "I guess the bastard took it. He was headed inside when I caught him. He has an AK-47. Knocked me on the head with it."

"Fuck. I gave my backup to Nate."

"No worries. I have mine." He bent and drew a small Glock from an ankle holster. When he straightened, their eyes locked. "Wait. Crane's here?"

"What choice did I have? I couldn't get a hold of you. No one knew your plan, and I couldn't exactly explain things to Liv. I... I...kinda freaked."

"Aw shucks, partner, didn't know you cared." One corner of his mouth shot up.

Lee glared. "Of course I care. We need a plan, now."

"Where's your witness?"

"I left him in the car with a gun, like I said." She swallowed a wince. "Don't worry, he's not going anywhere."

What would her partner say if she admitted to cuffing Nate to the steering wheel?

She cleared her throat. "Team's been mobilized, but they won't be here for about forty-five minutes, an hour at most."

"Stewart's going to kill Caselli."

"We have to stop him." She made a fist with her free hand.

"Agreed."

"Whose handiwork are the dead guys at the gate?"

"Not mine. I assume Stewart killed them. When I got here, they'd already decorated the snow red."

"Perfect," Lee spat. She looked up at the massive house. Even rows of windows stacked on top of each other suggested there were at least five floors. "Ever had a look at the inside?"

"No."

"Shit. So we're going into a humungous building blind, after a guy who shot his partner and killed a witness. He's got FBI training and an AK-47. We have no idea how many thugs are in there. Annnnnnd we need to stop him from killing a bastard *dead* wouldn't look that bad on. Because it's the right thing to do."

"That about sums it up, partner."

She arched a brow. "Something funny, Downs?"

"Nah. Just not often you think before you leap."

Lee rolled her eyes. "Wanna wait for backup?"

"I don't think we can. No idea how long I was out. Stewart's already inside with a nice head start. We need to get him before he kills Caselli. Hopefully he's as unfamiliar with the venue as we are."

"Hmmm, wouldn't that be *reckless*, Special Agent Clinton Downs?"

Clint chuckled. "I guess I deserved that."

Echoing gunshots shattered their banter.

Lee's gaze darted to the house then back to her partner.

All traces of amusement were gone from his expression. "Let's go," Downs barked.

She raised her Glock and nodded.

Chapter Twenty-Two

T he guy went ass over tincups down the stairwell without so much as a holler. His mug shattered, brown liquid that had to be coffee splattering far and wide as much as the blood that'd exploded from his chest.

Jeremy watched him tumble, a mess of crimson ichor, arms and legs. He bounced off the small landing then continued downward.

The rustle of fine fabric and the *thud* and *thump* of his body faded the further he went.

He landed hard on the balcony, neck at an awkward angle, one leg bent backwards.

If the bullets hadn't killed him, the fall had.

Jeremy lowered the AK, waiting to feel *something* as he looked at his handiwork. Body number three for the day.

Camera Guy and Downs could've made it five, but he didn't regret not killing them.

Was it some sort of redemption?

"Hell no." He snorted.

Numbness and desperation were the only emotions he could sense about himself. Well, determination to kill Caselli, too.

That was something, wasn't it?

Still won't make Evan be okay.

Shaking his head, he turned from his latest disaster and shut down what was left of his conscience. No place for it here, and certainly not *now*.

He held the rifle high, slinking close to the wall as he traversed the wide corridor. The naked women on both sides of the corridor taunted him, their somber eyes following his path.

Jeremy tried not to look at the paintings.

They weren't classics or anything he could remember from what little art history he'd been exposed to. Each woman — girl really — was on display, posed on a bed or a chaise, some standing. Nude, for the world to see, but with yards of fabric draped around her. Covering nothing. The opposite of modest.

Where they real girls?

Caselli's trophies?

Guido One had said Caselli had thrown a birthday party for his favorite girl the night before. The paintings were probably all Caselli's victims.

"Sick fucker."

At the end of the hallway, Jeremy ran into a set of mahogany double doors. They were oversized and as opulent as the rest of the place.

Lending to the theme of the blood-red walls and naked women, there were carvings on the four panels of each door. But unlike the taste level of the paintings, sex acts were displayed before him.

Graphic.

Resembling something that would've been painted on the bath-house walls of ancient Pompeii.

He'd seen a documentary about it once. Sex everywhere. And phallic symbols etched into the sidewalks to lead men to the whores.

Definitely his private quarters.

Caselli might as well have put a sign up.

"Fucker really *does* have a den of sin."

Two chairs sat up against the wall on either side of the doors. Like the asshole usually had twenty-four/seven guards.

Was the guy he'd just killed supposed to be on bodyguard duty?

He'd left to get some coffee.

Poor bastard.

Then again, it didn't matter. Jeremy still would've killed him, had he been at his post. Too bad the bodyguard hadn't had a chance to drink his coffee, though.

He backed up and sucked in a fortifying breath.

This is it. Hope his sheets are red, too. Blood will blend in.

He rushed the doors, using his foot as a battering ram. First kick didn't do jack shit, so he tried again.

Crack splintered through the air.

The door on the left protested when he kicked it again. Pieces of one of the lewd acts went flying but the rest of the wood held together.

One more kick.

Jeremy threw his shoulder into the door. Pain shot back, but the door opened.

The decorative handle glared up as if it was pissed he'd broken through.

He grimaced and rotated his throbbing arm, but gripped his rifle at the ready. His body spilled into a front room.

Bright and welcoming. Set up as a sitting room, but there was a giant TV in one corner and a brick fireplace opposite it. The styling was eclectic, full of antiques, from the Victorian couch to the painting on the wall.

Maybe he could cut parts of Caselli's body off and burn them in that private fireplace. Make the bastard watch while each finger and toe burned. Then hands, arms and legs. Torture before death could be a good thing.

Muttering to himself about the possibilities, Jeremy continued down an interior hallway. With no hesitation, he kicked open another set of double doors.

They were plain and white. Wood shards went flying as they offered no resistance.

"Where are you, Caselli? Come out and face me, you fucker!"

Screams greeted his ears as a naked girl darted out of the huge bed in front of him. She cowered in the corner, her dark hair partially obscuring her face.

Another girl hovered in what had to be the bathroom doorway. Also naked and shaking, a hand covering her mouth. She was a redhead—naturally, evidently. She made no effort to cover her nudity.

He looked away.

The girls were both young, couldn't even be legal.

Jeremy scowled.

Fucking sicko.

It wasn't a secret Caselli liked them young, and had kept females for sex-slaves as well as selling more girls than the FBI even knew about.

He wanted to assure them he'd get them out of

here—he meant them no harm—but he had to deal with *the boss* first.

The man himself lay back against a large headboard reminiscent of the carved doors to his wing. As if he had no cares in the world. A huge, chrome, fifty caliber Desert Eagle handgun was trained on Jeremy's chest.

Raising the AK-47, he squinted.

Stepped closer.

Dared Caselli to pull the trigger.

A blood-red sheet was slung low on Caselli's hips and his chest was bare. Fucker was probably naked, too.

Score another one for me being right about the bedding.

"Hello, Special Agent." The deep voice was even and calm. Familiar.

The nonchalance made Jeremy's blood boil. "I'd say it's nice to see you again, but, well, that's a fucking lie."

Caselli chuckled, but his aim didn't waver. His dark hair was sleep-tousled and his expression was pleasant, a small smile curving his lips.

Most women would consider him handsome. Strong jaw and a trim, muscular frame. Charming, too, when he needed to be.

Nothing fixed the evil asshole's other traits.

Murderer. Rapist. Drug dealer...

The list went on.

He was in his mid-to-late forties, but his career had started long ago, following in the footsteps of his father, deep into organized crime.

"Looks like your sweet, sick mother ran out of etiquette lessons for you. I hope your lovely Beth has had better luck with your daughters. I'd hate to have to *teach* them manners."

"Fucking leave them out of this. This is between you and me. *Just* you and me."

Caselli threw his head back and laughed. "Oh, Special Agent. How mistaken you are. When I get done with you, Beth and the girls will be mine. I'll be sure to remind them of your poor choices."

Jeremy growled. "I came here to tell you the FBI has a warrant for your arrest. For the murder of Angelo Fiato. I'm sure my unit will be here shortly. Was gonna try to help you get lost. I think I'll just kill you instead."

"You killed the men at my gate. I only assume my cousin in the camera room suffered the same fate. Not to mention my bodyguard, Dante. He was my favorite, too." The asshole's voice was sharper than it had been; deadly.

One of the girls whimpered, but neither the mobster nor Jeremy spared her a glance.

"I find it hard to believe you came into my home so harshly with *pure* intentions." The man's gaze was shrewd, the big pistol still aimed for a kill-shot.

Harshly?

Caselli sure as shit had a way with words. Did he think he was Shakespeare or something?

Jeremy ignored the surprise that rolled over him at Caselli's wealth of information.

Of course the bastard knew.

He'd seen him coming somehow. Had let him

come.

So much for a real ambush.

Did he know about Downs being on the property as well?

"Fuck you, Caselli."

Caselli laughed again, his lips twisted in a smirk. "How eloquent, Special Agent."

"Stewart, drop your weapon." The order was staunch.

Female.

With the AK still trained on his enemy, Jeremy didn't pause to look over his shoulder at Dawson, or stop to contemplate how the fuck she'd arrived at Caselli's mansion.

He pulled the trigger and held it down, spraying bullets at the mobster.

White-hot pain exploded in his shoulder.

Then his stomach, but he fought to remain upright.

His ears rang with the sound of gunshots.

More than the AK-47 in his wavering arms.

More than the big fifty-cal Caselli had.

Was Dawson firing?

Where was Downs?

An anguished yell breached his lips when his knees buckled and Jeremy hit the expensive oriental-looking rug beneath his boots.

His head spun as his cheek smacked the carpet. Vision danced, and his ears pounded as the room echoed.

Agony engulfed his form, flames burning his arms, his chest, even his legs. Numbness was chasing it away, sucking him in like an embrace, and he blinked.

Was it finally over?

"Stewart!" The dirty FBI agent didn't respond to her shout.

"Get him, partner. I got Caselli." Clint rushed to the bed.

The mobster wasn't dead, if his moan was any indication.

Two naked girls hovered in each other's arms in what had to be the bathroom doorway. One sobbed while the other held her.

Lee couldn't concentrate on reassuring them now. "Find a phone and call 9-1-1," she barked. "Then get some clothes on and get back here. Don't run off. If you do, you're looking at jail when I get you."

Nice. Threatening victims…witnesses now.

She had to.

The redhead nodded and they dashed out of the room hand-in-hand.

The brunette's sobs were still audible from the other room.

An expensive-looking and now blood-soaked rug cushioned Lee's knees when she holstered her Glock and lowered herself beside Jeremy Stewart. She nudged the AK-47 away with her foot. Better not to touch it with bare hands for now.

"Stewart."

Nothing.

She grabbed his shoulder and rolled his body over.

Jeremy's back landed on her bent legs, nestled against her thighs.

Lee sucked in a breath as she took in the three holes in his chest and one more in his collarbone on the right side.

He was hit in the leg as well.

"Jeremy," she whispered his first name.

Something she'd never called him before.

Her fellow agent's mouth moved, but no sound came out. His eyes were heavy-lidded. Brown irises seemed to be fading as she watched.

Lee's heart skipped. She'd never been close to him, but—

"Stewart, stay with me." She grabbed the collar of his black leather jacket. Her hands were already covered in deep red stickiness, and his blood had seeped into her jeans below.

A moan fell from his mouth. "Dawson…" Her last name slipped from his lips with breath he couldn't afford to lose.

"Don't speak. Stewart, just stay with me."

"Cas… Case… Caselli…"

"You don't worry about that bastard. You got him. Leave the rest to us." Her voice shook as she held him.

The man was dirty.

She shouldn't give a shit about him. But Jeremy Stewart was still her teammate. They'd worked cases together for almost two years.

"Partner, how's he looking?" Clint's question jolted her.

Lee looked up. She couldn't speak, so she shook

her head.

Her partner's mouth set in a hard line and he gave a curt nod. "Caselli's alive. Hit three times. Nothing looks vital."

She dug for something to say. "Of course the asshole's made of steel."

"He's out cold, but I cuffed him."

"Good."

Clint made it to her side in moments, kneeling. He pressed two fingers to Stewart's neck. "Pulse is thready." He didn't stay down long, though. Weapon still in hand, he loomed close, ready to protect them if necessary.

"He's not going to make it, Clint." Her statement was just above a whisper, and she looked up to meet her partner's gaze. A tremor shot down her spine and she gripped her injured co-worker closer.

"D-D-Dawson." Stewart's eyes flew open wide, and he gripped her wrist with surprising strength.

"Rest, bud. Ambulance will be here soon," Downs urged.

"No…time…" He was more breathless with each word. Stewart's chest heaved. His face was drawn and gray, his lips turning blue as she watched. His body shook. "Tell…"

"Stewart—"

"Tell Beth I love her. Mom, too. My girls…" He coughed and jolted. Blood shot out of his mouth.

Emotion threatened to bowl Lee over and she sucked her cheek in, biting hard. Pain grounded her, but she couldn't stop shaking. She was trembling as much as the dying man on her lap.

"Dawson." The light was fading even faster than before from his brown gaze. His expression was urgent and his bloody fingers flexed on her wrist with surprising strength. "Tell Evan I'm sorry. He...has to...live."

Lee almost gave in to a sob when his last breath exited his mouth on a whoosh and Jeremy Stewart's eyes slipped closed.

His arm went slack, his fingers falling from her jacket's sleeve.

"Damn..." Clint whispered, but she couldn't look up at him.

Nate. I want Nate.

Chapter Twenty-Three

The anguished look on her face made Nate's anger dissolve and panic rise. He frantically skimmed her petite frame.

She was pale. Her shoulders were slumped. No weapon in her hand, either.

He tugged against the steering wheel for the hundredth time, but the handcuffs only offered a *clink-clink*.

Holy shit.

Lee was covered in blood.

His heart took a dive for his stomach and he yanked away hard, wincing when steel bit into his wrist.

Her partner beat her to the Accord's driver-side door and wrenched it open. "Here. I have a key." Downs dipped into the rental, one knee on the driver seat. "She told me just how she got you to stay put."

The big man kept talking, but Nate couldn't hear it.

His eyes were glued to the love of his life.

She stood like a zombie only a few feet from the car.

"Lee," he breathed.

"Hold on a sec. Be still and I— There ya go."

Nate fled the car, leaving Downs there without even a thank you.

Lee fell into his arms, burying her face against his

puffy jacket.

He didn't give a shit about the blood; gathered her closer when a muffled sob greeted his ears.

Her team was bustling around, as well as paramedics and local uniformed cops. No way she'd want witnesses to any tears.

"What the hell happened?" Nate asked, meeting her partner's gaze as Downs got out of the Honda and shut the door.

He crossed his arms over his massive chest, studying them. "Stewart didn't make it. He died in her arms."

Fuck.

Nate looked down at the petite woman plastered to his chest. Lee Dawson was one of the strongest people he knew. She was more than entitled to *feel.* He'd hold her until she regained her composure. He burned to reassure her.

"Angel," he whispered above her ear.

She didn't look up, but she stilled against him.

"It'll be okay. I'm here. Your partner's here, and you're both in one piece. You found him. You saved us both."

Dark eyes locked onto his face. Her gaze darted back and forth, up and down, frantically, as if she'd suddenly remembered where she was.

Or who he was.

"Are you all right?" Lee demanded. Her mouth was a hard line and she was all FBI, not the soft woman with tears streaking her cheeks.

"I am. You kept me safe, angel."

As much as it pained him to admit, and took a sizable bite out of his pride, Nate would probably have rushed into the mansion after her. That would have endangered them all.

Standing tiptoed, she crashed her mouth into his, wrapping her arms around his neck. She pushed her tongue into his mouth before he could pause to consider their audience.

Lee was kissing him?

With other FBI agents around?

Not to mention her partner ten feet away.

Damn, he loved this woman.

He kissed her back, swallowing the sounds of desperation she emitted.

She squeezed his neck and kissed him harder, burrowing even further into his body.

Before he could get lost in the movements of their mouths, Lee pulled away. As if she'd realized where they were and who was around. She slipped from his arms and he let her go without protest.

His love didn't go far, looping her arm in his. As though she needed to touch him.

Fine with me.

Nate squeezed her arm, holding her as tightly as she was clinging to him. When he met her partner's gaze, the guy had an eyebrow cocked.

His ice blue orbs held an amused twinkle, and his moustache twitched.

He stared, daring him to say something. Hoped he kept his mouth shut. Needed her partner to cut her a break, considering their circumstances. Kissing in public wasn't a problem for Nate, but it went against Lee's very private nature.

"Hey, Downs. Dawson." A dark-haired agent strode over, thumbing toward the ambulance behind them. "Looks like Caselli's gonna make it."

"Good," Lee snapped. "He needs to rot in prison." She started to walk and Nate went, too so he didn't have to let her go.

They closed the distance to the two men, her hand still tucked into his elbow.

"They need someone to ride to the hospital. I'm gonna go with," the other agent said.

"Not a problem for me." Downs spoke before Lee or Nate could.

The agent jogged to the waiting red and white vehicle.

"Hey, Smythe," Downs shouted as the guy climbed in the after the paramedic.

"Yeah?"

"Keep me posted on the bastard's condition."

"You got it."

They watched until the doors shut and the ambulance pulled off, heading down the long driveway.

"Did you speak to the girls?" Lee asked her partner.

"No. Ortega and Morris took over for me when I followed you out. Ortega said she'd handle things. You know it's usually easier for a female agent."

"Yeah, well I'm sure they don't want to talk to me. I threatened them."

"You did what you needed to do, partner."

Nate watched, letting them talk, despite the questions stirring in his thoughts. He'd talk to her later.

"Wish it didn't make me feel like crap," Lee said.

"Nah, you're good. You covered my ass. Thanks."

She nodded. "That's what partners are for."

Silence descended as the three of them watched people bustle around the scene.

The county Medical Examiner's van pulled up and the three-man team got their gear and headed inside.

A local detective chatted with another of Lee and Downs' teammates, and a few uniformed cops were setting up yellow perimeter tape.

Flashing red and blue lights from a few cruisers reflected off windows as well as the snow.

Chaos was paramount, and didn't fit the peaceful, rural setting. Tracks marred the thick blankets of snow as everyone went to and from the house.

The local cops were in an excited frenzy, because Caselli's entire inner circle had been *rudely* awoken, and most arrested for outstanding warrants.

Probably not for anything major, but maybe the annoyance of a holding cell would encourage loose mouths that would help the case.

Nate sighed and ran his hand through his hair. "I need to call my brother."

"Lucas is gonna want to know about Caselli, too," Lee remarked.

"Without a doubt," Downs said. "The guy'll probably require crime scene photos as proof."

She smirked and shook her head. "Only because he

wasn't here. He'll be jealous as hell. But let me tell you, he's gonna want a verbal recital. Don't give him a call without having a speech prepared."

"Oh, I know. No details can be missed."

The two FBI agents looked at each other and laughed.

Nate shook his head. "Hey now, dude's not even here to defend himself."

His stomach flipped when Lee flashed a lopsided grin. Considering what she'd just been through, he was pleased she could focus on something, even if it was teasing their mutual friend in absentia.

"You've known him a few years now. Sure you worked with him on a county case or two."

"Right." He fought a grin and nodded.

"Then you know we're right." The twinkle was back in her dark gaze, and her cheeks were stained pink from the cold wind.

God, he wanted to kiss her, but didn't. She was back in control, which was great. She'd kick him in the balls for a PDA now.

Her partner chuckled. "Yeah, he knows. Not gonna admit it?"

Nate laughed. "Ya'll are right. I'll admit it. He's passionate. Hardworking. I'd never complain when he's the investigator on a case I pick up. So there."

Downs winked and Lee shook her head.

"Dawson. Downs." Another agent strode over to them.

He was a tall, black guy with attention-catching hazel eyes that popped against his dark complexion and bald head. His expression was hard.

Great. Bad news.

"Morris?" Lee asked, one dark eyebrow arched.

"Barnes wants you to head back to the office. Now."

"Shit," Downs spat.

"I guess we got some 'splainin' to do," she muttered.

Her partner threw her a look, but there was no amusement in his expression.

"Wanna talk about it?"

Lee jarred in the driver's seat, even though Nate's inquiry had been soft and even. She shook her head.

"It might help you process it all."

"I'm good."

"No, you're not. You're shaking from head to foot."

She sighed, gripping the steering wheel tighter.

Downs' Charger was in front of them on the freeway. Her partner wasn't speeding. Stuck in the right lane, going exactly sixty miles per hour.

Neither of them was looking forward to the ass chewing that awaited them in their boss's office. No doubt Liv would have some extra special touches for Lee, considering she'd not only left a safe site, but a witness *to* the man who wanted him dead.

Yay. It's gonna be fun.

She cleared her throat in lieu of rolling her eyes at herself. "Nate… Can you just…leave me be?"

Her lover was silent and she chided herself for the dose of honesty.

She'd just hurt his feelings — again.

When he'd only been trying to help.

As usual.

She didn't want to talk about seeing Jeremy Stewart fall to that Oriental rug in a mess of limbs and blood.

He'd been a dirty FBI agent that had worked *for* their enemy — a man the whole unit had been chasing for years.

Lee shouldn't care that he was dead.

Too damn bad she did.

At one time, he'd been a good agent. A good man. Had a family. People he cared about.

Why had he crossed the line? And *when?*

What'd made him kill a witness?

Shoot his own partner?

Sad thing was they couldn't ask him now. Jeremy Stewart's motives had gone to the grave with him.

When the dust settled, their whole unit would be left reeling...and wondering. No doubt asking. Pointing out times when things *'just didn't seem right'*.

Hindsight being twenty-twenty and all.

Maybe when Evan Roberts woke up they could get his insight. Did *he* know something about his partner no one else did?

Although, the emotion and anguish on Jeremy Stewart's face at the end had told her he regretted *everything*.

Maybe death was a gift. He wouldn't have done

well in prison. Ex-law enforcement never did, unless they were placed in protective units.

"Tell me what you're thinking."

Nate's whisper broke into her thoughts.

She shook her head. "I *really* don't want to talk about it."

"I just want to help. You need to be okay. So *I* can be okay. I lo—care—I *care* about you."

Her heart plummeted to her stomach and she started in her seat. Plastered her focus to the snowy road in front of her. Her tongue was frozen to the roof of her mouth, but Lee wouldn't have responded anyway.

He'd stopped short of saying he *loved* her.

Shit.

Just. Shit.

No way.

All the convincing in the world couldn't change what he'd almost said.

Her gut tightened.

She didn't—couldn't—look at him. Heat crept up her neck, scorching her cheeks. Lee kept herself busy by reciting Clint's license plate over and over again in her head.

Letters and numbers forward, then back, until it was all a jumble in her head.

The only sounds in the car were the wiper blades and the low hum of the radio. The music faded in and out. Like it was far away.

"Don't shut me out for caring."

She ignored Nate. Her pulsed thundered, rushing

her ears like a typhoon. Until her heart pounded so fast it left her chest with a physical ache.

God, just let me get to the office. Now.

Lee contemplated whipping around Clint's car, driving eighty or ninety, but then Nate would know he was getting to her.

"Lee." His hot hand clamped down on her thigh, but she didn't move.

Still didn't look at him.

"Why do you always have to push me?" The demand tumbled out. She cursed her shaky voice. "I said I don't want to talk about it. Not everything is about you, Counselor."

What a copout, Selena Dawson.

But it worked.

Nate pulled his hand off her leg. Said nothing, but her peripheral vision told her he'd turned to look out the passenger window. His strong jaw was clenched, and both hands were tight fists in his lap.

Great.

Keep piling on the hurt.

It was for the best, though.

He could go home now. Get back to his life; back to work. Back to the job he was passionate about.

Caselli would have to recover before they put him on trial for Fiato's murder. Likely months would pass before Nate would have to be back in New York to testify.

The state wasn't going to fight federal jurisdiction, so the mobster would be tried for capital murder as soon as he was back on his feet.

After all, they'd got a federal judge to sign the warrant, so the county District Attorney wouldn't have had a leg to stand on anyway.

As for killing Stewart, two FBI witnesses would expedite things.

Caselli would likely be arraigned on both charges at the same time.

Her lover could leave as soon as her boss and the prosecutor on the case gave the all-clear. No doubt Liv would let them know the status when they got back to the office.

Lee swallowed against the lump in her throat. A sob threatened and took her by surprise. She bit the insides of both cheeks, then her bottom lip.

Wouldn't cry in the car. Where there was nowhere to run.

She couldn't take sympathy in those hazel depths.

So she'd rather have him pissed at her.

She regretted hurting him, but at least it meant silence.

It'd make parting easier.

Chapter Twenty-Four

T he meeting in her boss' office was after a quick shower in the locker room and a change of clothes. Thank God she always kept jeans and a T-shirt at the office.

She'd thrown her soiled clothes out. Didn't want to wash them. Wouldn't wear them again, even stain-free.

Lee closed her eyes against the memories of the blood rinsing from her body only to go down the drain. Watered down crimson burned into her brain. Like the man who'd died in her arms had been nothing.

Liv's gaze had held real sympathy when she'd inquired if they were okay after what they'd witnessed.

No, I don't need a shrink.

She hadn't said it, but she'd wanted to.

As soon as her and her partner's well-being had been established, Liv had started in on them. Harsh admonition with a side of *'don't-even-think-of-doing-something-like-that-again'*, mixed with praise that'd they'd finally gotten Caselli, albeit wounded.

Special Agent Olivia Barnes' pep talk wasn't nearly as bad as she'd anticipated.

Thank. God.

The boss had even made a joke that Lee had rubbed off on Clint—in a bad way. They weren't fired or arrested, so her day wasn't as bad as it could've been.

Their whole unit was indeed reeling over Jeremy Stewart. No one had had a clue about his dealings with

Caselli, proving just how smart he'd been.

Caught between grief and shock, her teammates were very vocal about their loss. They'd be talking about him for a long time to come.

As his supervisor, Liv informed them all she'd be doing the death notifications.

Lee was relieved. She'd told her whom he'd spoken of as he'd lain dying. Didn't think she could face anyone who loved Stewart. His family knew him as a hero, in a way. Working for the FBI, catching the bad guys.

Did they have any clue what he'd been into?

Until they were able to talk to Caselli, there were too many questions they could plan the *when* and *how* they were going to tie loose ends. She and Clint were still the lead agents, despite the boss' displeasure.

Liv was in agreement with Lee and her partner—they'd head to the hospital the moment the bastard was awake and they could talk to him.

Neither would let any stupid doctor be overprotective and prohibit them from entry.

They *would* get the asshole to talk.

She couldn't wait to look the mobster in the face and tell him he was under arrest for murder.

Nate had been told to wait at her desk until the meeting with Liv was over, but she didn't want to face him.

Too bad there was no reason for her boss to chew on her and Clint for a while longer. The remainder of the day would've been nice.

Or all night into the next morning…

She hadn't been able to look her lover in the face since she'd pulled the Accord into the parking garage.

He hadn't said much after her snarky remark—not that she blamed him.

Who wants to talk to a bitch who does nothing but hurt you, anyway? And besides, his silence was what you wanted.

Right?

Clint had taken one look at the two of them before they'd entered headquarters, and had shaken his head.

Perfect that her partner could see it too.

"Why don't you go home?" Clint's deep voice made her jump as they walked down the hallway headed away from their boss's office.

"Nah. Tons of paperwork to handle."

"First of all, you don't have to do it all yourself. *And* it doesn't need to be today."

The federal prosecutors had either drawn straws or had lain in wait. Either way, the guy—Eric Bray— who'd been saddled with the Angelo Fiato murder had already contacted Liv and requested initial reports from NYPD as well as FBI.

Clint had written their report, so Lee hadn't worried about it, but she needed to write an addendum to the narrative with her take on the scene.

It didn't *have* to be today.

She sighed. "I need to work."

"Yeah, yeah, so you always say. But you're not alone in this. Besides, Crane is waiting for you."

Don't remind me.

"If nothing else, the counselor understands the value of hard work."

Clint pinned her with a sharp look. "Right."

She couldn't tear her eyes from his. "Clint—"

Her partner put a large palm up, making her pause before him.

Lee's gaze darted to their open office door, about twenty feet down the corridor. Her stomach flip-flopped.

She couldn't see Nate inside, but she could feel his proximity.

"Go. Home. Relax." Her partner's voice dropped and his harsh expression loosened. "Spend what time with him you can."

Shaking her head, she ignored the threatening mixed emotions. "It's not like that."

"Liar." His retort was quick.

"I—"

"Don't feed me your bullshit, Lee Dawson. Not about this. Won't work." He crossed his arms over his chest.

She felt about five years old. Lee cursed the tears burning her eyes.

"You wanna tell him he's cut loose 'til the trial, or should I?"

Eric Bray was satisfied with Nate's written statement, and confident if he needed her attorney he could get a hold of him—even in Texas.

So her lover could go.

Home.

Sixteen hundred miles away from her.

Her heart missed a beat.

Probably some stupid form of professional

courtesy.

Jerk.

Lee didn't know Eric Bray. But she didn't like him.

"Lee?" Her name on Clint's lips made her jump.

"What?"

"You got me on ignore now?"

She scowled at the amusement in his expression. "No. Just thinking."

"Wanna share with the class?"

"Hell no."

He chuckled. "There's my partner. So, you tellin' him, or am I?"

"I'll handle it," she snapped, and marched to her office, leaving her partner in the corridor with a smirk on his face.

One she'd pretended not to notice.

Lee's whole body stuttered at first sight of Nate, even before she stepped into the small room. His strong back was to her, and he was on the phone. She slipped inside, studying his profile.

"Great. Thanks." He jotted something down on her notepad and smiled. It was serene, free and something almost private.

'Intruder alert' from some space movie played on a loop in her head.

Her stomach somersaulted. "Nate..." The whisper was unintended.

His smile faded. "Are you all right?" Concern enveloped his demeanor.

She couldn't speak, so she forced a nod.

He was on his feet in seconds. "Sorry, I didn't ask

to use the phone."

Lee cleared her throat. "Oh, it's no problem."

Nate reached for both her hands and squeezed. "You're pale, angel. Tell me what's wrong."

"I'm good." She made her lips curve up. "Promise."

He scanned her face, but his shoulders loosened after a moment. "Good. How'd your meeting with Special Agent Barnes go?"

"I'm still gainfully employed." Her joke missed its mark, but her smirked.

"Well, I'm glad to hear that. Your partner in the same situation?"

"Yup."

And I need to thank him for giving us a moment alone.

"Listen. I have to tell you something." The rest of what she needed to tell him fizzled. She licked her lips.

Nate waited, his expression open to the bomb she was about to drop.

"The prosecutor for Fiato's case said you can go home. My boss agreed, since Caselli's in custody."

He was silent for a while, but his eyes spoke volumes Lee tried not to see.

"It's safe now, huh." More statement than question.

"Maybe not completely, but yes. For a little while, his organization will be in chaos. He never replaced his right-hand man after Bruno Gallo went to prison, and the inner circle is all in New York jail cells. As long as he's unconscious, he can't bribe anyone to get orders—death or otherwise—out of the hospital. Knowing his father, Antonio Senior will make a go for his assets. I'm not sure we put them out of business today, but we're a hell of a lot closer. So…you can go home." Her voice cracked on the last word and she cringed.

God, please don't react.

Nate squeezed her hand. "I'm not sure—"

"I'll call your brother and Lucas and brief them so you'll have adequate protection if need be." She forced the rest out faster than her brain formed the sentences. Her tongue stumbled.

She couldn't take it if he was worried about leaving.

Or if he told her he didn't want to leave *her*.

"I'm not worried about not being protected."

"Dawson."

She could've kissed her partner for the well-timed interruption.

His oversized frame filled the doorway, and she was more than glad to rip her gaze away from Nate's to meet Clint's eyes. "Yeah?"

"Eric Bray's on the phone for Crane. Wants to talk to him before he skips town."

Nate answered before she could. "Where do I take the call?"

"When are you leaving?" Her head spun when the question slipped out. Lee's chest *hurt*. Like her heart and lungs couldn't get enough air.

"Tomorrow. I have a meeting in the morning, but then…" Nate's gaze locked onto hers.

A tremor shot down her spine and she looked away. She wanted to ask him, 'but then…*what?*' She didn't.

Couldn't.

Am I supposed to ask him to stay?

God, stop looking at me like that!

Her eyes darted around the apartment that'd been *home* since arriving in New York City two years before. The décor was sparse at best—she'd never been a *thing* person.

No pictures on the walls. Only essentials as far as furniture—a dark brown, microfiber overstuffed couch and matching loveseat. Mahogany coffee table she'd bought at a local consignment store. At least it looked good with the standard issue, tan apartment carpet. Television was small, too. She hardly ever watched it anyway.

Lee hadn't brought anything from Dallas except clothing. Hadn't been able to stand the memories of the things from the house she'd shared with Russ. She'd sold the house and moved into an apartment after he and Dylan had died. Had put everything in storage, and left it there. Didn't really care if her mom paid the bill or let *Storage Wars* have at it.

She cleared her throat and squared her shoulders. "Do you need a ride to JFK?"

"Only if you don't mind."

"I don't. I'll let Clint know I'll have to leave."

"Lee—"

"Don't. Please. Just…just—let's enjoy our last evening together."

"I can call a cab."

Emotion threatened to close her throat, but she managed a head shake. "No. I can take you. I want to."

"All right." Nate took a step closer, but she backed up.

She couldn't have his hands on her.

His face fell. Like usual, he was great at reading body language and no doubt he could tell. He didn't move toward her or push the issue.

Thank God.

"What time's your meeting?" Lee forced the inquiry past her lips.

Normal. Be normal.

"Nine." His broad shoulders scrunched up and Nate buried his hands in the front pockets of his jeans. He reclined into the wall of her small living room, knee bent and cowboy boot propped up.

She didn't ask with who or what the meeting was about.

Don't wanna know.

She had unit debrief at the same time. Then she and Clint had planned head to the hospital to try to get Caselli to talk. The doc said he was stable. He was in the prison unit with a twenty-four/seven guard.

According to Smythe, the bastard was coming around nicely after surgery.

Stewart had hit him three times. Once in the gut, a right shoulder through-and-through wound and grazed his left side.

"What are we doing?"

"What'd you mean?" Lee swallowed hard.

"C'mon. Don't give me that crap. You're tense. Surprised you're not pacing. Tell me what you're thinking."

"Nothing." She sighed.

"Bullshit. I thought we were past this."

"Past what?"

"After all we've been through together, you *still* won't let me in?" He stalked across the room.

She looked up into his face when he stopped in front of her.

Nate still didn't touch her, but he didn't have to. The intensity in his eyes made her spine tingle and her body warm.

Desire she wanted to resist settled low in her belly. "I'm not going to fight with you on our last night together." It came out as a pained whisper.

"I don't want to fight with you, either." He rested his hands on her shoulders. Dipped his head down to brush his lips against hers. "I just want to be with you."

"I want that, too."

"*Completely* with you, Lee. Don't treat me like a second-class citizen. Let me know what you're thinking. What you're feeling."

I can't.

When he searched her face again, Lee ignored the lump in her throat.

The expression he wore told her he'd picked up the two-word phrase even though she'd not spoken.

Like he was a grade-A mind reader.

She couldn't deal with this.

Wouldn't deal with it.

Standing tiptoed, she pressed her mouth to Nate's, praying he'd just shut up about things she couldn't say.

Kiss me, Nate Crane. Just kiss me.

Lee repeated it over and over until she couldn't think anymore, because he was doing just that.

He plunged deep into her mouth, twining his tongue around hers and hauling her flush to his chest.

She wound her arms around him and rocked her hips into his.

Nate moaned first, pressing back into her pelvis. An erection was evident and she rubbed against him, kissing him harder.

Lee didn't want to think...because it hurt. She didn't want to feel the loss that was already settling over her.

He was leaving.

Tomorrow.

You knew this wasn't permanent.

Not that she'd wanted it to be.

Right?

She burrowed into his chest, slanting her mouth under his again and again. Prayed he didn't sense her desperation, but saw — felt — the desire and passion she had for him.

Nate continued to kiss her back with the same fervor. He held her tightly, caressing her back and cupping her ass. Holding her upright like he always did. Protecting as he controlled, plundering her mouth and making her crave his touch.

When things slowed down for the sake of breathing on both their parts, Lee rested her forehead against his, panting in rhythm with him. "Let's go to my room," she whispered into his mouth.

Chapter Twenty-Five

Nate stared down into her face. His cock pounded against the zipper of his jeans and he teetered between lust and coherent thought.

What do you want from me?

He couldn't ask. Pushing her got him nowhere. She wouldn't open up. When he got close to demanding, she shut down. Shut him out.

Shut up *is what you need to do right now, Nate Crane.*

Kiss her again.

Take her in her own bed.

Remind her how of it was with them.

Them together would be the last thing on her mind tonight and the first thing she thought of the next morning.

Maybe *seeing* him in her bed would jolt her into wanting to keep him there.

Permanently.

He couldn't tell her his plans for the morning. It didn't matter — for now. Nate would have to be smart. Let his case rest *before* the argument.

Get things all lined up so Lee didn't have a choice.

Because now that he had her back, he wasn't letting her go, no matter what she said.

No matter what she *thought* she wanted.

He'd dabbled with the idea of moving back to New York before he'd left Texas for his annual trip. He'd paced his office at home, staring at his flight itinerary and thinking of her.

When he'd discovered her past, it wasn't a shocker she could never be FBI in Dallas again. So maybe the fantasy of living with her in the city had started six months ago — almost seven now.

It hadn't solidified for him until their eyes had met in that hotel bar. He hadn't looked back as of that moment — not really.

Nate hadn't foreseen losing Angelo and being with her for weeks. However, he wouldn't have traded the unplanned time with his little FBI agent.

He'd miss his frat brother for a long time. Wished it hadn't happened. Or that 'Lo hadn't made the choices he had.

Lee.

He'd got time to really get to know her better.

Fallen even harder for her.

He couldn't lose her again.

Go back home and pretend they'd never been — again.

Nate had no illusions about Lee. She was deep and caring, though she rarely showed it. She was funny and gorgeous, and he loved her more than anything.

Under the surface, he sensed deep hurt.

Anger.

She'd lost her family six years ago, and her downward spiral had lasted more than three years. Despite being two years past the DWI and settled into the New York office of the FBI, she wasn't over losing her husband and son.

How could he tell her he knew it all?

This moment was like the dozen other times he'd wanted to open his mouth over the course of staying at the house in upstate New York. Nate couldn't find the right words.

Lee had never made him any promises.

He wasn't foolish enough to expect them. Just wished it didn't hurt like a bitch. Or make his chest burn and his eyes smart, even though he couldn't remember the last time he'd cried.

His love was no better about feelings than he was about telling her he knew about her past.

The only time she was honest with him was in bed. When she let her body communicate for her. It was pure. Beautiful.

She never held back.

"I don't want to talk anymore," Lee whispered, spreading little kisses all over his mouth. "I just...need you. Need *this*. Before you go."

Nate shivered and chided himself not to contradict her. Wanted to tell her she wasn't getting rid of him that easily. Declare he wasn't leaving The Big Apple; he had a job interview in the morning, but he didn't.

She wasn't ready to hear it.

Stop thinking. Concentrate on the love of your life. She's in your arms.

"Take me to bed."

"You read my mind, angel." He dropped his head low for a kiss.

Lee jumped up into his arms, wrapping her legs around his waist. Her body hit his in all the right places, but they had too many clothes on.

He held her, deepening their lip-lock and sucking on her tongue until she groaned. She ran her hands up and down his back and he fought a tremor. He needed her fingers on his bare skin.

Nate was going to taste every inch of her body. Brand her like she had him—make her realize she was his without telling her aloud.

Her apartment was small, and the bedroom was only a few steps from her living room. As Spartan as the rest of her place, there was only a double bed, an armoire and a nightstand.

Unlike the rest of the apartment, this room was more Lee. She had a few framed photos on the walls, and her closet door was open. Clothes were piled on the floor just inside the door, showing she wasn't always a neat freak.

Nate liked that. It made her more real.

When he laid her at the center of her bed and followed her down, she was already writhing beneath him.

"Don't tease me. Lose the clothes."

He laughed, nibbling on her bottom lip before nipping her chin and dragging kisses downward.

Lee hissed, but tilted to give him access to her neck. She buried her hands in his hair and tugged, but he didn't care.

He wasn't going to hurry, no matter the demands of his impatient angel. Thrusting his hips resulted in his denim-clad erection hitting her jeans-covered sex.

She moaned and rocked under him, lifting her hips and mock-glaring. "What are we? Teens dry humping?

Get naked. Now, Counselor."

Nate chuckled. "Awfully bossy, angel."

"I'm FBI. Comes with the territory." She pushed him off her and yanked her shirt up and over her head the moment there was space enough between their bodies. She made quick work of her bra, tossing it fastball-style to the carpet of her room.

He watched her, taking in every inch of bronze skin she'd bared. He licked his lips.

"Now you," Lee ordered, but she'd already tugged his tee from his jeans, her fingers teasing his abs as she went.

His muscles jumped, and he groaned as her caresses spread to his pecs. She pinched his nipples. Biting back a moan, Nate let her push his shirt up and off.

She tossed it over the side of the bed and skimmed his shoulders and back, adding kisses across his collarbone until a tremor shot down his spine.

"I can't concentrate when you do that," he whispered into her hair.

Lee flashed a signature smirk. "Good. Concentration isn't required when I'm trying to get you to do what I want."

Laughing, he shook his head and grabbed her hand, smothering her knuckles with kisses. He dragged his fingers up her wrist, then her arm, caressing as much of her soft skin as he could. Craved more.

"Hmmm, that tickles," she whispered.

He cupped her face and pulled her closer for another kiss.

Their mouths melded. It was tender and held none of the urgency as the one in the living room had.

Nate hauled her onto his lap, wrapping his arms around her.

Her full breasts pressed into his chest as they came together, and she rocked in his lap, reminding him they both still had jeans on.

His cock throbbed, begging for freedom.

"Angel, you were right." His speech was muffled against her luscious mouth. He felt her smile before he saw it.

"I'm always right."

He grinned and kissed her again. "Don't you even want to know about what?"

Lee undulated and they both groaned. "Think it has something to do with this." She slipped off his lap and covered his erection with a palm.

He lifted into her touch, burning for her fingers to free him, encircle him, stroke him.

"Oh, I see you like that, babe. Well, lose the pants and I promise there's more." She stood, a teasing smile on her lips that turned his insides to mush. Her nipples were hard, her gorgeous breasts begging for a caress, but she swatted his hands away when he reached out. "Stay there." Lee opened her belt and took her holstered Glock off, setting it on the nightstand next to her bed. She did the same with her magazine and handcuff cases.

Nate was torn between being even more turned on and jealousy when he watched the care with which she handled her equipment.

When his lover's attention was back on him and she lowered the zipper of her jeans slowly—striptease style—his dick pulsed and he couldn't look away from the movement of her hips.

She circled and swayed as she pushed her pants down as if she had all the time in the world, revealing a black lace bikini inch by inch.

His mouth went dry as he stared. Didn't give a shit that she'd replaced the practical cotton underwear he'd grown used to seeing her in.

She wouldn't be in the little black number long enough for it to matter.

As if Lee had read his mind, she shoved the panties off one hip, then the other. Stepped out of them. She stood beside her bed, naked as the day she was born.

Perfect.

The most beautiful woman Nate had ever seen.

"Come here," he growled.

She grinned and shook her head. "I showed you mine. You show me yours."

"You've seen it before." He fought a smile.

"I want to see it again."

"Oh, you'll get to."

"*Now*, Counselor."

He laughed again, and licked his lips, then complied, pushing to his knees and opening the button on his jeans. He stilled, fingertips on the zipper pull. "I'm afraid I'm not as good as you are with the teasing thing."

Lee stepped closer but didn't reach for him. "Yes you are, babe."

The endearment rolled over him like a caress. When she'd said it in the car, it'd felt like she was mocking him.

Then she'd said it when she'd kiss-cuffed him.

Now…it felt real. As though she meant it.

His heart flip-flopped and he swallowed. Nate suddenly needed to touch her, hold her. Kiss her again.

Chiding himself to be patient, he unzipped his jeans and pushed them down. He yanked them off and tossed them away.

Even after he'd divested himself of the rest of his clothes, she didn't climb on the bed. He felt the heat of Lee's stare and it kicked his libido up a notch. She liked his body, and that made his blood run hotter.

"Angel, you're killin' me. Come to me. Be with me." He put his hand out, and knelt on the bed at the same time her palm grazed his. He pulled her to him the rest of the way and Lee straddled his lap.

They sat facing, breasts to chest, sexes touching and arms around each other.

She pressed her mouth to his and he returned her kiss, cupping the back of her neck to tug her even closer. He buried his hands in her long, dark hair.

Lee pushed her knees into the bed for leverage and started to rock in his lap.

Nate groaned into her mouth as her core rubbed his cock. The friction wasn't nearly enough.

She moved back and forth, driving him crazy.

He ended their kiss and they panted against each other. "I need you," he confessed.

"Just warming you up, babe." The statement was a

tease, but her voice was deeper, thick with desire.

"Oh, angel. I'm already there. I want you. Inside you."

Lee swallowed and he kissed her throat.

Nate ran his hands down her back, until he splayed them both at her slender waist. He lifted her and she slipped a hand between them.

He grunted when she gripped him. Pleasure enveloped his dick, shooting into his balls.

He *needed* inside her.

She impaled herself on him. She was wet, welcoming and took all of him at once. Lee whimpered as her bottom hit his thighs.

"You okay?" The inquiry was strained to his ears, but he needed to make sure he hadn't hurt her.

She kissed him in answer, starting to thrust gently.

He rocked beneath her, deepening their kiss and urging her faster.

Lee ignored him, moving her hips in a too-slow pace. She braced her hands on his shoulders and undulated.

Nate tightened his grip at her waist and lifted her up and down.

Instead of fighting him, she threw her head back and pushed down faster every time he moved her away.

The sounds that breached her lips made his blood boil. Little whimpers and whines, mixed with deep moans and groans.

Nate kissed her over and over, nipping and sucking on her bottom lip.

She was right with him as they went higher and higher. Touches, kisses, tasting each other's sweat-kissed skin. Her nails bit into his shoulders as their strokes became frantic.

His spine tingled and his thighs burned as climax started to crest.

She was close too, her body giving him clues as her thrusts became jerkier and her hands opened and closed on his shoulders.

Orgasm crashed over them at the same time.

Lee writhed in his lap as his cock jerked inside her. She whimpered, burying her face in his neck. Her sex clenched him tight, holding him as her inner muscles pulsed.

He pinned her to his chest, caressing her back in long circles. Her skin was damp and overheated, but Nate didn't want to be parted from her — ever.

'I love you' was on the tip of his tongue, but he held back like before.

Telling her how he felt would ruin the moment.

She'd pull away from him — physically and mentally.

Lee hadn't lifted her head from his shoulder, and she was spreading warm, wet kisses on his neck, his throat and under his chin. Her palm rested against his cheek and her thumb teased his stubble.

He laid his hand over hers. He'd never get tired of her kiss. Her touch. He pressed his lips to the crown of her head before cupping her face and making her meet his gaze. "I'm glad I'm spending my last night in New York with you."

His heart stuttered when he saw the brown depths of her eyes shine with tears.

Lee sighed, her breasts heaving against his chest. She smiled softly. It was tremulous and endearing. *Honest.* "I'm glad, too. You'll stay with me all night, right?"

"Of course, angel. Where else would I go?"

She didn't answer. Just nestled into his torso.

He laughed. "Are we going to sit up all night?"

Her expression was torn between amusement and…hurt?

Nate swallowed, trying to focus on anything other than serious emotions that would force her retreat. He kissed her nose. "I want to lay with you, hold you."

Nodding, she flashed a smile that was almost shy. "You're privileged, you know."

"How's that?"

"You're the first guy to sleep in my bed."

And the last.

He grinned. "Oh? You don't bring boys home? Surprising, because you're not really the good girl type."

She scrunched up her nose and laughed. "Really? I thought I was good." She tilted her hips, intentionally grinding against his softening cock.

Nate groaned. "I'll show you *good*." He grabbed her and pushed her down into the bed, settling on top of her.

Lee yelped and let out a giggle, but didn't fight his kiss when he crushed her mouth with his. Their tongues danced and dueled, and she wrapped her arms and legs around him, burying her hands in his hair as she kissed him back.

He wished his dick was ready to go again.

When the kiss ended, she stared up at him. Her tanned skin glowed from exertion, her high cheekbones were flushed pink and her dark hair was mussed, spread out on her pillow.

Her beauty took his breath away.

Mine.

Lee Dawson, you're mine.

She caressed his shoulders and back as if she couldn't stand not having contact with him, and Nate once again stalled words of love from tumbling out.

Lee reached for his face, caressing his stubble.

He shivered. "I can't get enough of your touch."

She gave a sexy smile. "Good."

He dipped low for a kiss, but it was too quick.

Her eyes bored into his and he fought another tremor.

"I'm going to miss you, Counselor."

You don't have to. I'm not going anywhere.

"I'll miss you, too, angel."

Lee urged him to his back and dragged her fingers down his chest. She teased his pecs and abs, following up with kisses along the expanse of his chest and stomach.

Nate's dick twitched, already starting to harden even before her hand surrounded him. Her hair tickled his stomach and thighs as she moved downward. "Show me what I'll miss out on," he groaned.

Her eyes danced when their gazes met. "You

telling me what to do again?" She pumped him two quick times and he cried her name.

"Never," he panted.

"Good. In that case, I'm happy to show you what *I'll* miss." She winked.

His retort died on the tip of his tongue when she sucked him into her mouth.

Chapter Twenty-Six

"W here's Crane?" Clint shot a dark brow up, pushing off the wall next to their office. He'd been waiting for her to return from the restroom so they could head to the hospital.

Unit debrief had gone off without a hitch, but it'd lasted about an hour too long. Left her twitchy, more than ready to get out of the office.

"You made it all the way through briefing without asking me that *burning* question?" Lee kept her inquiry dry, trying to avoid his keen gaze.

Her partner shrugged. "You know, a time for everything and all that."

"He said he had a meeting. I didn't ask."

"What time's his flight?"

Dammit, Clint. Leave me alone.

Her heart galloped and she concentrated on giving a bland expression. She sighed. Didn't want to tell him. "Not 'til this evening."

"Well, when we're done at the hospital, I got you covered for the rest of the day."

"Clint—"

"*Lee*, don't be a shit. See your man off. Hell, take vacation and go with him. I know you got family down there and you stayed here for Thanksgiving *and* Christmas."

"Damn, you keep better track of my hours than I do. He's not my man. And don't tell me what to do,"

Lee grumbled.

"Geeze. What the hell am I gonna do with you?" His exasperation came out on a sigh.

"Let's go to the hospital," she barked.

"Don't tell me what do to," her partner returned, giving a fair impression of her voice.

She glared. "Really?"

"You can't pretend the last few weeks didn't happen. You're...different. I need to shake the guy's hand. I wasn't sure my partner was human."

"Totally not doing this." She stepped into their office and whipped her bomber jacket off the back of the computer chair. Stalked past him, continuing down the hallway; heading toward the elevators without waiting for him. "I'm going to the hospital. Come with or stay here, train's leaving now."

Clint didn't argue when she wrenched the driver-side door of the navy blue Charger open and got in the car.

Lee tried not to think of Nate arguing with her over who'd drive the rental car that day, which now seemed forever ago. She sucked her bottom lip into her mouth and ignored the pain inching up from her gut. Banished the memories of the times they'd made love the night before. How he'd held her. Kissed her. Looked at her like she was some precious gem.

Nate hadn't uttered words of love, though.

That was the only thing getting her through this morning.

Her partner shut the passenger door, silently stretching the seatbelt across his considerable chest then snapping it in place.

Good, he's not gonna be chatty. Way to alienate another male in your life, Lee.

She growled and started the car.

"Something wrong?"

"Nope."

Clint didn't answer, which was fine with her.

Her phone chimed and she dug it out of her pocket before she had a chance to back out of the parking spot.

Good luck with Caselli.

Seeing the text from Nate made her eyes burn, but she gritted her teeth and shoved her cell away.

Being an emotional wreck was new. Very, very unwelcome.

After cranking the car on and gunning it, she turned the wheel and drove toward the garage's exit, chiding herself all the way.

Her mouth was dry.

Like she needed a drink.

Whisky.

No. Get that shit out of your head.

Now.

"He's at Bellevue."

"I know." Lee tried to temper her affirmative, but the statement still passed her lips as a snap.

Thank God Clint didn't call her on it.

They didn't talk on the drive. All for the best.

She didn't want to be a bitch to her partner all day long. It wasn't his fault she was a total head fuck.

The guy cared about her. Not a bad thing, even though she had a shitty way of showing it.

Downside—the chaos in her head about Nate wouldn't quiet. All she could see were those hazel eyes. Hear words left unsaid. Fantasize about how she could—or would—have reacted. Remember his touch. How real it was, snuggled up against his chest. Arguments. The push and pull of a real relationship. How he made her feel—

"Lee."

"What?"

"You missed the turn."

"Fuck. Shit— I mean, I'm sorry."

Damn, her voice trembled. She cleared her throat and turned around as soon as she got the chance.

Lee parked the Charger, chanting, *'leave me alone, leave me alone'.*

Her partner's intuition must've been fully operational because he didn't speak as they got out of the car to head into the hospital.

Clint held the door open and waited for her to walk in front of him.

Too bad her knees wobbled and her stomach caved in on itself. Bile rose out of nowhere and her coffee-eggs-toast-bacon breakfast threatened to switch from digestion mode to *eject.*

Dizziness swamped at the same time and Lee crashed into the wall in the lobby of the big hospital.

No finesse. No playing it off.

Dammit.

"Whoa." Clint's large hand swallowed her left

biceps as he steadied her from falling on her ass. "Dawson?"

She swallowed a few times and cleared her throat, blinking until she was able to refocus on the man staring down at her. "I'm good."

"Bullshit. What happened?"

Lee shrugged his hand off. "Nothing. Just lost my balance. I'm fine."

Clint arched an eyebrow. "We're at a hospital. Should we stop at the ER?"

"God no. Let's get this shit done."

"Only if you promise to go home after."

"Nope." She whirled away from him, fighting a renewed wave of nausea.

What the hell is wrong with me?

She commanded herself not to throw up and slammed the *'up'* arrow when they reached the elevators. Her thumb smarted, but she ignored it, going through the mental list of all the foods she'd eaten the day before.

Chinese food. Maybe the General Tso's was bad.

They'd ordered in. Lee would have to see if Nate's stomach was off, too.

Stupid restaurant.

She distracted herself with duties, going through the check-in process with her partner when they reached the prison ward of Bellevue Hospital.

Special Agent Bobby Smythe met them outside Caselli's room. He'd ended up staying the night after leaving the mansion with the paramedics.

"They arraigned him this morning via video. He

was already hollering for a lawyer from the moment he woke up. Some wet-behind-the-ears kid showed up."

"From Fiato's firm?" Lee asked.

"Not sure. Speaking of Fiato, the plea was not guilty to the murder, of course." Smythe shook his head.

"What about Stewart?" Clint asked.

"You don't have to guess. Not guilty to second degree manslaughter. Trying to spin self-defense."

"Fuck me," she spat.

"Caselli won't talk to me, you or anyone FBI. *And* he was telling his attorney what to do," Smythe said.

She threw a look at her partner. "Wanna try anyway?"

His mouth was a hard line. "Let's at least say hi. We came all this way."

Yeah, all of a ten-minute drive.

She smirked and nodded.

"Well, he's secure here. I'm gonna leave you guys to it and head to check on Roberts."

"He wake up?" Lee asked.

"Not that I heard. Morris is with him now. I need to stop by the office, too, before I head home to crash."

"Take it easy." Her partner shook their fellow agent's hand.

"Good morning, Special Agents." Antonio Rodolfo Aldo Caselli, Junior, had a deep voice and a handsome face that made Lee cringe.

He sat, the bed propped up at his back. Dark hair neat and trimmed. His hands were folded on his lap.

Serene.

The bastard was wearing silk pajamas with a *C* monogram on the breast pocket instead of a hospital johnnie.

His expression was pleasant, and no bandages from his recent surgery or wounds visible. The blanket covering his legs wasn't hospital standard issue, either.

"I see you've had a visitor," she said.

"My attorney has ensured my accommodations are to my caliber, yes."

Lee snorted.

"Cut the crap, Caselli," Clint barked.

Caselli smiled, as if her partner hadn't spoken harshly. As though the guy didn't understand English.

She snorted. "Where's a good pair of handcuffs when you need one?"

"I got two, partner." He patted his double handcuff case at his waist.

"I assure you, I'm in more danger *from* you than I am *to* you, Special Agent Dawson."

Didn't surprise her the gangster knew her name. She squared her shoulders and tried not to show a reaction.

"Right. You're as harmless as a kitten."

Caselli glared at Clint. His face changed in a split-second — bi-polar style. "What can I do for you, Special Agent Downs?"

"Well, since we have you dead to rights on Fiato's murder, we thought you might want to share the deets with the rest of the class. So we're sure we have it right from your perspective and all that," Lee said.

His dark eyes pinned her as Caselli refocused his

glare. "Perhaps you weren't properly informed, so I shall forgive your overstepping, *this* time."

"Overstepping?" Her partner laughed.

"I didn't realize you were so proper, Caselli," she drawled. "I've only ever seen the *fucks-little-girls* side of you. Manners? Who knew?"

"I've invoked, bitch. So you can go to hell. You can't fucking talk to me without my attorney."

Clint whistled and snapped his finger.

"Oh, there's the Caselli I know," Lee said, staring back at the man with the same intensity he'd paid her.

The mobster cleared his throat and tugged his pajama shirt straight. He averted his gaze.

She'd seen him in court dozens of times, and had heard both personalities on many a recorded phone call.

Equal parts charmer and psycho.

"I think he's nervous, partner," Clint said.

"Yeah, I'd say so." Lee didn't miss a beat. "There's no superstar to *fix* it for him this time."

"Maybe he shouldn't have killed him."

Caselli looked back at them and glared. "We're done here. You can go."

She laughed. "Will you look at that? We've been dismissed."

Her partner nodded, a smile making his moustache shift.

"On the other hand, the FBI *is* good at wasting federal resources, so you can stand there all day and do what you do best. I'll have my attorney file a complaint about your coercion attempts and harassment."

Clint snorted.

"You don't give a flying fuck about federal resources." Lee shook her head. "I'm surprised you realize there's life outside Caselli-land."

"Oh, of course he does, partner. He has to get little girls to sell from *somewhere*."

"That's right. How could I forget?"

"And the harassment continues." Caselli's statement was even, nonchalant.

Wow. Dude probably is *bi-polar.*

"Tell you what. Here's my card. Have your attorney call me and we can discuss your *ill-treatment* by the FBI." Clint left his card on the end of the bed while she called for the guard.

She scowled when they were outside the secured area and reholstering their weapons. "That was a fucking waste of time."

"Well, honestly, we knew it would be."

Lee sighed and opened the exit door before Clint could. "I guess so."

"I, for one, liked seeing the bastard confined to a bed. Weak. Only his mouth to run."

"Yeah, I guess that's the plus side. I should have kicked him in the balls."

Clint *tsked* and waggled his index finger. "Now, now, Lee. Not around the cameras."

She laughed. "Don't do that. It reminds me of my mom."

"Are you calling me a woman?"

"When you *tsk*? Yeah, close."

"Hmmm, your mom lives in Texas, right?"

Not only had he let her jibe slide, he was talking about family again? "Yeah, in Plano... North of Dallas. Why?"

"Take some time. Go see her. Hell, take Crane to meet her."

Blowing out a breath, she left her partner in the prison ward entrance the same way she'd abandoned him outside their office.

Ignored Nate's smiling face as it danced through her head.

Her mother would adore Nate Crane.

Lee's phone chimed with a text right after she'd unlocked the Charger. She thumbed across the touchscreen and the message filled her vision.

Dinner in or out before I leave tonight?

Her heart galloped. Couldn't answer him. Scrolling through the messages, she counted.

Five gray bubbles on the left sign of the screen.

No green ones on the right side, because she hadn't responded to any of his messages since they'd parted ways at her apartment four hours before.

The idea of going home only to see him take his duffel and garment bag out of her closet made her chest burn.

Nate was getting on a plane today.

Leaving her.

Tell him you don't want things to end.

She couldn't. Long-distance relationships never worked.

Besides, Lee didn't do relationships anyway.

Her phone beeped again and she contemplated ignoring him.

When she looked at the screen again, she frowned.

When you and Downs get back, stop by my office. Thanks.

Liv?

What could her boss want?

"Everything okay?"

Lee jumped.

"Sorry." Clint's expression was apologetic.

"No problem, didn't realize you'd caught up."

"Ah. You good?"

"Yeah. Let's get back."

"I'd rather drop you off at your place. You can get your car later." Her partner was serious, his gaze narrowed. He was daring her to tell him no.

Saved by the text. Maybe.

"Couldn't if I wanted you to. Barnes wants to see me. Let's go."

Chapter Twenty-Seven

"**S**on, you have a job if you want it."

Nate beamed. "Yes, sir. Thank you for the opportunity."

"I should be thanking Dean for letting you go. You're gonna be a hell of an asset."

His new boss offered him a shake, and he took it, pushing to his feet when the man stood before him.

Lee consumed his thoughts, and he chided himself to focus on what the District Attorney, Mario Malcuri, was saying. Nate needed to know where and when to show up after he'd settled things back home.

His new boss had told him to take what time he needed to get himself—and his things—ready for a cross-country relocation. He had a place to stay, if he needed it, too.

Malcuri owned an apartment building in Uptown and he could use one of the units for as long as he needed it. The rent was going to be a steal compared to the going rate. The guy was thankfully cutting him a deal.

Maybe Lee wouldn't freak so much if she saw he'd planned to be *with* her, but not smother her. Ease her into the idea of him being in her life. Then they could talk about moving in together and…marriage.

Nate wanted everything. He already had plans to buy a brownstone in the city for them eventually.

Her inability to have kids was only a blip. He'd

always liked kids, but would be okay with or without them. If Lee wanted a child, they could always adopt.

She was the most important thing.

Nate needed *her*.

Workwise, he had a case to either wrap up or pass on to another prosecutor. He'd have to see what Dean thought when he got back to the office.

Two weeks, tops.

He wanted to be back in New York, start his life with Lee.

His woman sure as hell wasn't about to ask him to stay.

What would she say when he told her his fate was sealed?

He wanted to sweep her off her feet tonight. Tell her about the job, and that he'd be back in a few weeks.

Tell her I love her.

Somehow he had to balance it all. Convince her he wouldn't pressure her, but he wasn't going to retreat quietly and let her go this time.

Nate also needed to come clean that he knew about her loss, and what'd happened in Dallas. She was going to be pissed — mega pissed — but perhaps the time apart while he got everything in order would help her cool down...

Forgive him for keeping it from her.

Plans. Plans. Plans.

He was antsy, and he wanted to get back to her place before she did.

Lee hadn't answered his text about dinner, but Nate was going to stop by the grocery store and buy something to cook. Get some roses and sparkling cider. Prep everything so they had time before heading to the airport. His flight was the latest one available.

She'd given him her extra key that morning, because she hadn't been sure when she was going to get in, but she'd promised to leave the office by four at the latest. That would give them about five hours to be together before his flight.

"All right then, do you have any questions for me?"

Nate shook his head. "I think you've answered everything, but thank you."

Malcuri smiled. "Perfect. Let me show you where your office will be, and introduce you to the assistant the lead prosecutors share. Gina works for three—now four, including you—but she's fantastic. You'll have your own paralegal, Angi. She's great, too."

"Great, thank you."

Meeting the two ladies turned into a whirlwind tour of the whole office, and his new boss introduced him to a few would-be co-workers as well. The bunch seemed tight-knit, but welcoming to the new kid on the block.

Hope first impressions are right.

Coming onboard as a lead prosecutor might chafe if someone else had interviewed for Nate's new job.

The DA walked him to the elevators when they were done. The man offered him another shake. "Congrats, young man. I'm looking forward to working with you. Tell Dean I said hello."

"Thank you, and I will."

"See you in a few weeks."

"That's the plan." Nate smiled, his heart tripping as he stepped onto the elevator. He grabbed his phone. First text was to Pete to shout he'd got the job.

When his phone indicated it was sent, he went back to the menu and stared at Lee's name in his message menu.

Holding back his news was hard. She had yet to answer any of his messages, but she'd probably just been really busy at work. Hell, her cell could even be on silent.

He pictured her smiling face in his mind as he exited the building to hail a cab.

Here goes everything.

"I want you to take some time off." Liv's voice was as even as always, but the touch of concern in her light brown eyes made Lee's blood boil.

"I'm good. Don't need it." Her phone chimed and she ignored it.

If her boss heard it, she didn't react. "I disagree." This was harder. Liv leaned forward, both elbows on her desk.

Her short blonde bob didn't move at all. The cut made her look younger than her fifty-plus years, and she was still gorgeous. Looked younger than her age, anyway.

The woman had been that shade of blonde since Lee had worked for her, and she didn't have the guts to ask if it was from a bottle.

Special Agent Olivia Barnes had been with the FBI over twenty years, and she didn't pull any punches. Wouldn't have risen in the ranks if she had.

"Given what happened with Stewart, I also want you to have at least three sessions with Dr. Doran."

Aww, shit.

"I don't need a shrink, Liv."

"Nothing personal, Lee. Standard procedure for the whole unit."

"Then why're we having a little one-on-one?" She ordered herself not to glare.

Don't make the boss think you're crazy.

The older woman tilted her chin up. "Because *I* thought it was for the best."

Translation — I'm the boss and I said so.

Lee reclined in the chair and sighed. Planned a hundred different ways to kill her partner if he was the one who'd initiated this little pep talk. "How much *time* are we talking?"

"At least a week."

Fuck.

"No way. Two days."

"No way," Liv echoed fast. "Keep it up, and it's two weeks."

"Am I suspended or something?"

She steepled her hands and cocked her head to one side. "Nope. You have almost *two hundred* vacation hours. You need to use some."

"I really don't."

"This isn't a negotiation, Special Agent Selena Dawson."

Damn, title and full name? I'm screwed.

"This is the part where I point out how many leads I've personally tracked down. All the hours I've worked, and how many SOBs I've put away. How many little girls I've saved."

"Precisely."

Lee paused. "Those were supposed to be *positive* points."

"Oh, they were. I've never questioned your dedication. You're my go-to for the hard stuff. I know you work your ass off. But that also highlights how badly you need a break."

"Liv—"

"Do you need to go to a meeting?"

Whatever she'd been planning on saying dissolved.

Lee stared at her boss, her heart pounding.

Liv was always blunt. But calling her out like that?

"No." She clenched her jaw until pain shot into her teeth. For some fucking reason, she wanted to cry. She blinked and ignored how her gut tightened. Squared her shoulders, sitting taller in the chair.

Her boss stared for minutes that seemed like hours. "Okay."

Lee refused to sigh in relief. Reason battled with feeling insulted, but she respected Liv too much to let that tumble out. *She* was the shit, not her boss. "You win."

If Liv was surprised, or felt some sense of accomplishment, she hid it well. She offered a nod. "All right."

A part of her was *pissed* that Special Agent Olivia Barnes *always* let one come to whatever conclusion *she* wanted one to do so on their own.

Conceding *sucked.*

"I'll take tomorrow off, then the rest of the week."

"Not starting tomorrow. The rest of *today*. Keep going."

Lee groaned. "I'm coming back Tuesday. That's five working days."

"No weekends or sneaking emails."

"Shit."

A ghost of a smile played at her boss's lips. "I promise the office won't collapse."

"That's not the point."

I might collapse. If I have work, I can't think of Nate…

For about the hundredth time in the last two hours, emotion threatened to bowl her over. Her eyes burned. She fought the urge to suck in air.

"All right, Dawson. Get out of my office. Don't pass go, or collect two hundred dollars. Get your ass home. See you next week."

She forced herself to meet Liv's gaze. Cleared her throat. "One thing. Downs talk to you?"

The boss shook her head. "No. Why?"

"Hmmm, no reason." So Lee couldn't kill her partner, but she still didn't like this shit.

Liv wasn't a liar, and she wouldn't have covered for Clint if he had brought his 'concerns' to her. They would've had a meeting — the three of them.

Direct was how her boss rolled. She would've wanted Clint to air his issues with Lee present. Quash contention among the ranks.

Damn, for being away from the office with Nate for weeks, she was pretty damn transparent if Liv was kicking her out in less than forty-eight hours of being back.

Then again, they'd had a sit down like this one last month. At that time, her boss had ordered her to take it easy. *That time* she hadn't been exiled or sent to Shrinkville.

Had things snowballed?

I'm fine.

Right?

"See you next week," she muttered.

To Clint's credit, he didn't bat an eye or rub it in her face when she told him she was leaving for the day… For the week. He just nodded, told her he had things covered, and turned back to the report he was writing. Even tossed a "Take it easy" over his shoulder as Lee left their office.

By the time she made it to the Charger, her whole body was already trembling. Her hand shook so badly she missed putting the key in the ignition — twice.

That was when the water works started.

She cursed herself to hell and back. Bumped her head into the steering wheel a dozen times before the pain in her forehead made her stop.

Lee couldn't see she was crying so hard.

God, you're weak. A pussy. A wimp. Can't handle anything.

Images of Jeremy Stewart popped into her head. The look on his face, in his eyes when he'd begged her to listen to his dying declaration. The way he'd faded…becoming sallow, gray. Then his eyes had slipped closed for the last time.

Died in my arms.

She shivered in the driver's seat of her duty car. Rubbed her arms up and down her bomber, but it didn't warm her.

Right, 'cause losing Nate isn't enough. You need more reasons to feel like a crazy loser.

Lee made tight fists, but the tears wouldn't stop.

Everything whirled in her head, a chaos she couldn't shut out. Her throat burned, begging for alcohol.

Something.

Anything.

She needed to shut it all out.

Jerry's Fine Spirits.

The place was two blocks from her apartment.

She'd go there first.

Her conscience reminded her not to blow it. A drink wasn't going to fix shit—it never had. She ignored her do-gooder side *and* the statement that started out as a whisper in the back of her mind.

Go to a meeting.

What happened to being honest with herself? Lee had been so good at it over the last two years of recovery.

Go to a meeting.

She'd moved past feeling weak when she'd needed to seek the relief of AA when the urge to drink was overwhelming—or so she'd thought.

Since coming to New York, she'd held her crap together. Gone to work, played when she'd needed it— with guys like the cop Kowalski, no commitment. Hadn't even thought about drinking for the most part.

She'd even managed to forget about Nate—sorta— after their first affair.

Nate.

Lee could call him. Tell him how she was feeling.

Wouldn't even have to explain why she'd ignored his texts all day. He wouldn't push her. He'd hold her, listen to her. Wipe her tears if she cried. Whisper it would be okay.

No.

He didn't know about her past. The loss and the drinking. Why blindside him on his last day in New York?

New loss hit when she thought of losing Nate, too. *Grief. Sorrow.*

It all rose from her gut and seared her.

She closed her eyes, but all she could see were Jeremy Stewart and Nate.

Then Russ and Dylan entwined with them in her mind, making her thoughts a bevy of havoc that left her whole body a mass of nerve endings on fire.

White-hot pain caved her chest in.

Tears still flowed, but Lee swallowed against the rising bile and started the car.

Drove out of the garage.

Away from work.

Away from the stability she needed.

She looped around the block three times before she

had the balls to pull into the parking lot. *Jerry's Fine Spirits* flashed in a pattern of three different neon colors on the front of the stand-alone building.

Beckoning. Daring.

Do it.

Don't do it.

Go to a meeting.

Get a drink.

One little shot will help, not hurt.

No. Go to a meeting.

Have a drink. Then two, then three. Everything will melt away.

Like a demented comic strip, Lee pictured an angel and a devil on each of her shoulders, battling it out, whispering what she wanted to hear in one ear, and what she *should* heed in the other.

She craved the numbness of intoxication.

Wind whipped her hair and burned her damp cheeks. She wiped her eyes, giving a test sniffle and ordering her tears to go to hell.

Leave me alone.

Staring at the doorway that would release all her inner demons again, she shifted on her feet, embracing the cold of the winter day and forcing air into her lungs. It scorched her dry throat like a bitch, but unlike the debilitating pain of memories, this was good.

Focus.

Lee put one foot in front of the other, following a guy in a Carhartt jacket. She let him go into the store first.

The little bell jingling as he entered jolted her, but

she continued to look inside the window as though it was a Macy's Christmas display.

Signs for every brand of beer, wine and hard liquor fought for her attention as if they were shouting her name, but she already knew what she was buying.

She'd always been a Jack girl.

Fuck it.

Sucking in one last fortifying breath, she paid her shaking fingers no attention and opened the liquor store's door.

Chapter Twenty-Eight

"L ee?" His verbal call went ignored just like all the text messages for the entire morning.

Her car was in the vast garage attached to her building, so she had to be home. She wasn't supposed to be back yet—he'd wanted everything to be perfect.

It's only a quarter after one, why's she home?

Nate tried to tell himself it didn't matter, that they could prepare the meal together. Have an early dinner and spend the day, instead of mere hours together.

He wanted to make love to her at least once more before getting on that plane.

But why didn't she answer my texts? Why won't she answer me now?

She was avoiding him and it made his blood boil, especially after what'd been the perfection of last night.

Bags of groceries swamped his hands, but he managed to close the door to her apartment. He dropped the key and his burden onto the kitchen counter.

Nate carefully took the dozen red roses from one of the sacks and unwrapped them from their cellophane shroud. They weren't from a florist, but for grocery store roses they were still pretty. He grabbed a glass from the cupboard and filled it with water. He inhaled the light scent and smiled.

They'll do.

Lee didn't have a vase, but he hoped she liked his

efforts. Wasn't even sure if she was into flowers, but if he got even one smile, it'd be reward enough.

He couldn't wait to tell her his news.

Nate was bouncing in his cowboy boots like a kindergartener.

The speech was planned. He'd tell her he'd got a job, a place to live, and he loved her.

No pressure.

He'd have to emphasize that aspect and pray it was enough to keep her from freaking. Pulling away from him…crushing him.

Then he'd have to grit his teeth and admit he knew about her past. Adequately explain how much it *didn't* matter.

Could she love him someday?

Can I ask?

His heart tripped and he reached for confidence with both hands. Needed to picture walking into a courtroom with a well-prepared argument. Usually he prosecuted. With Lee?

Nate would have to defend.

"Angel, are you here?"

He hadn't been able to pick between homemade pizza and beef enchiladas, so he was going to let Lee select their meal, since she was home. It'd be fun to make either of the labor-intensive meals with her.

If she picked pizza, he'd have an excuse to have his arms around her, rolling the dough.

Hmmm, maybe I won't tell her I bought stuff for enchiladas.

He rounded the corner into the small living room.

Saw the bottle of whisky first.

His whole body flushed and he froze. Nate's pulse pounded in his temples and he made two fists to keep his hands from shaking. Blinked twice, but the scene before him didn't change. It wasn't a dream — *scratch that* — horrible nightmare.

Real. It's real.

Lee sat on the couch, head in her hands. The shot glass next to her poison was full of amber liquid.

His heart skipped then plummeted into his twisted stomach like a brick. "How many, Lee?" he barked.

Her shoulders caved in, but she wouldn't look at him.

Silence descended.

It was as thick as the mortar in his veins, and as palpable as if a wall was actually between them.

"Lee—" he croaked, her name forced out as his throat started to close.

"How long have you known?" His love's voice was low, but had a deadly edge. Lee's posture belied the rage just under the surface.

The anger he'd always seen in her eyes. She hid it so well, wrapped in the anguish she never showed the world. The constant humor was a cover she projected well.

If he didn't know her. If he didn't love her. It would've fooled him, too.

Guilt rose up and bit him. "Lee, I—"

"How fucking long, Nate?"

He stepped farther into the room, but she put her palm up.

Still wouldn't look at him.

A tremor shot down his spine and he felt her slipping from him.

She was never really mine anyway. No matter how I tried to convince myself.

Now she never would be.

Words dissolved on his tongue.

How many times had he wanted to bring up her past? Then she'd smile or laugh at something he'd said.

Happiness.

Lee wrapped him in it all the time. His greatest hope was that she'd felt the same way being with him.

He swallowed. *Nothing* he said was going to cut it.

"I asked you a fucking question, Counselor."

"After you left Texas." Nate was on autopilot.

Her dark gaze finally met his. She was as cold as ice.

He stared and locked his jaw to keep from showing any emotion. The look on her face ripped him in two.

"Why?"

"Because I wanted to know everything about the woman I lo—"

"*Don't* fucking say it." She made a cutting gesture with her hand. "I told you before I couldn't take it. Now, I sure as hell can't. It won't fix shit. You have some nerve, doncha?"

"Nerve?" Anger flipped his gut and he glued his fists to his sides. "Me?"

"You had *no* right."

"Maybe I didn't. But *you* have no right to throw my feelings in my face, either."

Lee laughed.

The bitterness rolled over him and Nate blew out a breath as his chest constricted. His knees started to shake, so he locked them. Tried to square his shoulders and failed.

"Just get out."

"Excuse me?" He croaked.

"Get. The. Fuck. Out."

He swallowed against the lump in his throat. It was either that or stand in front of her and cry like a ball-less wonder. He gripped his anger with both hands and locked the hurt in a vault. "I can leave now. If I never come back, it won't change a damn thing, Selena Dawson. You stay here, drink yourself to death. Hell, get in a car *again* and get yourself killed. Which is what you wanted in the first place, wasn't it? Doesn't matter to me. You'll still be *alone* for the rest of your fucking life. Stay cold and heartless. Add the drunk back in. It seems to work well for you."

When her face fell and those dark orbs misted over, Nate wanted to swallow his tongue.

Lee broke their eye contact and made a fist. "Get out before I shoot your ass."

Choking back an honest-to-God sob, he turned on his heel and walked out of the love of his life's little New York City apartment.

Slammed the door and didn't look back.

Lee refused to crumble. When the door to her apartment slammed, it rocked her to her very soul.

Tears cascaded.

He left.

No. You ordered him gone, what did you expect?

Nate had promised he'd never leave.

"Heh. You ruined that. Got what you wanted, right?"

She'd ruined it.

The one she actually wanted wasn't strong enough to put up with her shit after all. Why did it hurt so badly?

Doubling over on the edge of the couch, she grabbed her stomach and whimpered. Only in lieu of screaming.

She bit into her bottom lip until she tasted the metallic tang of blood, but the physical pain gave her something to focus on. However, it didn't even put a dent in the white-hot, searing hole that used to be her heart.

Lee didn't want him gone at all.

Wanted him on the couch right now. Holding her. Not judging her when she cried.

He'd listen when she complained Liv was making her take time off. Remind her she could use a break. Hell, maybe he'd even offer to stay in town… Or ask her to go with him back to Texas.

She could inhale his clean, masculine scent and clutch his shirt. Bury her face against his warmth. Feel his lips on her temple. He'd rub her back like he always did. Wipe her tears away. Kiss her when she was ready.

Realization smacked into her and Lee's body flushed with shock. Her pain sharpened like a slicing dagger. She couldn't breathe. Her vision danced.

I love Nate.

He loved her, too.

Nate had tried to tell her twice. What'd she done?

Ignored him the first time, and shut him down the second.

I love him.

He…loves…me.

Fuck.

She crushed her eyes shut, but it did nothing to stop the tears. Lee shot to her feet and grabbed the bottle of whisky, flinging it against the living room wall. It shattered, filling her nose with the sweet scent of *Jack Daniel's* as the amber washed her white wall.

She hadn't taken a drink.

Why was it always the anger first?

At the first sign of challenge, she always shut out all reason. Saw red and couldn't wade through it. She could've told him.

Explained she'd triumphed over temptation. Told the little devil to go back to hell and leave her alone. She wasn't going to throw her life away.

Beyond smelling the drink, Lee hadn't taken even one sip. As a matter of fact, the smell of the alcohol had turned her stomach instead of whetting her appetite.

She couldn't do it. Ruin two years of recovery from addiction—and the guilt of relying on what'd taken Dylan and Russ from her.

Lee couldn't shit on the new life she had in New York City, no matter how reluctant she'd been to leave Dallas. Couldn't disappoint Liv. Or Clint.

Her partner might not know of her past, but if she fucked up, he sure as hell would be clued in.

They were just starting to be real partners. She liked him…cared for him.

"Nate jumped to conclusions." Hearing her own shaky, fragmented sentence made her hurt even more.

Weak. Unacceptable.

She'd come to rely on him. Hardly even thought about Dylan and Russ when she was with him. Had started to forge a new…family with Nate?

"No."

Bile rose and her throat burned. Her stomach lurched and she made a mad dash into her kitchen and knocked the lid off her trash can just in time to lose the meagre contents of her stomach.

The early lunch of a bagel with cream cheese because she'd been starving when she'd walked in the door.

Lee vomited twice, hitting her knees hard on the linoleum, but she didn't care if she ended up with bruises.

Nothing less than she deserved.

After hugging her trash can and waiting for round three, she pushed to shaky legs and sucked in a deep breath.

She'd never been upset enough to make herself throw up before. She hiccupped and wiped her face.

Water.

Her mouth tasted like ass.

More tears were born when she saw the dozen red roses in one of the two real-glass glasses she owned.

He'd even taken the care to make sure they sat in enough water. The little packet of flower food rested on the counter.

Damn him.

Lee's fingers shook when she caressed one dark red petal. It was soft and made her ache all over again.

She swiped at her wet cheeks to no avail. She'd cried more tonight than she had in the last six years. Cursing herself to hell and back, she reached for the cupboard and tried not to think of the words he'd flung at her.

'You stay here, drink yourself to death. Hell, get in a car again *and get yourself killed. Which is what you wanted in the first place, wasn't it?'*

A sob ripped from her lips, even though she fought it. She shook from head to foot, leaning into her counter so she wouldn't fall on her ass.

Visions of Jeremy Stewart dying in her arms danced in her head.

"No!"

Lee didn't want to die.

She'd lost a man she'd loved, and a child who had been her life. If nothing else, losing them had taught her life was precious.

Not that her choice of alcoholism had proved it.

Now she'd lost Nate, too.

"Stop!" Her mind chose to ignore her shout. Her thoughts churned and no amount of closing her eyes was going to fix it.

She snatched a cup from above, yanked the faucet on and filled it. She downed two servings until she almost choked.

Her stomach jumped again, but she swallowed until the urge to puke again subsided. Lee dropped the cup into the sink and gripped the edge until her fingers whitened.

"What am I going to do?"

'You'll still be alone *for the rest of your fucking life.'*

No.

Lee didn't want to be alone.

She wanted Nate.

Chapter Twenty-Nine

esides the three AA meetings she'd forced herself to attend, Lee spent her *'vacation'* in bed. She couldn't stop crying and couldn't bear for anyone to see her as weak — even Clint.

So when the first week came to an end, she called Liv.

Her boss had about fallen over when she'd agreed to take another week off. She hadn't told her the *why*.

Lee was sick as a dog, too.

Experience told her she was an expert at making herself ill — she'd stayed in bed for the entire week after losing Russ and Dylan, but that wasn't like *this* time.

Losing Nate was sharper, of course, and made her a wreck, but the vomiting wouldn't stop. No matter what she ate or when she ate it, she had to run to the bathroom or the nearest receptacle.

It got so bad she'd finally dragged the trashcan from her bedroom and hauled it around the apartment with her.

Her head spun, she was dizzy all the time.

Welcome to the flu, Lee Dawson.

Just what she needed after losing the love of her life.

After a week and a half, Lee called the doctor.

Over the counter meds weren't helping.

She *hated* going to the doctor, and she'd been told over the years she was a horrible patient by family and the medical profession alike.

Go. Fig.

They should make a support group — Control Freaks Anonymous.

Lee needed to kick whatever bug she had going on so she could get back to work before anything Caselli court-related required her presence.

The bastard was recovering nicely, and even though the trial was likely months away, there was much prep to do. Both for the prosecution and the FBI. She felt like an ass; her partner had to handle it on his own for now.

Some of Caselli's guys had agreed to testify against him, so they were all in protective custody. They were added to the list that included Carlo Maldonado and Bruno Gallo, who were already in prison and had cooperated.

Eric Bray had left a message asking for a call to set up a meeting — she hadn't the strength to call him back yet. No clue if the prosecutor wanted to go over reports or prep her for the stand, but he'd have to wait until she didn't feel like crap.

Her partner had checked in a few times. She'd lied her ass off, told him she was enjoying the break and was indeed taking it easy. If Clint hadn't believed her, Lee couldn't tell.

Damn good thing he wasn't into Skype because she looked like death warmed over. Couldn't fake that on camera. Voice, however, she did okay with.

Thank God he hadn't asked if she'd talked to Nate.

Nate...

He'd been gone two weeks, and each day that passed, she died a little more inside.

He hadn't called, texted or emailed.

Not that she blamed him.

Lee owed him one big, fat apology.

Funny thing was the words he'd flung at her that day… Horrible *horrible* things to say, no doubt. But not even one ounce of her believed *Nate* had believed what he'd said.

It was just like her self-deprecation tendencies to stick up for a guy who'd crushed her on purpose, but it didn't change the way she felt.

He'd been angry. Hurt. *All* in reaction to what she'd said…

What she'd demanded from him. She didn't blame him.

If Nate owed her an apology, Lee owed *him* an even bigger one.

For stringing him along—both in Texas and in New York.

For not being honest with him *or* herself.

For giving him her body and withholding her heart.

Or so she'd thought.

Her heart had been his long ago. Waaaaaaaay before she'd admitted it to herself.

Too bad it's not fair to admit it to him now.

God knew she was going to love him for the rest of her life.

Even though she couldn't have him.

Understanding that made it easier to move on, in a

way. Lee was still hurt that he'd kept his knowledge of her past from her, but she kept asking herself *why* she was so upset, and the only answer was something would embarrass her to admit out loud.

You're one proud son of a bitch, Lee Dawson.

Pride.

Fear…that he wouldn't see her as the same person. Not that she was perfect, by any means, but Nate…

He was gorgeous, funny, idealistic. Caring. Loving. *Perfect.*

Basically, with all the skeletons in her closet, she wasn't good enough for Nate Crane.

No matter *how* she felt about him.

Lee sucked in her cheek and bit down when her vision blurred.

Jesus, get over yourself!

Her emotions were all over the place and she couldn't patch herself up. No matter how many pep talks she shouted in her head.

"Mrs. Dawson?" The young nurse looked up over a clipboard, a smile on her face.

"Ms., actually." Lee scrambled to her feet from the chair in the bright lobby. Prayed her stomach wouldn't revolt.

The drive over had been okay. She'd brought a bottle of water, the only thing her body could seem to handle.

"Oh, sorry about that." Tucking a blonde wisp behind her ear, the girl smiled again.

"No problem."

"Follow me; you'll be in exam four."

While going through the routine of vitals and general health inquiries, she made her shoulders loosen. She held her back straight, but not tensed. Shook her limbs out and took as many deep breaths as she could manage. It wasn't like she was dying or anything, just had a stomach bug that wouldn't quit.

"All right, hop up on the table, and Dr. Hawkins will be with you in a few minutes."

Lee nodded and thanked the nurse.

With a smile, the young RN slipped out into the hallway, shutting the door silently.

Nerves twisted her stomach every moment that ticked away at the loud clock on the wall. She studied the face to distract herself.

It was made for a doctor's office. Each of the numbers was represented by a tool of the trade—the twelve was a stethoscope, there was a Band-Aid, blood pressure monitor, etc. A red caduceus held the hour and minute hand on, which were both shaped like syringes.

The clock was nice—sort of. Although, watching the time go by was making her even more of a wreck.

She didn't do doctors. Unless she was passed out or bleeding from a bullet wound.

Lee actually jumped when he came into the room.

"Hello, Selena, I'm Dr. Hawkins." He was young, had a smile on his handsome face, and an iPad tucked under one arm. He threw his hand out for a shake, and she obliged, ignoring the tremor in her fingers.

Relax. He's not going to eat you.

"Lee, I go by Lee." She cringed; had been hurried

and cracked. She sat a little taller, trying not to wince as the tissue paper under her ass rustled.

"All right, Lee. What seems to be the problem today?" The doc took a seat on the stool and rolled closer to the exam table.

Her stomach fluttered and she launched into her issue — the physical one, anyway.

He nodded a few times and hit several places on the screen of his tablet.

She couldn't see the screen and it made her antsy. Couldn't sit still.

"Fever?" Dr. Hawkins asked.

"Not that I noticed. Didn't take my temp."

"No problem. Amanda noted your temperature's normal today."

Dr. Hawkins asked a few more questions, each one twisting up her stomach a bit more.

Lee screamed at herself to relax. It wasn't as though there was some magic answer.

He couldn't simply look at her to diagnose whatever was wrong.

"Well, let's do some blood work and see where we're at. I'm not liking that you can't keep anything down. You need to stay hydrated."

"Water's about the only thing my stomach doesn't revolt against."

He gave a small smile. "Good, at least you're drinking enough."

Drinking.

The word always zoned her mind right to the forbidden. Lee blew out a breath and forced a nod.

Ignored the memory of the amber liquid dousing her wall the day Nate had left.

She didn't miss the Jack Daniel's.

She missed Nate.

Three meetings had put her back on track mentally as far as being an alcoholic was concerned. It didn't fix her broken heart, or her regret.

"Do I have to go to a lab or something?"

"No, we can do it in office and get the results within about thirty minutes. One stop shop. I'll have my nurse come get you in a few."

"Thanks, Dr. Hawkins."

Once again the doctor smiled and offered a handshake. He glanced down at the iPad's screen. "Looks like I've been listed as your doctor for almost two years, yet this is the first time you've come to see me?"

Lee grimaced. "Well, I'm…pretty healthy. Usually."

"The older we get, the more important those yearly physicals are." He winked, but she heard the gentle admonishment.

"I'll keep that in mind, doc."

"Good. I'll send Amanda for you in a few."

Waiting for the results of the blood draw about killed her.

Amanda, the cute little blonde nurse, put her back in the exam room to wait for Dr. Hawkins again, and the only thing she could hear was the tick of that stupid clock.

It got louder with each passing second.

She glared at the stupid thing, but it didn't stop time, speed it up, *or* help the man appear any faster — damn him.

Lee wanted to go home.

Get the required meds for her tummy bug and be alone.

When he finally opened the door, she jumped again.

The grin on his face fell off a bit, and his brows drew tight. "Sorry, didn't mean to startle you. I should've knocked. I usually do."

"It's okay. Just wasn't expecting you. Lost in thought."

"Well, if you were worried, you can stop now. I've got you figured out."

She waited for him to continue, but he paused.

For dramatic effect or if the jerk just enjoyed it, Lee was *so* done. Tried not to glare, since he'd been kind to her. "Well, what's wrong with me?"

"Nothing." Leaning on the counter behind him, Dr. Hawkins crossed one leg in front of the other and flashed a grin.

"Nothing? Then why do I feel like ass?"

"You're not sick. But you might want to get a supply of saltines and ginger ale. It might make the coming months a little easier."

"What?" Lee's mind started to spin and her heart kicked into overdrive.

"Congratulations. You're pregnant."

"You sure about this, little brother?" Pete's words were a question, but his green eyes held pride when their gazes met.

Nate smiled. "Yes. Never been so sure about anything in my life."

His older brother threw his hand out, wearing a grin. "Good deal."

He took the invitation for a shake, but pulled the guy into an embrace, too. Pete's gorgeous wife, Nikki, stood to the side, also smiling in the empty foyer of Nate's huge house.

Nate released his brother, but Pete held his forearm and squeezed. "I'm gonna miss having you around."

"Me too." He smiled again, and hugged his waiting sister-in-law.

Nikki kissed his cheek. "I'll miss you, too. There'll be no one to help me and Andi keep Petey in check. We can't do it all. Big job."

His brother growled and grabbed her, laying a kiss on her mouth that made his gut ache with envy.

The redhead's giggle was cut off as she wrapped her arms around her husband and kissed him back with enthusiasm.

Lee.

Monday would make it four weeks since he'd left her.

A month that'd just about killed him.

He'd wrapped up his last trial in lieu of handing it off. Nate had won the case, too—put away two serial burglars being tried together. Wasn't a murder or anything, but it'd been quick and had helped him say a proper goodbye to Dallas—his office, co-workers and boss. He'd miss them, but he was looking forward to starting over in New York.

Starting over with the woman he loved.

Sooner than later, he'd get her back. Apologize for the horrid things he'd said that day.

He winced every time he thought about it.

Nate would try to convince Lee she needed him as much as he needed her. Admit how he felt, and promise he'd make up for his mouth. Give her the space she needed if she'd give him another shot.

A real shot.

Be her man, not just her lover.

"Give Mama and Pop my love. Thanks for talking her into not coming over here." He'd said goodbye to their parents the night before.

Their mother's tears had about killed him, but she understood his need to go.

She was fond of Lee. So things were in Nate's favor. Marilyn Crane was a hopeless romantic and wanted both her sons happy.

Although he'd said nothing, she'd noticed what a struggle the last month had been and she wished him good luck. Said Lee didn't look like a fool, so she expected an invitation to the wedding.

His heart leapt—*wedding.*

Nate could only hope.

Pete ran his hand through his fair hair, one arm around his wife's shoulders. "Well, that'll cost you later."

He grinned. "You can handle it."

One corner of his brother's mouth shot up. "We'll see."

Nate chuckled. "Just look at it this way—if you want to get me back, you'll have to hop on a plane."

The detective gave in to his smile, but it had a touch of sadness. "Don't remind me."

"You gotta visit, it's not an option."

"Oh, we will, don't worry," Nikki said, slipping her arm around her husband's waist.

Nate's gut ached. He wanted Lee. Wanted permanence with her like Pete had with Nikki. His ring on her finger and her glued to his side. In his bed.

He forced a smile, but his brother's keen gaze told him Pete saw right through him.

"It won't be easy, but I know you'll get her back, little brother. Lee Dawson is good people. Stubborn, but made for you."

"She cares for you," his sister-in-law whispered. "I saw it with my own eyes last time she was here. It'll work out, Nate. I believe that." She smiled.

Damn, I hope she's right.

He didn't want to talk about it, but Nate nodded. "I start the job on Monday. Gonna concentrate on that."

"She know?" his brother asked.

"I dunno. I told her partner I got the job and when I'd be back in the city."

"Nate, you should tell her you're coming back," Nikki said.

"I will. But for now, the ball's in her court. Pushing her gets me nowhere." Even as it passed his lips, his chest burned. He wanted to rub the spot, but hefted his duffel's strap to his shoulder instead.

Besides, I was a big asshole. She doesn't want to see me.

Nate hadn't told his brother exactly what he'd said to Lee that afternoon. Shame clouded his mind when he remembered. He'd be embarrassed to admit it out loud.

"How's that fair, if you're not sure she knows you're in New York?" Nikki asked.

"She hasn't called me since I came home." The cop-out flew out before he paused to think. Nate let it ride.

No way was he admitting his wrongdoing to the happy couple.

He didn't blame Lee for not contacting him.

Why *would* she after how they'd parted?

"Have you called her?" Pete asked.

I haven't had the balls.

"No."

Nikki shook her head and frowned. "Fricking Crane stubbornness."

His brother chuckled. "I have to agree with my wife, buddy. You should call her. Give Lee another shot."

No... It's more like — is she gonna give me *another shot?*

"It's...complicated."

"Then why are you going back?" Nikki's brown eyes were intense.

Nate frowned. How could he get away from their penetrating stares without telling them anything?

"I have to," he managed, several seconds too late.

"You should have a quicker answer than that, little

bro."

I don't want to talk about this!

"You guys are killing me."

Pete stepped forward and grabbed his arm. "If you love her, get her back. It's worth it." He threw a glance at his wife, his mouth curved in a tender smile.

"*She's* worth it." His answering whisper surprised him.

"Exactly," Nikki said.

He didn't know what he was going to do, but he didn't want them to know that, either. Nate burned for Lee. His fantasy was that *she* would come to him, but he didn't deserve that.

He was the one who had groveling to do.

Would she come to him if she knew he'd moved to the city?

Was her partner going to tell her he was back?

The guy had told him not to give up on her. That was why he'd called Clint Downs to tell him about the new job, that he was coming back.

"I suspected as much," Downs had said. He'd ended their call with, "see you next week." The big man hadn't said anything about Lee, and Nate hadn't had the guts to ask.

Time will tell. Be patient.

But how long?

"Well, I'll keep an eye on the house until it sells," Pete said, gesturing to Nate's large, empty place.

"All right. Thanks. I appreciate it. Already hooked up with Mason, the guy who sold it to me. He's scouting. Shouldn't be long. I'm asking under market."

"If it wasn't so far from Antioch, I'd buy the damn thing—you have good taste."

Nate smiled. "Mama would have a heart attack with both of us out of town."

"Right."

Silence settled over them and he fought the urge to hug his brother again. If he did, Pete would know just how freaked out he was.

Not about moving to New York. He was happy about the job.

What about Lee?

Chapter Thirty

Lee slipped into the memory from three weeks before. It didn't matter that she was at her desk. That she was supposed to be working on a report.

All she could do was play the conversation in an endless loop.

She could see it all in her mind's eye like it'd occurred that morning. No matter how hard she threw herself into work, into all that was required to get Caselli's case ready for trial, she couldn't stop thinking about the morning she'd found out her life was about to change dramatically.

"But I can't have kids." Her voice had sounded shaky to her own ears, but shock would do that.

"I read your medical history. Losing one fallopian tube and ovary doesn't make pregnancy impossible, just improbable, even with the amount of scar tissue you have."

"I can't even remember the last time I had a period."

Shit. What was it?

Three—no four—months. Never knew when to expect it. Had been like that since the ectopic pregnancy.

"Well, Ms. Dawson, sporadic menstrual cycles are also normal for your condition, but obviously your remaining parts worked. You are pregnant."

God, will you quit saying that?

Lee had swallowed, blinking against the sudden rush of emotion.

A baby.

Nate's baby.

"Are you all right? Do you want me to call someone for you?"

Nate. I want Nate.

"No. I'm…alone." She'd shaken her head. Her whole body had quivered, and it'd been a good thing her ass was still on the exam table.

The doctor had grabbed a cup from the water dispenser in the corner and filled it. "Here, drink this." He'd pressed the cup into her hand, but Lee hadn't taken more than one sip.

"I'm old. I'll be thirty-seven next month."

The concern in Dr. Hawkins' gaze had been chased away by amusement. "Well, as you've already pointed out, you're healthy. You are at what we call an advanced gestational age, or a geriatric pregnancy, which *can* place you at higher risk. But we'll keep a close eye on you and the baby. I'm not overly concerned at this point. If you need an OBGYN, we can find you a good one."

Lee had nodded numbly, gripping the paper cup tightly.

"Ms. Dawson, I'm sorry if this isn't good news. It's early. You do have options."

"No!"

The shout had surprised them both.

Her doctor's eyes had gone wide, and her hand had shot to her lower stomach.

She'd been told she couldn't have any more children. Yet, she was carrying a baby.

Nate's baby.

Even if it'd been someone else's child, she'd never believed in abortion. She wasn't a holy roller, but this child was a gift from God. A piece of Nate she'd hold in her arms.

She wanted this baby more than…anything.

Dr. Hawkins had nodded, a ghost of a smile playing at his lips. "Good. You sit here for a moment, sip that water, and when you feel better, you can go. I have your script for prenatal vitamins and I'll have Amanda give you the names of a few OBs."

The door to her and Clint's office opened, jolting Lee in her seat and yanking her from the play-by-play in her head.

Her partner closed the door, but she didn't look over her shoulder.

She turned back to the computer, hollering at herself to concentrate on the report she was drafting for the prosecutor, Eric Bray.

It was supposed to be a sequence of events from the day of Jeremy Stewart's death. She'd never documented her take on things, and since she'd been back at work for the last two weeks, Liv had asked her to finish it.

Too bad she'd been working on it over an hour and only had three paragraphs.

She didn't expect to make Clint believe she was busy, but she wanted him to leave her alone. She could feel his body heat at her back.

He loomed over, but not like he was trying to intimidate her. More like he was waiting for her to acknowledge him.

Lee fought the urge to close her eyes, ignoring him.

Clint didn't say a word, but set a *grande*-sized paper coffee cup from Starbucks in front of her.

"Thanks." She grabbed it and took a sip. Hazelnut, her favorite flavor of cappuccino, greeted her tongue. She took a second drink, savoring. Then she remembered the baby in her belly and pushed it away, hoping her partner wouldn't remark.

Coffee was her vice. If she didn't drink it, he'd want to know why.

She'd told no one of her pregnancy. She'd to tell Liv and Clint eventually, but she wasn't through the first trimester for two more weeks. Didn't want to jinx things. Nate should be the first to know, anyway. She'd been missing her baby's father for six arduous weeks now.

Lee was going to tell him—she really was. Just hadn't grown the balls to call him yet, not even after the shock of the pregnancy had settled.

He deserved to know.

She'd thought about flying to Texas, but her unit needed her right now. She'd have to tell Nate over the phone. The idea was killing her, and she was procrastinating.

When Clint perched himself on the edge of her desk instead of taking his seat, she was forced to look at her partner.

He arched one dark eyebrow, looked at the

discarded treat, then back at her. "Hmmm." He crossed his arms over his broad chest and she squirmed in her seat.

"What?" She bit back a wince.

Damn, that was defensive.

He appraised her. "No coffee?"

"Already had some," Lee muttered. "Have you talked to Roberts today?" She rushed the question, desperate for a distraction.

"No, but Liv did. He's doin' okay. Still trying to understand what all went down with his partner, like the rest of us. He's grieving, but I think the guy'll be okay. He should be back to work in a few weeks."

"Good. Glad to hear it."

Her partner nodded. Didn't call her on her coffee BS, but his gaze darted to the desk top before he looked her way again.

Lee glanced down and froze.

Clint had tried to slip her a business card.

It must've been under her cup.

Her hand shook as she reached.

'Nate Crane'. Embossed in black. Then under it was etched, *'Lead Prosecutor'.*

That wasn't what had caused the tears in her eyes.

It was the *local* New York City address and phone number that did it.

Fuck. Crying at work?

"Clint..." she croaked.

Her partner's hand swallowed her shoulder. Despite its size, his touch was gentle.

Thank God their office door was closed.

Not only was she crying at her desk, but Clint Downs was rubbing her back. One of the few times she could remember him touching her at all. She'd barely shaken the man's hand. Never even hugged him.

However, the comfort wasn't unwelcome. Lee could use a hug right about now, but she wouldn't ask.

"It's okay to cry once in a while." His statement was calm, even. Like they did this every day.

Lee shook her head. "Not at work."

"Just me and you here, partner."

His normalcy with her falling apart made the lump in her throat even bigger.

Weak didn't work.

Maybe he'd known how she'd spent her two-week break from work, after all.

"I don't think you're weak, Lee Dawson."

Shit.

She'd spoken aloud.

"As a matter of fact, you're one of the strongest people I've ever met. But that doesn't mean you're not human. You bleed red like the rest of us. And trust me, I've seen that."

Lee smirked. She took a breath and tried to ignore the business card on her desk. Like it had a spotlight on it, glaring up at her until she had to squint.

Why hadn't Nate told her about the change in jobs?

He'd moved to New York City without a word.

At least to *her*.

It doesn't matter.

Her heart cantered on its way to a full gallop.

Nate's here. In the city. Less than fifteen minutes away.

She popped up from her chair. "I have to go out."

"Oh?" Amusement rippled across Clint's face.

"Uh. Yeah." Heat crept up her neck and settled in her cheeks.

"Be gone long?" One corner of his mouth shot up and his moustache twitched. He reclined in his post on her desk and crossed his arms again.

Depends on what he says.

Lee couldn't—wouldn't—tell her partner that.

"Don't wait on me for lunch." She shoved her chair in until it *thumped* against her desk. Then slipped out the door.

Couldn't hold back the smile at his bark of laughter.

From the moment the blonde chick had said, "Around the corner, first door on the right," her heart had been in her throat, thundering in her ears.

The breakfast she'd choked down for the sake of the baby churned as her stomach played cement mixer. She swallowed and prayed she wouldn't toss her cookies in the hallway.

Too bad she couldn't blame it on morning sickness this time.

One look at the open door with his name etched on it, and she had to suck in a breath. Her whole body shook like a leaf, so Lee shoved her hands into the pockets of the brown leather bomber jacket. She made tight fists, wishing she had something else to hold onto. To hold her together.

His fair head was down and he was writing on a yellow legal pad. He didn't see or sense her hovering outside his office — which was funny, because she could smell his cologne all the way down the hall. Or maybe that was just wishful thinking.

Tears burned her eyes as she watched him.

Confident. Collected.

Perfect.

The pale green shirt would bring out the color in his hazel eyes, but would she get to see them up close and personal again?

Her knuckles brushed the open door.

He'd heard her, because the movement of the pen paused, hovering over the paper. "Gina, do you have that file—" Nate looked up.

Stopped talking.

Lee's voice caught in her throat.

"Lee…"

Her name was a breathless whisper, but she couldn't read his expression.

Fucking tears.

She swiped at her cheek, but her vision blurred again. Couldn't move from the doorway, screamed at herself to get it together. Lee made a show of looking around his office. "Nice digs. Lead Prosecutor, huh? Pretty cool since you just started. How long you been back?" Her words were rushed and her knees wobbled, so she shifted from foot to foot.

"Two weeks." Nate stood, straightened his tie. He shrugged.

She nodded.

Two weeks…

Why hadn't he called?

He motioned for her to enter the room, but she hesitated.

Until Nate came from around his desk, crossed the room and pulled her forward by her wrist. He shut the door.

Her skin tingled from his touch, but then his hand was gone.

He'd wasted no time breaking their physical contact.

She couldn't let that discourage her. Lee needed to be here, to talk to him. Fix things. Not *only* for the sake of the child he knew nothing about.

No matter the outcome today, she *would* tell him he was going to be a father. Even if he didn't want to be with her, he had a right to his baby. To help raise him or her, co-parent.

God, please let him want me…

Us…

She stood in the middle of Nate's office, fingers clutched in front of her body, fighting the urge to wring her hands like a kid in front of the principal.

He perched on the edge of his sizable dark wood desk, appraising her. Saying nothing. Arms crossed over his broad chest, his feet planted on the floor.

Nate wore simple black loafers, and it was the first time she could remember seeing him without cowboy boots on.

Tell him you love him.

Tell him about his baby.

Words deserted her as she stared at his tall, familiar form. Lee tried not to watch his thighs as the muscles shifted under his gray suit pants when he settled.

The garment implied more than displayed what was there, but it only made her think of them entwined. Moving together.

Making love.

Her stomach somersaulted and her nails bit into her palms.

"I'd ask how you found me, but you're FBI and all."

Nate's voice made her jump, and her eyes darted to his face.

A smile played at his full lips and her heart sped up again.

Emotion smacked into her and Lee bit her bottom lip. She needed to touch him. Kiss him. "I'm sorry. For everything."

He startled. As though he hadn't expected her to apologize. "No. *I'm* sorry. What I said the day I left… It's unforgivable. Surprised you didn't come in here kicking my ass." His gaze was pained, serious as he searched her face, but he made no move to touch her, like he was afraid.

"It doesn't matter," she said quickly, shaking her head.

"It does. I was an asshole. Saying that… Leaving you. Hurting you. Worst thing I've ever done in my life."

She had to make him understand. "No. I promise it doesn't. I hurt you, too. Over and over. Look, I came here—"

"God, I'm glad you did. We've been in the same city for two weeks, and every day I didn't see you... It killed me."

Lee took the hundredth deep breath of the day.

Here goes nothing. No. Here goes everything.

"I love you."

Nate blinked. But then his eyes went misty. He was off the edge of his desk in seconds, then she was pinned to the muscled wall of his chest. He held her so tight it was hard to breathe, but she didn't give a damn.

She buried her face against his shoulder and wrapped her arms around him. No doubt her tears already soaked his shirt.

"Do you have any idea how long I've wanted you to say that?" His warm breath tickled her forehead and made her hair shift.

Lee shook her head.

He cupped her cheeks.

She'd been right about the shirt. His hazel orbs stood out, a gorgeous mix of green, brown and gold. The tears making them shine were going to kill her.

"Angel, I fell for you hard. Last year. When you came to Texas after Marchetti."

"I love you," she repeated.

"I love you, too."

Then his mouth was moving over hers.

Her whole body stuttered. Knowing it and hearing him *say* it were two different things.

Lee kissed him back. She needed to hold it together, tell him about their baby. Couldn't get lost to his touch, his kiss, the feel of being in his arms again.

She pulled away on a gasp, her heart fluttering.

"Lee," Nate whispered, caressing her cheeks with his thumbs. He lowered his head to kiss her again, but she rested her fingertip against his lips.

She smiled when he kissed her finger. "I'm pregnant."

He blinked.

Silence.

Her stomach twisted, and she swallowed hard.

Good job, Lee. Blurting things out seems to be your new forte.

"I thought…"

"So did I. Promise. I had no idea I could get pregnant. Doctors told me I couldn't. I worried because my parts are messed up. But it's good. I'm okay. I mean…*we're* okay. Had my first ultrasound last week. The baby looks good, doc says. We're healthy."

Nate's Adam's apple bobbed, but he didn't release her. Or back away. Still held her against him. He touched her face.

That's good, right?

Lee chewed her lip, forcing her gaze to remain locked onto his beautiful eyes. "I'm sorry. I mean, I don't expect—"

His mouth crashed down on hers again, and he kissed her until desire settled in her lower belly.

Her sex throbbed and her breasts felt heavy. Her pregnancy-induced oversensitive nipples ached, rubbing the fabric of her bra in a pleasure-pain sensation. Heat suffused her limbs and her legs wobbled, threatening to dump her on her ass.

He was the only man that could make her feel like this.

Damn good thing he was holding her up.

Nate pulled away on a ragged breath, panting against her. His erection pulsed into her stomach, and she had half a mind to ask him if he wanted to christen his office.

"I'm not." He was breathless and rested his forehead against hers.

"You're not what?"

"Sorry. In the least."

His words sank into her passion-hazed brain and Lee's eyes blurred with tears again.

He was *happy* about the baby.

"We're having a baby." His smile was brilliant.

"We're having a baby," she repeated, her throat burning as she fought the emotion clogging it up. She blinked, but more tears were born. Cascaded down her cheeks.

Nate kissed them away before pressing a tender kiss to her lips. "I love you, Selena Dawson."

Lee smiled and snuggled close to his chest.

"Only thing better than having you back is this." He rested his hand against her still-flat lower stomach. "Now I have you both."

She shivered.

"Are you cold, angel?" The concern in his tone made her glance up.

"No. How could I be cold with you holding me? I'll never be cold again."

"Damn straight." He took a breath, and his gaze

bored into hers. "Marry me."

"Wh-what?"

"Marry me. Before the baby comes. We're already a family, but let's make it official."

Family.

The word used to remind her of what she'd lost.

Now… It was hope.

A *future*.

What Lee could have again.

She'd grab it with both hands and hold on for dear life. Life was indeed dear. Especially the miracle inside her. She closed her eyes and he thumbed her tears away again. "Fucking tears," she muttered.

Nate laughed. "It's okay, angel. Tears are good. Tears show you care."

"Care? I *love* you, Nathaniel Dennis Crane."

He laughed again and kissed her. "If you love me, what about an answer?"

She grinned. "Yes. Hell yes, I'll marry you."

When he laughed again, she joined him.

"Only my angel would curse when accepting a proposal."

Lee smirked. "Would you have it any other way?"

"Hell no."

She threw her arms around his neck and kissed him.

Epilogue

The baby kicked and Lee laid her hand on the spot, a smile curving her lips.

Nate grumbled something in his sleep, his cheek against her hip, but his face was down, buried in the pillow she had at her back. His warm breath tickled her skin.

She ran her hand through his thick blond hair, wishing it was comfortable to bend down for a kiss.

His arm was flung across her bare thighs as she sat propped against their headboard watching TV. The volume was low as to not disturb him, but it was really just background noise. She was too busy studying the man she loved.

Lee ran her fingers down his stubbled cheek, shivering at the memory of the rough feel on the tender skin of her inner thigh, but it turned her on.

His fingers twitched, tickling the outside of her leg.

She wiggled and Nate rolled onto his back with a loud yawn, flashing a sexy, sleepy smile when he blinked his gorgeous hazel eyes.

"Angel." Her husband's voice was thick with sleep.

"Hi." She caressed his naked chest, tracing his defined lines until his muscles jumped. "Did you have a nice nap?"

He grabbed her hand and kissed her knuckles, then sat up and pulled her into his arms. Against the hard chest she'd just admired.

"I did. Because you're here with me." He kissed her forehead and her cheek, until Lee met his lips with hers.

Nate took it from there, kissing her softly, but deeply, their tongues rubbing and dancing.

She moaned into his mouth, desire unfurling low in her belly.

When he tugged the sheets and blanket away, she didn't resist him.

They made love slowly, tenderly.

Nate worshipped her body, reverently caressing the curve of her belly, lavishing kisses on the place where their child grew. He was careful with her, but it didn't take much to please her these days anyway.

Hormones heightened lovemaking, and the further along her pregnancy got, the quicker she seemed to orgasm.

Today proved to be the same, and she climaxed twice before her husband grunted his release. Nate fused their mouths as they both came down from the edge, shuddering in each other's arms.

He slipped from her body and rolled to his back, nestling Lee into his side.

She sighed contentedly, resting her head on his chest.

He rubbed her back until Lee was lulled almost to sleep. However, one glance at the clock on her nightstand had her eyes flying open. She sat up. "We need to get up, babe. Shower, dress. You shave. Then we need to go. Clint and Robin are expecting us at five."

Nate pulled her to him and nipped her bottom lip.

A tremor shot down her spine.

"Angel, I thought we'd discussed this before."

Lee grinned, wrapping her arms around his neck. "Discussed what?"

"Your partner. Very patient man."

She threw her head back and laughed, and he wasted no time dragging warm, wet kisses down her neck. Biting her bottom lip to keep from moaning, Lee tugged his hair. "Right. Clint is. But it's rude to keep Robin waiting. I like her. And she's a damn good cook. Don't forget the girls, they like seeing us."

Nate laughed and rubbed her round tummy. "Ah, my wife and her cravings."

"Hey, talk to your kid. It's not my fault he makes me hungry all the time."

"She."

A tender smile curved her lips and she kissed her husband's cheek. "You're the only man I know that doesn't harp on about having a son."

"I want a baby girl that looks just like you."

They'd decided to be surprised about the baby's sex, but Lee suspected he was worried she'd be upset about having another son if the baby was a boy.

Funny, she'd always thought having another child would be an insult to Dylan. A replacement baby. She didn't feel that way now. Still felt Dylan's loss—always would—but her new baby was an individual. A child to be loved as much as she'd adored her son.

Nate's child would most definitely learn of the big brother he or she hadn't got the chance to meet.

Someday. When the time was right.

Her husband encouraged her to talk about Russ and Dylan if she needed to.

Lee had a few times. Nate was the only person on earth she'd uttered their names aloud to since they'd passed away.

His openness in regards to learning about the family she'd lost and his willingness to be there for her only made her love him more.

She'd talked about her alcoholism as well. Nate didn't think she was weak. He'd told her he'd never met a stronger person. She'd triumphed over a disease. He made her promise to tell him if she ever felt like she needed to go to a meeting. Offered to go with her.

"I don't care what we have, as long as he or she is healthy." Lee caressed his cheek.

"Right. I just hope she has your eyes." He flashed a lopsided grin that had her insides melting.

"I love you, Nate Crane."

"I love you too, Lee Crane."

She pressed a kiss to his lips, but kept it quick so he couldn't drag her back into the depths of desire. She really was looking forward to dinner with her partner and his family.

Nate groaned when she pulled away.

"You do realize we have all night. We're married. Live together and all that." Lee arched an eyebrow and scooted to the edge of the bed when he made a grab for her.

He chuckled and followed her. Hit his feet first and gently pulled her to hers. "I do realize this. But do *you*

know how irresistible you are?"

Heat crept into her cheeks and she rolled her eyes. "Right. I get fatter by the day."

"No way, angel. You're gorgeous." He rested both palms on her distended stomach. Nate bent to kiss her belly. "You know what the best part is?"

She rested her hands between his, smiling when the baby moved. "What?"

"In less than two months I get to meet my baby. You both belong to me. Forever."

Lee wrapped her arms around him and he pulled her close. Her firm tummy pushed into his abs and her smile widened to a grin. "I suppose I like your calculations. Guess that's not so bad, Counselor."

"Nope, not bad at all, Special Agent Selena Crane." Their gazes collided and they grinned.

The End

About The Author

USA TODAY Bestselling, award winning author of historical and epic fantasy romance, as well as romantic suspense, C.A. loves to dabble in different genres. If it's a good story, she'll write it, no matter where it seems to fit!

She's a hopeless romantic and always will be.

Risking it all for Happily Ever After is what she lives by!

C.A. is originally from Ohio, but got to Texas as soon as she could. She's happily married and has a bachelor's degree in Criminal Justice.

She works with kids when she's not writing.

WEBSITE: http://www.caszarek.com

BLOG: http://www.caszarekwriter.blogspot.com/

TWITTER: https://twitter.com/caszarek

FACEBOOK: http://www.facebook.com/caszarek

INSTAGRAM: https://www.instagram.com/caszarek/

GOODREADS:https://www.goodreads.com/author/show/5815085.C_A_Szarek

NEWSLETTER SIGNUP: http://blogspot.us7.list-manage.com/subscribe?u=296abc5983ebc51c1d4d0972b&id=fb22ce93be

EMAIL: ca@caszarek.com